Pra

Kathy's columns have entertained our newspaper readers for years, so it doesn't surprise me she'll now be entertaining the world with a new cozy mystery series.

— KIM LEWICKI, PUBLISHER, HIGHLANDS NEWSPAPER

Astonbury, the fictional Cotswolds village in this new Dickens and Christie series, much like Louise Penny's famous Canadian village Three Pines, will have you longing to visit and even live there. Something is amiss, though, in this vibrant village, and you'll find yourself trying to solve an unexpected murder. Highly recommended for lovers of cozy animal mysteries.

— KATIE WILLS, LIBRARIAN

An author whose books are set to become bestsellers.

— LONGTIME READER

PUMPKINS, PAWS & MURDER

A Dickens & Christie Mystery
Book II

Kathy Manos Penn

Copyright © 2020 by Kathy Manos Penn and
Manos Penn & Ink

MANOS
PENN & INK

Paperback ISBN: **978-1-7343226-4-4**
eBook ISBN: **978-1-7343226-3-7**

All rights reserved.

No part of this book may be reproduced in any form or by any electronic or
mechanical means, including information storage and retrieval systems,
without written permission from the author, except for the use of brief
quotations in a book review.

For my father, who never got to complete the book he started.

I have a certain experience of the way people tell lies.

— AGATHA CHRISTIE

CONTENTS

Cast Of Characters

Aleta "Leta" Petkas Parker—A retired American banker, Leta lives in the village of Astonbury in the Cotswolds with Dickens the dog and Christie the cat.

Henry Parker—Handsome blue-eyed Henry was Leta's husband.

Dickens—Leta's white dog, a dwarf Great Pyrenees, is a tad sensitive about his size.

Christie—Her black cat Christie is sassy, opinionated and uppity.

Anna Metaxas—Leta's youngest sister lives in Atlanta with her husband Andrew, five cats, and a Great Dane.

Sophia Smyth—Leta's younger sister is married to Jeremy and lives in New Orleans.

Bev Hunter— Bev is Leta's Atlanta friend who fosters dogs.

Martha and Dylan—The donkeys in a nearby pasture look forward to carrots from Leta.

Libby and Gavin Taylor—The Taylors are the owners of The Olde Mill Inn.

Gemma Taylor—A Detective Sergeant at the Stow-on-the-Wold station, she's the daughter of Libby and Gavin and lives in the guest cottage behind the inn.

Paddington—Libby and Gavin's Burmese cat is fond of Leta.

Beatrix Scott— Owner of the Book Nook, she hosts the monthly book club meeting.

Trixie Maxwell— Beatrix's niece works in the bookshop.

Max Maxwell—Trixie's husband is a magician who performs at the Fall Fête.

Wendy Davies—The retired English teacher from North Carolina returned to Astonbury to look after her mum and has become good friends with Leta.

Peter Davies— Wendy's twin and owner of the local garage, Peter is a cyclist and cricket player.

Belle Davies— Mother to Wendy and Peter, Belle lives at Sunshine Cottage with Wendy.

Tigger—Belle and Wendy's cat is a recent addition to Sunshine Cottage.

Rhiannon Smith— Rhiannon owns the Let It Be yoga studio where Leta and Wendy take classes.

Jill and Jenny Walker—Jill works at the Olde Mill Inn, and her sister Jenny is a barista at Toby's Tearoom.

Dave Prentiss—A journalist from the States, he and Leta hit it off when he stayed at the inn.

Toby White—Owner of Toby's Tearoom, he gave up his London advertising job to pursue his dream of owning a small business.

George Evans—George is the owner of Cotswolds Tours.

Constable James—Constable James works with Gemma.

The Watsons—John and Deborah live next door to Leta with their little boy Timmy.

Summer and Sparkle—The two Fairy Hair ladies have a booth at the Fall Fête.

Phil Porter— Phil is the bartender at the Ploughman

Barb Peters—Barb is a barmaid who works with Phil.

Brian Peters—Barb's cousin Brian is the gardener for The Olde Mill Inn and several country estates

Chapter One

"Yes I can, yes I can," I chanted under my breath. Standing in front of the garage looking at my bicycle, I knew I needed to make the leap. Well, not literally. I wasn't going to leap onto my bike, but I had promised myself today would be the day I'd get back on it.

With the leaves turning and the sun trying to break through the clouds, it was a perfect fall day for a ride in the Cotswolds countryside. My shiny red bicycle was tuned up and ready to go, thanks to my friend Peter Davies who'd taken it to the bike shop in Bourton-on-the-Water. I had no excuse, except for the one I'd been using for nearly two years.

I hadn't been on my bike since Henry's accident in Atlanta, and I was still haunted by vivid images of his crumpled body on the side of the road. Though I hadn't seen the collision, I'd glimpsed the red Mercedes convertible as it sped past me and rounded the curve where Henry pedaled up ahead just out of sight. I'd heard the crash, thrown down my bike, and run up the hill, but it was too late. It was a sight I'd never forget—my husband of twenty years lying dead next to his mangled bicycle.

"Stop it," I muttered. "Get on the darned bike."

Dickens cocked his head and barked. "You can do it, Leta."

Even Christie chimed in with a sharp meow. "Oh, for goodness' sake, get on with it."

"I'm trying, I'm trying," I replied.

There were times when having talking animals could be a real pain, but today I needed the encouragement. Fortunately, if any of my neighbors overheard me, they'd think I was talking to myself, not to my animals. Heaven forbid that I get a reputation as the village crazy lady who thought her animals spoke to her. I'd managed my entire life to keep my strange talent hidden, and I had no intention of letting the cat out of the bag—or the dog, for that matter.

I shooed my four-legged cheerleaders into the garden and swung my leg over the bike. I put one foot on a pedal, pushed off with the other, and wobbled down my gravel drive. Turning left into the lane, I checked my mirror to be sure Dickens and Christie weren't behind me. I didn't need a Pied Piper scene to complicate the morning's challenge.

Up ahead, I glimpsed Martha and Dylan in the field. It took the donkeys a moment to realize it was me on a bike—instead of on foot with Dickens by my side. When I stopped by the fence, the sight of carrots did the trick. The two trotted over and soon I was rubbing donkey noses and laughing.

One mile down, only one more to go to reach The Olde Mill Inn, my goal for the day. "The hills are alive with the sound of music," I sang. Only there were no hills and it would be a stretch to call the sounds coming out of my mouth *singing*.

I felt confident and comfortable on my bike. Still, I was relieved to catch sight of the waterwheel as I pedaled through the gates. Perched on the River Elfe, the old wheel was part of the flour mill that had operated from the early 1900s to the 1950s. Now, it was the setting for the popular inn owned by my friends Libby and Gavin Taylor.

I propped my bike on its kickstand and wandered in. "Libby, Gavin," I called.

"In the kitchen," called Libby.

"In the conservatory," yelled Gavin.

I chose the kitchen. "Hey, I did it! I rode my bike today, and here I am."

"Oh, I'm so proud of you," exclaimed Libby. "I know it wasn't easy, but now that you've done it, you'll be riding everywhere."

"I hope you're right. No backsliding. I can wander so much farther on a bike than I can on foot. Well, a bit farther anyway. I think next time, I'll try riding to Sunshine Cottage to see Belle and Wendy—except I'll have to explain to Dickens why he's not going."

Belle and Wendy Davies, mother and daughter, lived together in the family cottage now that Wendy had retired from teaching English in the States. Dickens and I visited often to see the ladies and their cat Tigger.

Libby laughed. "Dickens is quite the social butterfly, isn't he? Do you think he understands what's in store for him this weekend?"

I couldn't explain to Libby that of course, he did. He was beyond excited about accompanying me to the inn for the Astonbury Fall Fête, where there'd be people galore and plenty of children. My handsome white dog adored kids, and they couldn't get enough of him. A forty-pound dwarf Great Pyrenees, he was the perfect size for the munchkins. They loved to hug him and give him belly rubs and bury their faces in his soft fur. Come Saturday, he'd be in heaven.

"Hard to say," I said. "Now, I stopped by to see if you have anything last-minute I can help with. I'll be busy tonight with book club, but I'll be back tomorrow to help Beatrix set up her booth of used books, and I'll be here with bells on this weekend."

She shook her head. "Don't need a thing. Jill will be here all day Friday baking and helping to set up, and then on Saturday, she'll be a general dogsbody. I see her passing trays of pumpkin spice biscuits and scones and apple cider and handling whatever else needs doing. Jenny will be here Saturday too."

Jill and Jenny Walker were sisters. Though there was a year between them, they could have passed for twins with their light brown hair and hazel eyes. A godsend after Libby lost her last housekeeper, Jill was a great fit at the inn, and Jenny was a barista at Toby's Tearoom in the village. I'd hired them both for a party I'd thrown in September. "Those two are a delight," I said. "I only wish I could talk Jill into being my housekeeper too."

"Let her get her feet under her here, and she may take you on. Your cottage can't be much work except for the dog and cat hair, that is."

"Tell me about it," I groaned. "Okay, I'm headed home. See you tomorrow."

"You're back! How far did you go, Leta?" barked Dickens.

"Four miles round trip," I replied as I returned my bicycle to the garage. "Not far, but now I know I can do it. Maybe

Peter and I can go for a longer ride when he's up to it. A leisurely ten miles would be nice."

My friend Peter had broken his collarbone in a bicycle accident, and I knew he was eager to get back out. He kept threatening to ditch the sling the doctors told him to wear for four to eight weeks, but I and his twin sister Wendy were after him to stay the course.

"Good job," barked my boy.

When I unlocked the kitchen door, Christie strolled in behind me. "Pfft, only four miles? Back in Atlanta, you and Henry always rode at least fifteen. Tsk, tsk, such a slacker."

"That's rich coming from a girl who sleeps eighteen hours a day," barked Dickens. "Leta and I walk every day while you're stretched out napping. Slacker, indeed!"

I joined in the ribbing. "Gee, Dickens, do you think it's only black cats who sleep all the time?"

"Enough you two," huffed Christie. "Joke all you like, but I'm the trimmest four-legged member of the family. I'm speaking to you, Dickens. Now, it's time for someone to feed me."

Well, she was right about being a sleek beautiful feline. And Dickens's habit of scarfing her wet food wasn't helping with his tendency to be on the plump side. I kept her dry food dispenser in the pantry where only she could get to it, but when she turned her back on her dabs of wet food, Dickens gobbled them up in a flash.

I served Christie a forkful of food and kept an eye on Dickens when the princess turned her back. "Uh-uh," I admonished him when he made a move toward the dish. I fluffed the food and nudged the dish back to Christie. After several minutes of that routine, she cleaned her dish, much to Dickens's dismay. The things we do for our pets.

I fixed a cup of tea and called Wendy. "Guess what? I rode my bike today."

"Way to go," she replied. "You were beginning to sound like The Little Engine That Could with your constant refrain of 'I think I can, I think I can.' Henry's probably saying 'that's my girl.'"

"More like 'it's about time,' but I know he'd be happy I'm back at it. Now, about tonight. Are you still picking me up for book club?"

"Yes, I can't wait to see the gang. I'll honk the horn."

Book club had become one of my favorite pastimes since my move to Astonbury. Though I'd long been a bookworm, I'd traveled too much in my banking job in the States to commit to monthly meetings.

Beatrix Scott, owner of the Book Nook, kicked off the meeting promptly and introduced Rhiannon Smith to lead the discussion of our October book. Rhiannon had selected *Wicked Autumn* by G. M. Malliet as a seasonally appropriate choice. "What's not to love about a book that has a handsome vicar as the main character?" she asked.

Our lithe blonde yoga instructor gave us a bit of background on the author, and then we launched into a discussion of the similarities and differences between the fictional village of Nether Monkslip and our beloved village of Astonbury.

"Well, I for one would love it if we had a vicar like Max Tudor—a gorgeous, *single* vicar," said Wendy. "Though I'd like him to be a bit older so he'd be the right age for a few of the good-looking single women I know."

Rhiannon and I both laughed at that. "Hmmm," I said,

"Perhaps age 50 – 70? Would that do? I'm assuming you're counting Rhiannon, Beatrix, yourself, and me in that group, right?"

Gavin piped up. "Hey, if he were younger, he might suit Gemma. Doesn't my daughter get a vote?"

"Only if she comes to book club," said Beatrix.

We all knew that was unlikely given Gemma Taylor was a Detective Sergeant at the Stow-on-the-Wold police station. No way her schedule lent itself to making a monthly meeting.

We turned to a discussion of the Fayre held in Nether Monkslip and concluded our Astonbury Fall Fête would be more festive. Libby had asked several of us to come in costume, and we were counting on being a hit with the villagers and tourists. Since the goal of the Fête was to raise money for Breast Cancer Now, she'd come up with the idea to charge guests to take photos with us.

Wendy had organized a group of Peter Pan characters with herself as the lead. I always described her as petite and elfin, so she was perfect for the part, though I don't recall Peter Pan having spikey platinum hair.

I'd be dressed as Dorothy from *The Wizard of Oz* with Dickens as Toto, Libby as the Evil Witch, and other friends as the Tin Man and the rest of the cast. Thankfully, there was no mention of playacting, just good dress-up fun.

Gavin shook his finger at us. "Just be sure the Evil Witch doesn't wind up crushed beneath a house. Nether Monkslip may have had a dead body at their Fayre, but we'll have none of that."

A hush fell over the room when he uttered those words, and it took Gavin a moment to realize what he'd done. Given I'd stumbled across a dead body only a few weeks ago, his comment hit a bit too close to home.

He hung his head and stuttered. "Crikey, I'm sorry, I didn't think . . . I didn't mean—"

Beatrix stepped in. "Don't worry, Gavin. We know you didn't mean anything by it. A month ago, we'd have thought nothing of it."

"Right," said Rhiannon. "What we want is good weather, good fun, and lots of money for Breast Cancer Now. And an attractive single vicar showing up in Astonbury would be a bonus!"

The group broke up after that. I gave Gavin a hug and told him not to worry about his faux pas, and Wendy gave him a peck on the cheek. I was picking up teacups and wine glasses when Beatrix's niece approached me.

Trixie had only recently moved in with her aunt, and this was her first time at book club. The two had the same fair coloring and strawberry blonde hair, and I imagined a younger, slimmer Beatrix would have been the spitting image of her niece. "Leta, Aunt Beatrix told me about you finding the body. That must have been awful. Are you doing okay now?"

"Thanks for asking, Trixie. I'm fine. I think we all shudder when we think about it, but life goes on. By the way, I know Beatrix is happy to have you here. Are you settling in?"

"Yes, you know my mum named me for Aunt Beatrix, and we've always been close. It was only when I went to Totnes and married that we grew apart. Glad to say that chapter of my life is closing. I'm looking forward to working in the bookshop and starting fresh."

"Working in a bookshop sounds like heaven to me, but I'm afraid I'd spend every dime I have on books. I'm sure your aunt has told you I almost singlehandedly keep her in business —along with Wendy, that is."

"Ha! That she has. Well, I'll be holding down the fort here

tomorrow while Aunt Beatrix sets up her booth of used books at the inn, but I hope to see you Saturday for the big event. Bye now."

Wendy hustled me out the door. "Good grief, I can't believe Gavin said that about a dead body. I know he didn't mean to be insensitive, but still."

"This too shall pass," I said. "We managed to enjoy reading a book with a body in it, and eventually we may be able to watch murder mysteries on TV again. I doubt we'll ever joke about finding dead bodies, but we'll get through this."

I was up bright and early the next day to make the morning yoga class. I followed my routine of pouring a tiny puddle of milk for Christie, tossing Dickens a treat as he ran to the garden, and brewing coffee.

For once, Christie seemed satisfied with the appearance of her milk and quickly lapped it up. "You're moving awfully fast today, Leta. What's up?"

"I need to take your brother for a quick walk, get to yoga, and then over to the inn. No time to dilly-dally."

Dickens wandered in from the garden in time to hear the word walk. "Did you say walk? I'm ready."

He was disappointed we didn't make it as far as the donkeys, but he got over it when I explained I'd be taking him to the inn after yoga. In the kitchen, I grabbed a protein bar and my yoga mat and was off.

The yoga studio was located in a building that had been a

school in the early 1900s and had served over one hundred students in its heyday. Fifty years ago, when a larger school had been built in Cheltenham, this one had been broken up into flats and businesses.

Rhiannon had an end unit. When you entered the building, a door to the right opened to her flat, and a staircase directly ahead led to the second-floor studio. Rhiannon chose to make her home on the lower level so she could access the small rear garden from her kitchen. The large sitting room which fronted High Street contained a fireplace as well as wall carvings and niches left from the original structure.

I greeted the other students who were laying out their mats and gathering blocks and blankets for class. Every session was different, and I never knew which part of my body would ache the most when class ended. Those who thought of yoga as little more than stretching had no idea how intense a good class could be.

"Lordy, I'm going to be sore after this class, Rhiannon," I said. "I'm already feeling it . . . in a good way, of course."

Rhiannon chuckled. She offered an array of classes at her Let It Be yoga studio, and this early class was tougher than the one I usually attended. "Are you ready for a scone and a cup of tea or your usual coffee? One of these days, we'll get you hooked on tea."

"Yes, I am," I responded. "I like a cup of tea in the afternoon, but it's coffee all the way until lunch. I'll walk with you to grab a cup, but I've got to get a move on." Together, we walked to Toby's Tearoom further up on High Street, and Rhiannon found a seat as I ordered. In a reversal of Rhiannon's floor plan, Toby had his residence above the tearoom.

This morning, Toby was behind the counter while Jenny was busy baking. The shop was quiet, and he had time to chat. "You ladies look like you could use a cuppa—especially you, Leta," he said. "Did Rhiannon work you hard?"

"Yes," I groaned. "But I know I needed it. Make mine a large to-go cup, please. I'll need the caffeine boost to help Beatrix set up her booth."

"Sure thing. By the way, my scarecrow costume's ready to go. Jenny brought her glue gun and pinking shears to work yesterday and between customers, she added the finishing touches. She said I needed all the help I could get."

"You're cracking me up, Toby. Of course, you needed help, and who better than young Jenny, only a few years out of school? She and Jill have probably been pulling together costumes for years. Can't wait to see her handiwork. Oh! I almost forgot. I need to send an email reminding everyone to wear long underwear under their costumes. October can be pretty chilly."

I grabbed my cup, waved goodbye, and hurried to my car. I made a quick stop by the farmer's market for some pumpkins for my front walk and made it home in no time. Dickens yelped in excitement as I opened the door to my black London taxi and fastened him into his harness. I'd loved my red SUV in Atlanta but had grown quite attached to my new ride. Thank goodness Peter had alerted me to the fact that I could purchase a refurbished cab.

Beatrix was unloading boxes of books when I pulled up to the inn, and other vendors and volunteers were setting up booths in a large semicircle under Gavin's watchful eye. The annual Fête was one of his favorite events.

Dickens bounded out of the car and went in search of his pal Paddington, the Burmese cat who reigned supreme at the inn. I stood back and admired the colorful booths, some with flags flying from their tops, others with cobwebs and black cats decorating their awnings.

Phil Porter and Barb Peters, who worked at the Ploughman Pub, were planting the scarecrow garden in a circle around the tall rowan tree in the center of the courtyard. Its bright yellow leaves provided a picturesque backdrop for the colorful scarecrows, and a miniature white picket fence would be the finishing touch. The scarecrow creators had each paid a fee to enter the Scarecrow Contest to be judged by Gavin and Toby. The prize? Dinner for two at the Ploughman.

Barb waved me over. "Leta, what do you think? Can you believe the variety we have?"

"I think the selection is amazing. How will Gavin and Toby ever decide the winner?"

Barb laughed. "I wonder the same thing. Glad all I have to do is help stand 'em up."

Phil was staring at the sign he was about to attach to the fence. "Crikey," he said, "I think I misspelled the word *sponsored*. When am I going to find time to fix that?"

Sure enough, the sign read "*Sponsered* by the Ploughman."

Barb chuckled. "Tell you what. If you'll give me an hour off tomorrow afternoon, I'll paint a new sign and bring it over in the morning."

Further back, Summer and Sparkle were setting up their fairy hair booth next to Beatrix. I'd found Summer in nearby Cheltenham but hadn't met her business partner before. According to Summer, Sparkle lived in Totnes, and the two met up for festivals. They were walking advertisements for their trade. Summer's blonde bob was woven through with sparkly pumpkin and bronze silk threads, and she reminded me of an autumn elf in her olive green suede jacket and jeans. Sparkle had gone with a vamp look with her sleek shoulder-length ebony hair sporting purple threads. Black leggings and a long, belted V-neck black sweater completed the outfit. She resembled a voluptuous witch.

I planned to get fairy hair the next day. I'd discovered the fun look in the States on a visit to Black Mountain in North Carolina and loved the effect, though Henry'd said he felt like he was married to a hippie. He'd always been a tad more conservative than I was.

I waved at Beatrix. "Shall I grab more boxes or set up your tables?"

"I'm almost done with the unloading, so if you can set up the tables and start arranging the books by genre, that would be great. I've got a sign and some spooky decorations too."

"Okay. Do you have plenty of Halloween and autumn themed books? They're sure to be a hit."

"Oh yes, I made a special trip to the Manchester flea market to stock up. And I snagged three copies of Agatha Christie's *Hallowe'en Party* with Hercule Poirot. I don't care that the critics said it wasn't one of her best. Anything by Dame Agatha is good by me."

I chuckled. "Well, I know a black cat who would agree with that. Halloween is Christie's season, you know."

"And," added Beatrix, "I have Mary Shelley's *Frankenstein*, Shirley Jackson's *The Haunting of Hill House*, and Bram Stoker's *Dracula*. Oh, you'll love this! Have you read any of the laugh-out-loud reviews of *Dracula*? The ones written by young adults who grew up with the *Twilight* series? They complain that the book is boring and written in flowery language that's difficult to understand. They have no idea Count Dracula was the beginning of vampire fiction. Imagine!"

"That's hilarious. I never taught *Dracula*, but I did assign *Frankenstein* to my tenth graders, and they loved it. Of course, I only taught a few years, and that was over thirty years ago. Who knows what they'd think today? We'll have to ask Wendy, since she just retired from teaching last year."

I spread black and orange cloths on the tables and went to work arranging books, but I was hard-pressed to accomplish much because I kept stopping to thumb through the merchandise.

Summer saw me and came over to chat. "Hey there, I'm looking forward to doing your hair tomorrow. Are you going with pumpkin?"

"Oh no, that's not my color at all, but those pumpkin and bronze strands look smashing in your hair. Perfect for this time of year. My favorite color is red, so I think I'll go for silver with a few red strands. Might as well highlight the natural silver that's beginning to appear in my brunette locks. If I'm lucky, I'll sparkle all the way to Christmas."

Out of the corner of my eye, I caught Sparkle gesturing to Summer. "Look who's here. It's Max."

Sparkle was grinning. "Max? I didn't know you'd be here. Thought you were working at the magic shop this weekend."

The young man dressed in black jeans, a black tee-shirt, and a black leather jacket was the spitting image of Johnny Depp with his dark good looks and slim build, but it was more the actor's bad boy look than it was his role as the lover in *Chocolat* or the charming playwright in *Neverland*.

He looked surprised to see Sparkle. "Didn't expect to see you either. Didn't you tell me you were booked in Burford?"

"That's next weekend. Leave it to you get it confused."

"Just caught me off guard. I'm a last-minute fill-in for the local guy who broke his wrist. Can't do magic tricks with your wrist in a cast. They needed a magician, and here I am. My caravan's parked in Bourton-on-the Water. Where are you staying?"

"I'll be at Summer's place in Cheltenham."

"Well, want to have dinner tonight in Bourton?"

Sparkle looked at Summer. "We don't have plans, do we?"

"Nope, you go on. You know me. I like to have an early night before these all-day events," replied Summer.

I lost track of their conversation and continued sorting books. When Beatrix walked up with the last load, she was huffing and puffing. "Phew, I forget how hard it is to haul books, but I'm done now."

"What do you think of the booth? I think we need a few miniature pumpkins for the table, don't you?" I asked.

"I've a box of those around here somewhere," she said before glancing over at the Fairy Hair booth. "Is that who I think it is?"

"If you mean Summer and Sparkle, yes. Have you met them before?"

"No, I mean that sleazy-looking guy in black. Only met him once, but if I'm not mistaken, that's Trixie's lout of a husband, all the way from Totnes. What's he doing here?"

I turned to look at him again. "He's not my type—I prefer the Sean Connery and Tom Selleck look—but I wouldn't describe him as sleazy. Do you think Trixie knows he's here?"

Beatrix thought for a moment. "I don't think so, but I'll be sure to ask her before I send her over tomorrow. That's all she needs—an encounter with her worthless soon-to-be ex. Though it'd be an opportunity to press him again to sign the divorce papers, something he's been putting off for months."

"Is he just irresponsible or is there some reason he doesn't want to sign?"

"Who knows? If he doesn't sign by the end of the month, she'll either have to endure two years of separation to be rid of him or refile on grounds of unreasonable behavior and do it soon. I'm sure he's been verbally abusive, possibly even physically, either one of which fits the bill.

"She just wants out. I'm happy to have her at my place, but she wants to be on her own to start a new life. She doesn't want to be tangled up with him for two more years."

I was processing this whole divorce thing. "Wow, sounds way more complex than it is in the States."

Dickens ran up with Paddington close behind. "Leta, we're having great fun. Jill let us play in the pile of dirty linens and now we're going to see the scarecrows."

Paddington took off, meowing, "Bet I can climb to the top of one before you can."

Uh-oh, it was time to keep an eye on those two. The scarecrow garden wouldn't last long if Paddington treated the crops as cat trees. I ran after them, yelling "Come back here, you two!"

I got to the garden in time to peel Paddington from the librarian scarecrow before the frisky feline could knock the poor lady's glasses off. I was laughing at his antics when I saw Max walk up to Barb.

"Don't I know you?" he asked. "Barb? What are you doing here?"

Barb seemed taken aback. "I could ask you the same thing. I *live* in Astonbury. What are you doing here—all the way from Totnes?"

He was explaining how he'd come to be in Astonbury for the weekend when I heard someone call my name.

George Evans needed help with a tent pole, and I ran over to lend a hand. "Phew," he said. "The whole thing almost came down. Can you take a minute to look over my new brochures and tell me what you think? I'm hoping some of the tourists will sign up for driving tours. It's the perfect time of the year, and since I'm short a bicycle guide at the moment, I need to beef up the driving side."

"Sure, George. You know Henry and I enjoyed your tour and told all our friends to look you up if they ever made it to the Cotswolds. Didn't my sister Sophia hire you when she visited?"

"Oh yes, she did, she and her husband Jeremy. Even though he's a Brit, I think he learned lots he didn't know about the area. They seemed especially taken with Stow-on-the-Wold and St. Edwards Church. Apparently, your sister is a Tolkien fan."

That made sense. Ever since Sophia read *The Hobbit* as a child, she'd been enamored of Tolkien. I remembered now that I'd told her about the church and its fairytale back door flanked by two yew trees, a sight thought to have inspired Tolkien's design for the entrance to Moria. That would have been right up her alley.

I looked at George's flyers and suggested he put some in Beatrix's booth and in the sitting room in the inn.

George nodded. "I'll do that. I didn't print all that many because I may have to change up part of the tour, and that would mean revising the brochures. Remember, you and Henry toured Astonbury Manor?"

"Oh yes, it was an amazing place. As I recall, it's only open to the public part of the year, right?"

"Yes, and now that the Earl has passed away, no one knows for sure what the situation will be. Rumor has it some American offspring may have inherited."

That sounded like a juicy bit of local gossip. With the estate located just across the river from the inn, I figured Libby and Gavin would know what was going on. Plus they were friends with Lady Stow and the late Earl, so I suggested to George that he ask them what they knew.

Regardless, speaking with George made me think my editors in the States might be interested in a column about George and his tours. That thought reminded me I needed to edit next week's column and start a new one, so I grabbed a flyer and called Dickens.

He barked as he ran up. "We don't have to go home, do we? I haven't visited the river yet, and there's way more to see."

I rubbed his head and scratched his ears. "Sorry, boy, no way I'm letting you get wet and dirty today when you have a starring role at the Fête tomorrow. Let's go."

Judging from the plaintive meowing that greeted us before I could unlock my cottage door, Christie wanted lunch. "For goodness' sake, where have you been? I'm starving."

"What? You couldn't eat the dry food I left you?" I responded as I obediently gave her a dab of wet food.

She licked it up and ran into my office as though she knew I needed to get to work. After a salad for lunch, Dickens and I joined her. He wriggled into position beneath the desk where I could rub his belly with my feet, and after knocking a few unnecessary items off the desktop, Christie curled up in the file drawer. All was right in the world.

I'm a "work before play" kind of girl, so first I edited my "Parker's Pen" column for the following week and sent it off to the two papers I wrote for in the States. Then I started one about the Astonbury Fête. I'd add more detail to it on Sunday after the festivities were over. When I'd had a demanding corporate job, my columns had been a welcome break from the more serious writing I did for work. Even though I'd retired, I couldn't imagine life without writing and was pleased to find my readers had taken to my dispatches from England.

With work done, I emailed my sisters Anna and Sophia. I knew Sophia would get a kick out of George remembering her and Anna would laugh at the story about the *Dracula* reviews. Anna was a *Twilight* fan, but that didn't stop her from appreciating good literature. They'd both get a kick out of Paddington climbing the librarian scarecrow. With five cats of her own, Anna would especially enjoy that tale.

Time for an afternoon cup of tea and a few games of Words with Friends. I was addicted to the online word game and played regularly. I saw that my 95-year-old opponent from North Carolina had played her turn on the five games we had going. I'd never met Martha, but when she read in one of my columns that I liked WWF, she contacted me to see if we could play. She was one sharp gal, and we were pretty evenly matched.

I added a log to the fireplace in the sitting room and pulled out my new book. Beatrix had discovered I'd never read Agatha Christie's Tommy & Tuppence mysteries, and she'd pointed out *The Secret Adversary*, the first book in the series. The story began just after WWI, and I was eager to get into it.

The phone rang before I could get beyond the title page. It was my friend Dave Prentiss calling from New York City. We'd met and gone out a few times when he stayed at the inn in September. We were both avid readers and enjoyed writing, so we had lots in common. "Hi there," he said. "Are you ready for your starring role as Dorothy?"

"You bet. My red shoes are polished and my pinafore is starched. How's your Peter Pan article coming along?"

"I've been putting the finishing touches on it this week. I'll send you the link to it as soon as it goes online."

"You know I can't wait to read it. What's next? Your article on Arthur Conan Doyle?"

"Yes, my editor at the *Strand* wants to run it in the December issue, so I need to immerse myself in my notes and start pulling it together. Speaking of December, do you still plan to spend Christmas in England?" Dave asked.

"That's what I want, but my sisters have stepped up their campaign to get me to Atlanta. I'm torn. I'd like to see them, but I'm eager to start my own Christmas traditions here in Astonbury. Chances are I'll see Sophia and her husband Jeremy in the new year when they visit London, so it's just Anna and her husband Andrew I'd miss."

"Well, keep me posted. If you come to the States, maybe you could plan a detour to New York City—you know there's nothing like the city at Christmas. We could go ice skating at Rockefeller Center, take in the Rockettes, see all the department store windows . . ."

A visit to New York for the holiday season sounded delightful. "Ooh, that's awfully tempting. I'll keep that idea in mind, and I'll let you know soon."

"Okay. Time to get back to work. Say hi to the gang and give Dickens and Christie each a belly rub from me. Bye now."

I thought about my holiday dilemma, my sisters, and Dave as I made another cup of tea and returned to the couch. I was attracted to Dave, but I wasn't ready for a serious relationship. I looked at Dickens. "I still tear up over Henry. How can I even consider a relationship with another man?"

Dickens cocked his head and studied me. The question seemed to stump him.

Christie, on the other hand, was ready with an opinion. "Seems to me you have the perfect setup with Dave. Since he lives across the pond, as they say, what's the harm in seeing him every few months?"

She was probably right. Who knew a cat could be a relationship expert? I sighed and opened my book. Nothing like reading to clear my mind, but it was not to be. When the phone rang again, Christie jumped from my lap in a huff. Clearly, she'd had it with the interruptions.

I'd barely said hello before Beatrix declared, "I knew he'd be trouble."

"Huh?"

"That worthless Max Maxwell. Whatever were his parents thinking when they named him Max? If that's even his real name. Never mind. When I told Trixie he was in town, she wasn't happy. Then she bucked up and said it would give her a chance to ask him about signing the divorce papers one more time without making a trip to Totnes."

"Uh-huh, so when's she going to do that?"

"Her first thought was to go straight to the caravan and have it out with him, but I convinced her it wasn't a good idea to be alone with him. Then she decided she'd leave a note on his door telling him she'd meet him at the Fête tomorrow. That way she can read him the riot act in kind of a public place. Just what we need, right? A scene at the Fall Fête?"

I tried to respond, but Beatrix didn't take a breath.

"So, here's the plan. When Trixie comes to relieve me

tomorrow, I'll motion you over to the booth. Then, can you go with her to get Max's attention and take him off to the side for a conversation? She'll be safe out in public, and I know you'll keep them civil."

I was almost speechless, but not quite. "What? Why me? Why not you?"

"Oh, come now, I'm hardly a neutral party, so he's more likely to get on his high horse if it's me. You're so good at calmly speaking with people and getting them to be calm in turn. Don't forget you told me all about that conflict resolution work you did in your corporate days. I know you're the best person for the job."

"Whoa, wait a minute, Beatrix. I've never mediated a domestic dispute, for goodness' sake. Getting two professionals to work something out is an entirely different ball of wax."

Beatrix bulldozed right over my rationale. "Doesn't matter. I need you to do this for me. Please."

There was no convincing her otherwise, and I asked myself for the umpteenth time whether I would ever learn to say no to my friends. Instead of a fun-filled day dressed as Dorothy, greeting visitors, and laughing with my friends, I had this drama to look forward to.

Chapter Two

Saturday dawned crisp and cool, a day made for a fall fête, and I could almost forget what lay ahead with Trixie and Max. I couldn't help grumbling as I ushered Dickens into the car.

Dickens was puzzled at my sour mood. "What's up with you?"

"People! Why can't they be more like dogs?"

He cocked his head. "You're not serious, are you? I like people, especially you."

I looked down at my blue-checked dress and white pinafore and sighed. "Never mind. We're going to have a super day. What do you think about my outfit? Do I look like a young girl?"

"Sure you do, Leta," said my ever-faithful dog.

"Ha! Maybe not, but I *feel* young. Do you feel like Toto?"

"Can we talk about this Toto thing? I'm not brown, and I'm certainly not tiny. I'm much bigger . . . and much more handsome."

Dickens had a thing about being called small, maybe

because as a *dwarf* Great Pyrenees he was so much smaller than full-sized Pyrs. I tried to cajole him. "It's all about your *big* personality. You know everybody's gonna love you, and with your scarf that says Toto, they'll know exactly who you are."

He was pretty much always chipper, and he was easily distracted, so by the time we pulled up to the inn, he was chomping at the bit. "Ooh, I see Wendy and Peter, and I just glimpsed Paddington running under a table in the face painting booth. Hurry!"

As he scampered off, I looked for my Wizard of Oz cohorts. Our plan was to position ourselves next to the Scarecrow Garden. The garden had blossomed since I'd seen it yesterday. Today there were nearly thirty scarecrows with pumpkins scattered among them. There was even a Humpty Dumpty scarecrow sitting on a bale of hay.

Barb was positioning the correctly spelled sign against the white picket fence. Today, the tall, athletic blonde was dressed in a crisp black skirt and a white top, ready for her long day at the pub. "Phew," she said. "That should do it."

As she waved at me and walked toward the parking lot, I saw Max the Magician try to intercept her. She made a rude gesture with her hand, and he smirked and said something I couldn't quite catch. *Odd*, I thought, as I turned back toward the Scarecrow Garden.

I heard Gavin before I saw him. He wore a silver vest and gallon paint cans up and down his legs and arms. With his face painted silver and a tin funnel on his head, he was somewhat recognizable as a Tin Man—maybe one crossed with the Michelin man.

He clanked toward me, followed by Toby as the Scarecrow and Peter as the Cowardly Lion. Rhiannon's Glinda the Good Witch costume sparkled in the sunlight as she exited the inn arm in arm with the Wicked Witch of the West. With her green face paint and big fake nose, Libby was almost unrecognizable. What gave her away were the salt and pepper curls peeking out from beneath the black hat.

I clapped as the group came together. "If there were a costume contest, I'm sure we'd win. Too bad Dickens doesn't look much like Toto, but he'll just have to do."

I never ceased to be amazed at how well Dickens could hear. He came dashing toward us from the garden, barking. "Hey, what do you mean I'll 'just have to do?' I'm made for this part."

"Well, you've certainly changed your tune, young man," I said.

I'm sure my friends wondered what I was talking about, but they didn't ask. Everyone was too busy taking in the sights and sounds of the Fête and greeting friends.

"Look, Leta, your neighbors are here—Deborah and John Watson and their son Timmy. Let's see if Timmy wants his picture made with us," said Gavin.

Wendy had recruited Timmy to play Michael Darling with her Peter Pan crew. Dressed in footy pajamas, he threw his arms around Dickens as Deborah and John greeted us.

"No dental emergencies today, John?" I asked.

"Hush, don't jinx me," said our village dentist. "Getting out of this Captain Hook outfit to repair a tooth wouldn't be easy. I'm keeping my fingers crossed." He dropped a pound in my straw basket while Deborah took a picture of Timmy posed with the gang.

John pointed out the Peter Pan team across the courtyard and moved that way. His sword clanked as he walked, and he periodically removed his pirate hat and waved at the crowd.

Deborah tagged along as the official family photographer for the day.

I spotted Belle getting her face painted. Belle was all about fun and had volunteered to sell tickets for cornhole. It was set up on one side of the apple-bobbing bucket, and the Peter Pan team was stationed on the other side. "Oh my gosh, Peter. Your sister's costume is perfect. Did Belle make it?" I asked as I caught a glimpse of Wendy.

"Of course," said Peter. "Just like she fashioned this lion suit for me. She had the darnedest time making my tail."

Next to Wendy, a.k.a Peter Pan, stood Gemma in a blue empire waist dress, the spitting image of Wendy Darling with her blonde hair down on her shoulders. When Captain Hook and Michael Darling joined them, the ensemble was complete. Kids and parents started lining up to have their photos taken, and there was a line forming in front of the Wizard of Oz cast too.

When there was a momentary lull, I asked Peter to take a pic of me with Dickens, so I could send it to my friend Bev in Atlanta. She'd kept both Dickens and Christie while I was househunting in the Cotswolds, and she and Dickens had formed a special bond.

I told the gang I'd be back in a bit and went to see Beatrix. "How's it going? Selling lots of books?"

She beamed. "Yes. It always cheers me up to see kids picking up books and asking their parents to buy them. I've even sold some classics to a few teenagers."

I looked over at the Fairy Hair booth but saw only Summer. "Are the girls taking shifts today?"

"I don't know. Max the Magnificent, as he bills himself, was over here trying to chat with Sparkle as I was hanging my sign, but I haven't seen her in a bit."

"Ugh. Well, what time will Trixie get here? I want to be on the lookout."

Beatrix looked at her watch. "Not until 1 pm, so you've got some time yet."

I glanced back at the Oz group and saw there was still no line, so I stopped by the cornhole setup to see Belle. "Oh, look at you. Is that Tinker Bell on your cheek?"

"Yes. Since I'm named for that mischievous fairy, I think it's only appropriate. A bit of sparkle on my cheek is as close as I can come to dressing the part."

"Shoot, Belle, maybe we should get you some fairy hair too. Wouldn't pale blue look good in your white hair? I'll see if Summer and Sparkle can fit you in today."

Belle may have been near ninety, but she never missed an opportunity to try something new. She grinned and agreed, and I went to confirm my appointment and get one for her too.

Summer, dressed in a purple bell-sleeved top with the phrase Fairy Hair embroidered on the pocket, was working on a little red-haired girl so I approached Sparkle. She was wearing a Fête sweatshirt over her brightly colored skirt. I would have thought she and Summer would be dressed in matching blouses. Perhaps she was chilly, but as I drew closer, I could see it was more than that. Her hair was wet, and her face was flushed.

"Are you okay?" I asked.

She acted as though she hadn't heard me and busied herself sorting the colorful silk threads on the table. I took the hint and shifted to talk of appointments for me and Belle and how the booth was doing.

She perked up. "We're doing well. Both Summer and I have been booked back to back. I mean, it only takes about fifteen minutes for ten strands, but lots of the young girls have wanted twenty. They're all into either pumpkin and gold for the season or the rainbow look."

"Sounds like a good day, then, and it's early yet. The crowds will probably pick up as more folks arrive from farther away. We've got mostly locals right now." I saw a crowd forming near Dickens, who for some reason had decided to bob for apples, so I scurried off, promising to return later.

"What's going on over there?" I called.

I heard a voice from the crowd. "I've never seen a dog bob for apples before."

By this time, Dickens had his front paws and his head in the bucket with his hind legs dangling above the ground. He popped back up and barked. "Leta, look at the balls. Can I have one?"

I laughed at my dripping wet dog. Fortunately, only the front of his body was soaked. "Dickens, those aren't balls, you silly boy. They're apples."

"Yup, I tried to tell him that," said the teenager in charge, "But he's a determined little thing. Guess I'll have to rinse out the bucket and start fresh."

The crowd chuckled as I led him away. Somehow Jill had anticipated the problem and came running up with a towel. "How'd you know I'd need this?" I asked.

Jill grinned. "Well, Dickens isn't the first visitor to get soaked today. A few of the smaller kids lost their balance and all but fell in before their parents grabbed them. And Sparkle must've tipped in too. I handed her a towel when I spotted her off to the side dripping.

"Look for the kids in Fête sweatshirts. They're the ones who got soaked. The sweatshirt business is booming, and I think next year we should sell towels too."

28

That explained why Sparkle was wearing a sweatshirt. "Why didn't she just tell me that?" I mumbled to myself. Strange to be secretive about it.

I did my best to dry off Toto so he'd look good for the photos. The problem was he had such thick hair, my task was almost impossible.

The Cowardly Lion waved us over and tried to look stern, but he couldn't quite pull it off. "We're gonna dock your pay if you wander off again. Look at the line of fans waiting for photos."

Dickens barked and I joked, "Hey, you in the lion pajamas, where were you when Toto decided to bob for red balls? Someone had to rescue him."

The photos resumed, and my basket was getting heavy with donations. Though we were only charging a pound per photo, plenty of visitors were dropping in more. It was going to be a good haul. The crowd began shifting to the food booths around lunchtime, about when Trixie showed up to spell Beatrix.

She approached me hesitantly. "Thank goodness you're willing to stand by me. Max sometimes goes off without warning."

"What do you mean 'goes off'?" I asked.

"He has a bit of a temper. That's one reason I filed for divorce."

"Trixie, you're not telling me he gets violent, are you?"

She hesitated. "Well, not exactly. He never hit me, just kinda grabbed me and pushed me."

It amazed me that she defined grabbing and shoving as not exactly violent. "Maybe we need to bring Gavin or Toby with us too," I said.

"No, no. That will make him think we're ganging up on

him. Yesterday, I left a note in the caravan saying I wanted to speak with him here by the waterwheel, so he's expecting me. Look, he just waved."

I saw Max performing in his spot near the apple-bobbing bucket. I had to admit he looked dashing in his tux jacket, his red scarf, and his top hat. He'd just pulled flowers out of the hat with a flourish, and the crowd of children was clapping. He moved to a little girl and pulled a coin from behind her ear, making her giggle.

When Trixie, Dickens, and I walked that way, he gave a deep bow and snapped his magic wand. A small flag with the words "Back in a Magic Minute" unfurled from it, much to the disappointment of the children.

He made his way to the waterwheel, and we followed with Dickens at our heels. "Why did you suggest we talk by the river, Trixie?" I asked.

"I didn't want anyone to overhear us if Max created a scene. It's more private there but still in sight of the crowd."

Max opened his arms wide for a hug when we got there, but at the same time, he looked at me curiously. "What are you doing here, Dorothy?"

Maybe I was biased, but the question sounded snarky. "Oh, I'm a friend of Trixie's. Just want to be sure everything is okay."

"Why wouldn't it be? We're going to have a friendly chat, right, Trixie?" he asked.

Trixie avoided his arms. "Yes, but since it's about our divorce papers, I doubt it's a chat you're happy to have."

He smirked. "Not that again. What's your hurry about divorce? I'm thinking you'll miss me before long and come crawling back. And if you're really sweet about it, I might have you."

Dickens picked up on his tone and barked. "Hey, watch it."

I don't know what reaction Max expected, but what he got was indignation. "Come back? Are you kidding? Don't hold your breath. If I have to, I'll refile and charge you with unreasonable behavior. You know I can find someone who will attest to you sleeping around while we were still living together. All those weekends away? You think I didn't know?"

"Oh, come on. Those girls were just a bit on the side. Nothing serious."

Oh, for goodness' sake. He acted as though cheating on your wife was okay. Was that what he thought? It was time to move this conversation along. "Max, Trixie is giving you fair warning. No matter what you call it, adultery is adultery. I understand Trixie could charge you with that and be done with this. So, please, don't be unreasonable."

Probably not the calming influence Beatrix was thinking of when she asked me to get involved, but enough was enough. We could stand here listening to this jerk insult Trixie or we could get down to business.

Max had a wicked laugh. "Unreasonable, my arse. She walked out on me. That's unreasonable."

Good grief, verbally abusive and not the brightest bulb in the pack. "Come on, Trixie, he's not listening," I said.

Before I could usher Trixie back to the crowd, Max grabbed her arm and spun her around. "Listen here, you cow, I'm your husband. You don't walk away from me."

Trixie tried to jerk away, but Max tightened his grip. With her other hand, she hauled off and smacked him across the face.

Stunned, he let go. "You'll pay for that. You wait."

This time it was me who grabbed her. She was sobbing, and Dickens was growling.

When Beatrix caught sight of us, she came dashing out from the booth. "What now? Did he hurt you?"

Trixie gasped and sobbed. "Aunt Beatrix, I can't believe it. Max thinks I'll go back to him. He has no intention of signing the divorce papers."

Sparkle must have overheard Trixie. "Max? Divorce papers? You're . . . you're his ex-wife?"

"I wish it was *ex*. He *told* me he'd sign the papers, and I've been waiting nearly six months for him to do it. If he doesn't sign by the deadline, I'll have to wait even longer."

Sparkle looked shocked. "He told me he was already divorced, the filthy liar. As though I'd have anything to do with a married man."

"What?" yelped Trixie. "You know Max? How?"

It turned out Sparkle had known Max longer than Trixie had. She explained they'd been in school together in Totnes, and they'd only recently reconnected and started dating.

The girls were sharing their stories when Barb hurried up. "Hi ladies. I'm here for my appointment, and I don't have long. Got to get back to work."

Sparkle looked flustered. "Um, yes, you're Barb, right? If you'll have a seat and look at the color options, I'll be right with you."

Barb seemed to pick up on the atmosphere. "Um, is there something going on? I'd say I'd come back later, but this is the only time I have off today."

"No, no," said Sparkle. "I can do your hair. Trixie and I've just had a bit of a shock."

As Barb unloosed her ponytail and chose the colors for her long blonde hair, Sparkle elaborated about Max. *What a mess,* I thought—*an estranged wife and an erstwhile girlfriend stumbling across each other at the Fête.*

That seemed like drama aplenty until Barb interjected, "Max? That plonker? You girls know him too?"

He sure gets around, I thought. I wondered how Barb knew him and then recalled the encounter I'd seen this morning. Sounded as though Max's ears would be burning all afternoon at this rate. Who knew? Maybe Trixie, Sparkle, and Barb would be comrades in arms before the day was done. I would have loved to have heard the rest of the story, but I had to get back to my group. Beatrix gave Trixie a hug and then accompanied me to the Scarecrow Garden.

In the distance, I saw Max entertaining the crowd. The children were bouncing up and down in glee as he pulled a chain of red scarves from his top hat. It was as though he'd thrown a switch and turned his charming side back on.

Gavin and Toby were discussing the entries for the contest, and I didn't envy them the job of deciding on the winner. The designs were creative and included a doctor, a nurse, a chef, a handyman, a constable, and Raggedy Ann and Andy in addition to the librarian and Humpty Dumpty. After the judging, they'd be auctioned off to raise even more money for Breast Cancer Now.

Beatrix, Libby, and I weighed in with our votes. "No matter who you chose as the winner, Gavin," said Libby, "we've got to have Raggedy Ann and Andy for the inn."

Beatrix looked longingly at the librarian with her wire-rimmed glasses and armful of books. "I wonder if there's a way I could prop her up in the bookshop?" she said.

"Well, if you don't bid on her, I might want her for my garden," I chimed in. "I have fond memories of all the librarians who recommended books to me when I was a child, and in Atlanta, I loved putting library books on hold online and getting the emails that said, 'come get me' when they came available."

We three continued our banter, and before Beatrix left, I reminded her we were all meeting at the Ploughman when the Fête was over. We suspected the pub patrons would stand us a few rounds of drinks when they got a load of our costumes. Dickens would have his pick of dog beds, and I was sure he'd be tuckered out by then. My boy was having a ball.

By the time the festivities ended and the crowd began to disperse, Dickens wasn't the only one worn out. Still, we all pitched in to help take down booths and pick up trash. Libby had labeled a box "Lost and Found," and we filled it with toys, stuffed animals, and even a scarf someone had dropped.

When Rhiannon and Wendy saw the fairy hair Belle and I were sporting, they wanted in on the act, so Sparkle and Summer stayed late to squeeze them in. Rhiannon chose silver and gold for her long wavy blonde locks, and Sparkle suggested rainbow strands for Wendy. Jill and Jenny got in on the act with pumpkin and shiny bronze.

It seemed Trixie and Sparkle had bonded over their woes with Max, so I invited them both to join us at the Ploughman, and Summer tagged along. Though we all could have walked the path to the pub, some of us piled into cars and drove. Cheers went up whenever one of us entered, and sure enough, rounds of drinks ensued.

When the whole gang was gathered around our table, we congratulated ourselves on the money we'd raised. Libby was debating where to put her Raggedy Ann and Andy scarecrows, and Beatrix was crowing over winning the librarian. She'd enlisted Toby via cell phone to ensure she had the winning bid. Sparkle, Summer, and Trixie were standing at the bar chatting with Barb, and Dickens was passed out on a dog bed in the corner.

When Max walked in the door sporting his black coat, cane, and top hat, Beatrix nudged me. I wondered which side of Max the Magnificent we'd see. He walked straight to the bar and pushed in between Sparkle and Trixie. We couldn't hear what he said, but it must have been offensive because Barb snarled at him and Phil the bartender reached across the bar and jerked him up by the collar.

Max backed away from the bar, turned, and bellowed, "You lot want to drink here with these losers, go ahead. I'm outta here."

The crowd of regulars was stunned into silence, and a few of the men got to their feet, but Max made his way to the door before anyone could get physical. We were a close-knit village, so he was wise to leave before someone took action. He was sure to come out on the losing end of an altercation.

Barb high-fived Phil and Sparkle and Trixie grinned and turned back to the bar. Before we turned to more pleasant topics, Beatrix brought our friends up to speed on the saga of Max, Trixie, and Sparkle. I provided details about him grabbing Trixie and threatening her at the waterwheel.

Gemma went into full-on Detective Sergeant mode. "Beatrix, if that git gives Trixie any trouble, you call me right away. Men like Max tend to escalate, and she could be in danger. She may want to consider a restraining order."

Funny, I'd been thinking the same thing since I'd witnessed his behavior with Trixie. Hopefully, he'd return to Totnes the next day and be out of our hair.

After another round of drinks and a hearty dinner, our

group began to break up. It wasn't easy to rouse Dickens, but he eventually stood up and stayed awake long enough for me to get him to the car.

We dropped Rhiannon and Wendy back by the inn to get their cars and were home in no time. On the way, I spied a lone cyclist pedaling toward the village but couldn't make out who it was in the dark.

I felt exhausted after being on my feet all day and slept like a log that night. Only, of course, after I fed my demanding black cat, and Dickens and I filled her in on the day's activities. When I fell into bed, Christie snuggled against my back and Dickens stretched out in his dog bed.

Sunday morning, I was pouring my second cup of coffee and humming "Somewhere Over the Rainbow" when my phone rang. I was surprised to see Gemma's name pop up on the screen.

She got straight to business. "You'd better get over here. Mum just found Max the Magnificent dead by the river."

"What?"

"I know. It's unbelievable. Mum brought me a basket of scones and fruit like she does most mornings. When she went 'round to my patio to pop in the back door to the kitchen, she glimpsed the body between my cottage and the waterwheel."

Gemma lived downriver from the mill in a small building the Taylors had turned into a guest cottage. This would make two dead bodies she'd dealt with in less than a month.

"You want me to take care of your mum, right?"

"To start with, yes. And then I'd like to know what you saw and heard yesterday at the Fête."

"Okay, I'm on my way."

Christie and Dickens looked at me expectantly. I knew they'd heard both sides of the conversation. "You're taking Dickens, aren't you? And leaving me behind again," complained Christie.

"First, it's damp and drizzly, not a good day for kitties to be outside. Second, you've never been beyond the garden, and we're not going to start today," I replied. I'd been considering getting a backpack for her to ride in so she could accompany me and Dickens on our walks, but that wasn't yet a fully formed idea.

"Leta, I got a bad vibe from that Max guy," barked Dickens. "I didn't hear Gemma say what happened to him, but I bet someone threw him in the river."

"I'm as eager as you are to find out what happened over there, and you're going with me, Detective Dickens. While I'm tending to Libby, you can sniff around for clues, and you can also check with Paddington to see what he knows. Christie, I'll try to take some pictures to show you when we get back, though I'll have to be sneaky about it. I doubt Gemma would approve."

Constable James blocked my way when I pulled up until he recognized me. "If it isn't Miss Marple again. I know, bad joke. Gemma told me she called you," he said. "And you've brought that little hero dog too."

"What's with these people?" huffed Dickens. "I'm not little, I'm not tiny, I'm just the right size."

I laughed at him despite the serious nature of our visit.

"Simmer down, boy. I could be just as offended at being called Miss Marple. Seriously, I don't look *that* old."

As I unlatched Dickens, I stood for a moment and took in the view of the colorful trees on the river. The beech trees were cloaked in russet-brown and the chestnut trees in a mix of orange and gold. I wanted to soak in the peaceful scene before it was marred by the presence of a dead body.

Dickens went off to find Paddington, and I found Libby in the sitting room in front of the fireplace, her hands wrapped around a mug of tea. She looked at me tearfully and told me Gavin was busy with the guests checking out after the weekend. Most had come for the Fête and were on their way back to London or Heathrow. "I can't believe I found a dead body," she moaned. "And you know exactly how I feel, don't you?"

"Unfortunately, I do. Thank goodness it's not someone you really knew, much less liked. Do you want to talk about it? Or has Gemma asked you enough questions for now?"

"Yesterday was such a success. We took in lots of money for Breast Cancer Now, and you could tell everyone had fun. I can't believe someone died, even it was that nasty Max person. Why did that have to happen?"

I nodded as she sipped her tea. I knew once she started, she wouldn't need much encouragement.

"I was doing what I do most mornings, taking a light meal to Gemma. On the days she hasn't already left for work, she likes a scone and fruit after her run. Other days, I put it all in the fridge so she can have it as a light dinner.

"I went in the kitchen door and put the basket on the counter. Left to walk back to the inn. That's when I caught a glimpse of red. There were apples in the shallow part of the river, if you can believe it, but when I moved closer, I saw it was more than that. Several apples in the river, several on the bank, and a man."

"Was he in the river?" I asked.

"No, he was on his back very close to the edge."

I was getting a bad feeling.

"Somehow I knew he was dead. Maybe it was his color. It was a ghastly sight. I don't know how long I stood there, frozen in place. Long enough to notice an apple core on the ground and one rosy red apple in his mouth.

"And, you won't believe the image that popped into my head? I may never again see a picture of a roast pig on a holiday table without thinking of what I saw this morning."

"Are you serious? An apple in his mouth?"

"Yes. Gruesome."

Gavin came in and stoked the fire. "Thanks for coming, Leta. Most of the guests have checked out now, and Jill's started on the rooms, so I can sit awhile."

I told Gavin I was going to find Gemma but would be back to relieve him. I knew he had a mile-long list of chores to accomplish before the next group of guests arrived and couldn't relax for long.

I called Dickens, and he came bounding down the stairs, followed by Paddington. We all trooped through the garden to the river. Gemma was greeting the Scene of Crime Officers who'd just arrived. Guess there was no doubt this was a suspicious death and she'd called them in right away.

She motioned me over. "Careful where you step, Leta, and watch Dickens. I saw his apple-bobbing attempts yesterday, and I don't want him anywhere near the river or the body."

Paddington took the hint and climbed a nearby tree, while I positioned Dickens by the waterwheel and told him to stay. As was common with Great Pyrenees dogs, he often had a mind of his own, but *stay* was a command he mostly obeyed. *Come?* Not so much.

I approached cautiously and studied the scene. "Do you ever get used to this, Gemma?"

"No, and word is if you do, you're not long for the job," she replied. "I'm just glad it's not someone I know. I saw him yesterday performing his magic tricks, and I witnessed the scene at the pub, but at least he's not a friend. You interacted with him more than I did, so I'd appreciate your perspective. Is he dressed the same? You know, details like that."

"Give me a minute. I'm having a hard time getting beyond the apple in his mouth. That's an image I won't soon forget." I swallowed. "Okay, down to business. Still has on the black coat with the tails. And he's still wearing his jaunty red scarf. I don't see his top hat. Didn't he have it on last night at the pub?"

"Yes, he did. And he had a cane too, didn't he?"

I studied the scene. "He did, but I don't see it. What's that bottle say? Highland Black? What's that?"

Gemma knelt down. "Ah, not a whiskey drinker, are you? It's a decent cheap whiskey. You can find it at Aldi. As close as the bottle is to the body, I'm betting Max carried it over here. Looks like he was drinking and eating apples from the river. They seem to have been caught by that branch near the bank, but how on earth did half a dozen apples get in the river in the first place?"

"Dickens may have been the cause of that," I said. "After he went apple bobbing, they had to start fresh. Probably emptied the dirty water and the apples into the river before refilling the bucket. Couldn't have folks bobbing in water Dickens had been diving in. Nor chance anyone chomping into an apple he'd played with," I said.

She glanced over at Dickens. "Always in the middle of

everything, your boy, but he's being awfully good now. Let's give the SOCOs some space and then come back."

I called Dickens, and we three moved to Gemma's patio, where we could watch without getting in the way. "You know, this is really going to play hell with my enjoyment of the river view. Not sure I'll ever sit here again without seeing an image of Max the Magnificent with the waterwheel in the distance," she said.

"Not a happy thought. I'm assuming you think this is murder?"

"That would be my first guess, but I honestly don't know. It's why I called in the SOCOs. He pretty much looked the picture of health yesterday, so what happened? If we'd found him in the river, I might think he'd drowned. Instead, he's soaking wet only from the waist up. Could've leaned over the bank here in the shallow part to splash his face, I guess. And hauled himself up and passed out.

"I might think he'd choked on a bit of apple or a swallow of whiskey, but he sure didn't stick an apple in his mouth after he did that. Way too many things to look at it here. The medical examiner will have to make a final determination."

It sank in that I'd now seen two dead bodies in a month. I'd never thought of Astonbury as the murder capital of the Cotswolds. Never considered this charming village a dangerous place to live.

I shook myself and turned to Gemma. "As long as we're waiting, do you want to hear my memories of Saturday?"

"Yes, I've learned you're exceptionally observant. Just don't get any ideas about messing with my crime scene," she warned.

Gemma was referring to my unfortunate involvement with another violent death. Wendy, Belle, Dickens, and I had rushed to the victim's home to rescue her cat. Except we didn't only find the cat. We also found what I guess the experts call a secondary crime scene. I wasn't sure Gemma was ever going to let me forget that.

I started with my initial encounter with Max on Friday when I'd learned he knew Sparkle. "By now, I bet Trixie knows more about that relationship than I do. I couldn't tell then whether they were boyfriend and girlfriend or just friends. It wasn't until Saturday I learned they were dating." I shook my head at the thought. "Anyway, Max told her he was staying in the caravan park in Bourton-on-the-Water and invited her to meet him for dinner."

Gemma was taking notes. "And what about Saturday?"

"There's more to Friday, first. I was standing by the Scarecrow Garden when he walked up and spoke to Barb. I think they were both surprised to see each other. From there, the rest of what I saw picks up when Trixie and I met him at the waterwheel," I explained.

"Right," said Gemma, "here on the river."

"Trixie wanted to push him to sign the divorce forms or whatever you guys call them over here. He was taking his sweet time, and she was getting anxious. Lord, was he a jerk."

Though I'd told the story the night before at the pub, I went over it again—what he'd said to Trixie and how he'd grabbed her arm and gotten a slap across the face in return. I finished up with the conversation between Trixie and Sparkle at Beatrix's booth.

"A right rotter, that one," said Gemma. "Not that I haven't encountered lots like him in my time. Plenty wind up in jail, but not enough of them, if you ask me. They're bound to cause real harm sooner or later if they aren't stopped."

"I'm sure you're right," I said. "I'm curious as to how a girl like Trixie came to be married to him. She strikes me as young and naive. I bet there's a tale there. How did Trixie meet him, marry him, figure out she needed to be rid of him? Could shed some light on his death."

"What else did you observe on Saturday? Did you see Max performing?"

"You know, I didn't see much of his act, just glimpses in passing, but the kids seemed charmed by him. But wait a minute. I almost forgot I saw some interaction between him and Barb that morning as the Fête was kicking off."

"There's more with Barb? Good grief," Gemma said.

"Yes. He tried to approach her as she was leaving, and she gave him that universal rude gesture. He said something back, but I couldn't hear what it was. I thought that was an interesting shift from the day before. I mean they weren't chummy Friday, but there wasn't any tension."

"Fascinating," said Gemma. "Visiting from Totnes and runs into three women he knows? How does that happen?"

The SOCOs were preparing to move the body, and one walked over with several evidence bags. One held the apple core, another an apple, and a third a phone. The fourth held a wallet. "Odd thing about this apple. There are two sets of teeth marks on it as though it's been bitten by two people or this one tried twice to bite into it."

"Like he started to eat it. And was interrupted? Anything else of note?" asked Gemma.

"Oh yeah. Looks like he took a beating before he went in the water. His nose is swollen with a bit of dried blood around it. Don't think he walked into a door, so probably he was punched. And a handprint on his face, like someone slapped him.

"Funny that. No offense ladies, but it's typically guys who punch and women who slap. So, could be two different people had a go at him. That's about it. Won't know what all happened to him until the medical examiner has a look."

The SOCO was right about a woman leaving the handprint. I assumed the mark was from where Trixie had slapped him. As for who punched him, who knew?

Gemma frowned. "Not much by way of evidence, is it? Maybe you'll have better luck with his truck. It's over by the garage. And keep an eye out for a top hat and a cane."

I thought for a moment. "Gemma, if he had a swollen bloody nose and an apple stuffed in his mouth, could he have suffocated?"

"Hmmm, I guess that's a possibility. Someone could've stuck the apple in his mouth as a joke, and then the bloke couldn't get any air . . . "

"So it could have been a prank gone wrong?"

As she watched the SOCOS head to the drive, Gemma speculated. "Who knows? I need to wait to hear what the medical examiner has to say. Meanwhile, I know two women who had a relationship with Max and good reason to be furious with him, but angry enough to kill him? I'm not sure. And we know a third who seemed irritated with him, at the very least. Given the rule of the thumb is to look at the spouse, guess my first stop this morning will be the widow."

Chapter Three

I checked on Libby. She'd dozed off, so I felt comfortable leaving her. Rest would do her good after the shock she'd had. I nonchalantly walked to the waterwheel and snapped a few pictures of the riverbank and the surrounding area. Good thing the body was already gone. I would have been tempted to photograph it too, and Gemma would have had a cow.

As soon as I'd latched Dickens in the back seat, I called Wendy. "Good morning. Any chance I can drop by for a cuppa?"

"You know you're always welcome. In fact, Peter's coming for lunch, and I've made two quiches. Why don't you join us?"

"Sounds like my lucky day. Be there in a few."

I looked in the rearview mirror at Dickens. "What did you find out from Paddington?"

"Nothing useful. He comes and goes most nights, stays out catting around. Saw plenty of owls and mice out in the fields, but nothing exciting at the inn."

"Nothing exciting? Did he see anything at all?"

"Yes. When he climbed his favorite tree by the waterwheel,

45

he saw Max lying on his back. And when he set off down the driveway to resume his nightly patrol, he saw Trixie leaving. He was passing the truck when he spied the top hat and couldn't resist peeking in. Silly thing thought he'd find a rabbit, but no luck."

I thought about that for a moment. "Hmmm. So that's where the hat is. I guess the SOCOs will find it when they search the truck. I wish I knew what time Paddington saw all that."

"Paddington's a smart cat, but he doesn't wear a watch, Leta."

I was laughing at the thought of Paddington with a wristwatch when I pulled up to Sunshine Cottage, and Dickens had already moved on. "Look, Tigger's in the garden. Hurry."

He bounded out of the car to join his feline friend, and I stuck my head in the front door. "You guys in the kitchen?"

"Yes, come on in," said Belle. She gave me a peck on the cheek when I leaned in to give her a hug.

Wendy poured me a cup of tea. "What have you been up to today? A walk with Dickens?"

Their eyes widened in shock when I told them about Max the Magnificent. "Oh, poor Libby," said Belle. "For that matter, poor you. Another dead body?"

"Well, as I said to Libby, at least this time it isn't someone we know or like, but still."

"You've got to tell us everything, but maybe we should wait for Peter," said Wendy.

We agreed her suggestion made sense, so I wandered outside with my tea while Wendy set the table and made a salad. The drizzle had stopped, and Dickens and Tigger were chasing each other in and around the woodpile. It was fortunate Peter had laid in a supply of logs before breaking his collarbone.

When Peter drove up, Dickens greeted him with an ecstatic bark. Both he and Christie had grown attached to my tall lanky friend, and I suspected it had something to do with his resemblance to Henry.

"Peter, let's go for a walk! Want to?"

Peter chuckled and responded as though he'd understood what Dickens had said. "Hello, boy. You looked exhausted last night at the pub, but you're awfully frisky this morning."

I gave Peter a hug, careful not to jar the bad arm. "Lucky me. I called at the right moment to score an invitation to lunch. Come on in."

The homey kitchen decorated in cheerful reds was always spotless, and today was no exception. It was as though the meal had miraculously appeared on the counter. A pot of tea, a crock of butter, and a jar of jam were already on the table surrounded by red checked placemats. Wendy served from the counter, and I handed around plates of quiche, salad, and scones.

When I took my seat, Belle and Wendy looked at me expectantly. I took a bite of quiche and went through the phone call from Gemma, what Libby'd said, and what I'd seen. I suggested we finish lunch before I recounted my discussion with Gemma on the patio.

Peter and Belle moved to the sitting room while Wendy and I cleared the table and washed up. Seeing Tigger on the window box outside the kitchen window made me think to bring the animals in, and we all made ourselves comfortable in front of the fire with our four-legged companions in their favorite positions—Tigger in Belle's lap and Dickens on the hearthrug.

I sighed. "Beatrix and I brought you up to speed about Max, Sparkle, and Trixie over drinks last night. Gemma and I rehashed that as we watched the SOCOs at work. The interesting bits of evidence were the apple in his mouth and the bloody nose."

Peter frowned. "Well, it doesn't seem like an apple in his mouth would kill him. Unless the Wicked Stepmother poisoned it."

"More likely one of the women he mistreated, but no, it wasn't a poison apple, that I know of. Still, it would appear someone stuck the thing in his mouth. And turns out it had two sets of bite marks on it."

I closed my eyes as I pictured the scene. "Oh, and there was an apple core too. I guess someone will figure it out. And the medical examiner will let Gemma know whether Max was punched in the nose. Could have tripped over his own feet, right? And fallen flat on his face? But how likely is that?

"I wonder who else Gemma plans to interview. I should've suggested she speak with you, Belle, since you were pretty near to Max the Magician all day while he was performing."

Wendy gave me a questioning look. "You should have *suggested*? Leta Parker, don't tell me you're thinking of getting involved with another investigation."

Belle piped up. "Why not? We might never have solved the last case if not for Leta."

"You know," I said, "I haven't consciously thought of myself as involved, but . . . I guess I am, if only unofficially. I mean Gemma *did* want my input."

"Oh, let's get involved, please," barked Dickens.

I smiled at my four-legged partner. It was at times like this I had to be extra cautious not to let on that he and I conversed. I worried that one of these days, I'd pop out with a

"Dickens says" comment. I could only imagine what would happen then.

Wendy chuckled at Dickens. "I wonder what Dickens is thinking. I know he's a little hero dog, but we don't want him having to reprise that role, so if you're planning to nose around, I want in. You need a partner to keep you out of trouble."

"Don't forget me," said Belle. "It's a wonder what people will tell a little old lady."

Peter looked askance at the three of us. "You've got to be kidding. What exactly do you think you're going to do? Interrogate people?"

"If you'll recall, I didn't *interrogate* you during the last case. We had a conversation over dinner, and before I knew it, you'd told me things even your mother and sister didn't know," I reminded him.

At that, mother and daughter crossed their arms and stared at him, the expressions on their faces identical. If I were writing a novel, this is where the two would have said, "Don't you worry about us. We can take care of ourselves."

"And, you know what?" said Belle. "I *did* see something."

"You did? What?" I asked.

Belle shook her head in disgust. "That scoundrel! If I were more spry, I'd have come out of my chair and given him a piece of my mind. I saw him shove Sparkle's face in the water with the apples and hold it there while she tried to get up."

"I wondered how she'd managed to get wet bobbing for apples. Never thought about Max being responsible for that."

Wendy came up with the obvious connection. "Oh! A possible motive for Sparkle."

"Yes, but who kills someone because he's mean? Well, mean and he lied to her about being divorced, but still. And we need to remind ourselves that Gemma doesn't know for sure it was murder, though I can't see how it could be anything else. I mean, who sticks an apple in his mouth and lies down?"

We hadn't spoken to anyone beyond our little group, and already we had ideas. I suggested Belle let Gemma know about the confrontation between Max and Sparkle so she could follow up on it.

I looked at Wendy. "I can tell from the expression on your face that you've had a brainstorm."

"Well, I was thinking 'the early bird gets the worm.'"

"Huh?" I said.

"While Gemma's waiting until it's officially been declared murder, she might miss something. Something no one saw as important, like Mum seeing Max shoving Sparkle's face in the water. We could nose around. What's the harm?"

"What do you have in mind, luv?" asked Belle.

I had an idea. "We can get Peter to help. It would only take a quick conversation. Peter, are you visiting the Ploughman any time soon?"

"Crikey," he said. "What do you want?"

"Sit at the bar and chat up Phil. Find out what he said to Max last night when he jerked him up. You'll be surprised how easy it is to get information. I bet Phil has plenty to say about Max, and he'll be more forthcoming with you than he would be with one of us."

"Well, if it will keep you three from making a spectacle of yourselves at the pub, I'll handle it. But that's it. I'm not getting involved beyond that."

Next, I looked at Wendy. "What say you and I talk to Beatrix to get the backstory on Trixie, how she wound up in Totnes, and why Max? I want to know how she got hooked up with him and what made her come to her senses. I don't see Gemma having that conversation, do you?"

"I was thinking a chat with Beatrix would be the logical first step. Dinner out, or maybe at your place? And what about Mum?"

"I'll do dinner, and I'll call Beatrix. Belle, you had a long day yesterday, so what if Wendy and I carry on this evening without you? Tomorrow, we'll put our head together and draw up a plan."

"That's fine, girls," Belle replied. "Meanwhile, I'll think back on what I saw yesterday to see if I can remember anything else helpful."

I had a sudden thought. "Wendy, if you get a chance, can you browse the *Astonbury Aha* for photos the villagers posted online from yesterday? Someone could have inadvertently caught something on camera. You know what I mean? Like the police studying CCTV video?"

"Yup," she said. "Too bad there's no CCTV at the river."

As I drove to Sainsbury's for groceries, I called Beatrix. She was at the Book Nook and told me Trixie had come in late the night before and had been asleep when Beatrix left mid-morning. She was shocked when Trixie called with the news about Max and said Gemma had come and gone. The girl was in quite a state, and her mother was on her way from Manchester. To top it off, Gemma had asked Trixie not to leave Astonbury, a request that didn't bode well.

Beatrix didn't see how she could come for dinner with her sister and her niece at her flat, though after hearing I'd been to the crime scene, she was eager for news. When I suggested we move dinner to Monday evening, she was all over it.

Sitting around twiddling my thumbs seemed less than efficient, and I pondered next steps as I shopped. I'd planned a simple meal of baked chicken and my Greek salad, but with our dinner date delayed a day, I had time to make spanakopita instead of chicken. With a name like Leta Petkas Parker, it was only natural that Greek dishes were my go-to, and my new friends in the Cotswolds had come to expect them when they dined at my cottage.

Driving home, I called Trixie on Beatrix's home line. She was sniffly but seemed comforted to hear my voice. "Trixie, when is your mother due to arrive? Would you like company until she can get here?"

"Oh yes, Leta. Aunt Beatrix offered to close the shop and come home, but I couldn't let her do that. It's bad enough that I'm in no state to go in to help her today. I don't expect Mum until after dark, and it's awful sitting here by myself."

I told her I'd be over after a quick stop at my cottage, and then I called Wendy to alert her to the change in plans. She agreed it was a good idea for me to see Trixie on my own, since I'd established a relationship with her.

I made my stop by home as speedy as I could. Given that Christie was demanding to know where we'd been and what we knew, it wasn't as fast as I would have liked. With Dickens' help, I told her what we'd discovered as I was putting groceries away.

She was none too pleased with our haste. "Mee . . . oow," she screeched. "Did you get pictures? Tell me you at least brought me pictures."

During the last sleuthing adventure, I'd had lots of photos, and my intelligent black cat had been instrumental in discovering clues I hadn't noticed. All I had to do was set up the slideshow on the computer and leave her to it. She was disappointed I had so few this time.

Dickens tried to explain. "Christie, she couldn't help it. Gemma and the SOCOs were there at the scene, and they'd have noticed if Leta pulled out her phone. Can you imagine her snapping pictures of the body and them saying, 'Sure, take all the pictures you like?' Not likely."

She ran to the office and leaped on my desk, scattering paper and pens. "If you're taking off again, at least transfer the ones you have. I can't very well help with this investigation if you don't get on the stick."

My girl. She hated being left out, and I realized I needed to try the backpack idea sooner rather than later. When I returned, I'd order one from Amazon and see whether I could convince her to ride in it so she could accompany me and Dickens out and about.

Trixie opened the door and threw her arms around me. "I'm so glad you're here, Leta. I can't believe Max is dead, and I can't believe Gemma told me not to leave Astonbury, as though she thinks I could be responsible."

Dickens positioned himself protectively at her feet. He could tell she needed comforting. I sat on the couch next to her and rubbed her back. "Did you explain to Gemma you had nothing to do with it? You saw him at the pub, and that was it?"

She gulped. "That's the problem. I saw him later."

That was news. I realized Gemma had to question her because she was the spouse, the most likely suspect. And she'd had a nasty encounter with Max yesterday, but it hadn't occurred to me she might have been involved. "You did? Where?"

"Summer, Sparkle, and I rode to the pub in Summer's car, but I was ready to leave before they were. Goodness, those girls can drink. I took the walking path to the inn to get my car. Max's truck was still there, and I looked inside thinking he might be passed out—a common occurrence when he drinks. No sign of him.

"But I saw his top hat in the bed of the truck. Like it had been tossed there. He's awfully particular about that thing, so I was worried. I may have been furious with him, but I had to be sure he was okay. I wandered the grounds and finally found him by the river between the guest cottage and the waterwheel.

"Sure enough, he was out cold, a bottle of Highland Black by his side. He was hanging over the bank with his face almost in the water . . . like he'd tried to get a drink from the river or maybe splash his face."

"Did you see anyone else?"

"No, just Max. I pulled him back from the edge and rolled him over. He was a muddy mess. I figured he'd be okay there. He was far enough from the water that he couldn't accidentally tip himself in. And he'd sober up soon enough."

"Sounds like you did him a good turn. So you left?"

"Yes, Leta. I was already later than I'd told Aunt Beatrix I would be, and I needed to get home. I'd had a lot to drink, and I had to concentrate to drive here."

I only had to nod and more came tumbling out.

"If only I'd stayed with him at the river, maybe he'd be okay. I mean, I didn't want to be married to him any longer,

54

but I didn't *hate* him. Might have if I'd stayed with him long enough, but I wised up and left him."

"Trixie, it's not your fault. Most women, including me, wouldn't have gone anywhere near him after the way he behaved."

"Maybe not, but in some small way, I still cared about him. I can't believe he's dead. And how did he die? Gemma wasn't clear about that, or maybe she said and I couldn't take it in."

I had to think for a moment. Was it okay to tell her Gemma didn't know for sure, but suspected foul play? "The medical examiner will have to say for sure. It's hard to say."

"He was out cold when I left. How can he be dead?"

Something was niggling at me. Something about the scene. Then it occurred to me. I didn't want to mention the apple in Max's mouth, but I could ask about the apple core. "Trixie, was there an apple core on the bank?"

"No, not that I noticed. Only a handful of apples, whole apples."

So, who ate an apple and tossed the core aside? Who was there after Trixie?

I'd known Trixie maybe two weeks, and I thought I was a good judge of character. Nothing she'd told me changed my perception of her as an innocent young thing, and I felt she was telling me the truth about Saturday night. How on earth had she gotten tangled up with Max?

"Trixie, your aunt told me you went to Totnes only to take a class. How'd you wind up staying? Was it because you met Max?"

"Oh, Leta, you can't believe how magical Totnes was after living in a city like Manchester. It was small and friendly. I'm a shy person. I love books and art and took art lessons all through school. If I didn't have my nose in a book, I was drawing or painting. More school wasn't for me, so I went to work at an art supply shop when I graduated. I loved it there and became fascinated with papermaking.

"When I found there was an eight-week program in Totnes on book and paper arts, all I could think about was finding a way to go, even though I'd never been away from home. The class covered designing handmade books, papermaking, printing, and bookbinding—art and books combined. It sounded like heaven."

"I bet Beatrix would have loved attending too, since she keeps her eye out for old books. I can see why you two were close."

"Yes, Aunt Beatrix encouraged me. Mum and Dad were hesitant, but in the end, they paid for the class and a place for me to stay. I found a walkout flat in a family home. The mother and I hit it off, and sometimes I even babysat the kids in the evening. It was perfect. Taking the bus every day from my flat to Sharpham Hall for class was super convenient. It was a wonderful summer, and I chatted off and on with Aunt Beatrix about someday working for her and combining my two loves—books and art."

"So, what happened, Trixie?"

"I fell in love with the town and being out on my own, but I couldn't ask Mum and Dad to keep supporting me, so when the course ended, I kept my flat and found a job at the book-shop in Totnes. Suzanne, the owner, let me make cards to sell in the shop, and they were a huge hit with the customers."

"And Max, how did you meet him?"

"The White Rabbit, where he works—worked—is just up High Street from the bookshop, and I'd met the owner's daughter at Sharpham Hall. She introduced me to Max one day, and we kept running into each other. I'd never had a real boyfriend at school, and Max was so attentive. I know it's hard to imagine after the way he acted yesterday, but he was charming. He must have bought a card a day, and he surely didn't need all of 'em. And, you know, he's handsome beyond words. Guess I read too many romance books for my own good."

Trixie broke down and sobbed, prompting Dickens to put his paws in her lap and try to lick her tear away. That brought a tremulous smile to her face. "I wanted a dog, but Max wouldn't have it. One of the many edicts he issued once we were married."

What's the saying? "Leopards can't change their spots?" He dazzled the poor girl and swept her off her feet, and then revealed his true self. I could just see him buying the cards she made, pulling flowers out of his sleeve, and more to win her heart.

"Leta, I loved him, but I'm not stupid. Well, I guess I was for a few months, but he changed. He drank. He was jealous, and he belittled me. He said my artwork was amateur and he was the true talent in the family, things he never said when we were dating.

"And I was pretty sure he cheated on me when he went off to festivals and I stayed home to work. All that's why I filed for divorce after the first year and moved back to the flat I'd rented before."

I could only imagine how he took that, given what I'd seen of his ego. Must have been a real blow to his masculinity. "Let me guess," I said. "He wouldn't leave you be, and you felt it best to move here or back to Manchester."

"How'd you know, Leta?"

"He fits the pattern of an abusive man. In a small town like Totnes, he'd have known your every move. You made the right decision to leave. I wonder if he took the job at our Fête because you were here?"

"Don't know, didn't ask. It's all too much to deal with," she mumbled.

"Trixie, I know your Aunt Beatrix must have some brandy in the house. Let me fix you a cup of tea with a shot in it. I know from experience it's good for shock."

Preparing the hot toddy gave me a moment of quiet, and questions crowded my brain. If Max was fine when Trixie left, someone had to have been there after her. According to Paddington, he *was* fine and lying on his back by the river *after* Trixie left. That was confirmation of at least part of her story, not that anyone besides me was going to take the word of a cat.

Who went to the river after Trixie left? Who put the apple in his mouth? Who wanted him dead?

Or maybe I was being naive. Was Trixie lying to me? Did she go back later? Wanting out of the marriage was a motive, and he wouldn't sign the divorce papers. Plus he'd threatened her. Was she so desperate to be rid of him that she killed him? And how did he die? Gemma didn't know for sure it was murder.

I could hear my sister Anna whispering in my ear, "Right, Leta, you're one to see only the best in people. You never believe anything bad until it slaps you in the face, and even then you give 'em the benefit of the doubt way too long." I'd heard that lecture for so long, you'd think it might have done some good. But no, I was trusting to a fault.

I made sure Trixie drank her tea, and then I tucked a blanket around her on the couch. She had stopped crying, and with her mother arriving shortly, I felt sure she'd be in good hands.

Belle's story about Max holding Sparkle's face in the water made me want to see Sparkle and find out where she'd been late Saturday night. But I couldn't think of any reason she'd talk to me. Questions were flying in and out of my brain, and I needed to figure out how to get answers.

Chapter Four

I spoke to Dickens as we drove home. "Where do we go from here, boy? What would Nancy Drew do?"

"I bet Nancy Drew would revisit the scene of the crime, so how about we check on Libby tomorrow?" suggested Dickens.

"You know, I was going to call tonight to see how she was doing, but visiting tomorrow is a better idea. Wonder what Gemma's found out today. If we get to the inn early enough, maybe we can *bump into* Gemma before she leaves for work," I mused.

Christie greeted us at the door, stretching and yawning. I felt like yawning too. It was my habit to take afternoon naps, and I hadn't had one in several days. Not to mention I'd been on my feet most of Saturday and out later than usual. It was past five, though, and I deemed it too late for a nap. Bummer.

Christie meowed as I put a dab of wet food in her dish. "Thanks. Studying those photos wore me out, and I didn't spot a thing. Guess the SOCOs carried it all off. I was hoping they'd missed something—something that would crack the case wide open."

I laughed at my petite black cat. "Now, now, don't take it too hard. You may be named for Agatha Christie, the Queen of Crime, but even her detectives never get results that easily."

I opted for a glass of red wine and a phone call to Anna in Atlanta. It was lunchtime there, and as a small business owner, Anna was usually in her office doing paperwork on the weekends.

"Well, if it isn't my favorite *oldest* sister," she said. "How was the Fête? I was sure I'd get an email with pictures last night."

"Oh, the Fête was a huge success. We were a hit in our costumes there and at the pub afterward. Dickens tried to bob for apples. You should have seen the crowd that gathered to watch that act. I got fairy hair again, as did most of my girl-friends. Everyone enjoyed themselves."

"Sounds like the festivals we're having here every week-end," she said. "Except you and I used to shop them together. We didn't participate. I wish you were going to be here for the St. Simons Art Festival this year. I could use your help selecting the perfect painting to hang over the bed in the blue guestroom."

I laughed as I thought of our many shopping expeditions. "The good news is I didn't succumb to shopping at *this* Fête. The bad news is something dreadful happened today—well I guess it happened last night, except I didn't know about it then."

"Uh-oh, are you okay?" she asked.

"Fine, and I can't believe I'm saying this, but . . . my friend Libby found a dead body today."

"What?" blurted Anna. "A dead body? You can't be serious. You're supposed to be living in a quiet country village, not someplace that's crime-ridden. What on earth?"

"I know. At least this time it wasn't someone we knew. Not someone we'd even met until this weekend. Still, a dead body is a dead body."

I told her the story and answered the questions she posed. Anna was a detail-oriented businesswoman, and talking it through with her helped bring some semblance of order to my jumble of thoughts. Once upon a time, I'd been a detail-oriented businesswoman too, but those skills had dulled since I'd retired.

Anna couldn't miss an opportunity to press me about Christmas. "This is all the more reason for you to come home for Christmas. I need to lay eyes on you after this crime wave."

I laughed. "I appreciate your concern, but you know this situation has no bearing on Christmas. I still haven't made up my mind, though Dave's mention of a detour to New York City for the Christmas lights and decorations makes the trip awfully tempting."

"That's a great plan. See your family, enjoy the holiday spirit in New York City. Two birds with one stone. Not to mention I'll bake all your favorite desserts."

Anna was the number one baker in the family. I could almost taste her pound cake, pecan pie, and brownies. Soon, I'd have to make a decision, at least by the end of the month. I promised to keep her posted on that decision and any additional information about the murder in the village.

Sitting with my phone in my hand reminded me that I needed to send the picture of Dorothy and Toto to Bev in Atlanta. I missed her, and I knew Dickens did too. I fired off an email with the photo attached and told her what fun we'd had on Saturday. No need to mention the dead body.

Taking another sip of wine, I rang Wendy. I thought of her as my partner in crime, but that phrase sounded inappropriate in the present circumstances. When she answered, she asked me to wait while she put her phone on speaker and got Belle's attention. Come to think of it, I had two partners in crime, and they were all ears as I relayed Trixie's tale.

"Sounds like something from a Halloween tale," said Wendy. "A pretty girl out on a dark night, a victim . . . the only thing missing is a werewolf."

I stated the obvious. "And the killer, since according to Trixie, Max was alive when she left him."

Belle had a good chuckle. "Well, you know in the best murder mysteries, the killer's identity isn't revealed until later."

I acknowledged Belle was right. "And it's early days yet. I know, I'm just impatient. By the way, Belle, did you get hold of Gemma?"

"Oh yes, and she was quite interested. Said she'd have Constable James locate Sparkle and speak with her. So, what's the next step for the Leta Parker Detective Agency? We're going to tackle Beatrix tomorrow night, right? Any other ideas?" asked my octogenarian partner.

"Yes, we'll have dinner here and see what more Beatrix can tell us about Trixie, and I have a tentative plan for early in the morning. Barring rain, Dickens and I will walk to the inn to check on Libby, have a cup of coffee, and maybe chat with Gavin too. Chances are Gemma's let slip a detail or two to her mum about the investigation. And, if I'm there early enough, I'm likely to catch Gemma in person. I mean, she *did* invite my input today, so perhaps she'll share her progress. I sure would like to know what she heard from Sparkle."

My partners agreed it was a good plan, and Wendy offered another idea. "Do you suppose Gemma's planning to talk to Summer? Maybe I should find a reason to visit her in Cheltenham. Doesn't she offer fairy hair in one of the shops?"

"Now, that's a thought," I replied. "During the week, she works in the soap shop, and the owners have set aside a small space for fairy hair customers. She has a local clientele and travels to festivals on weekends. You can drop by to tell her how much you love your hair."

Not to be left out, Belle spoke up. "Don't think you're leaving me behind. Let's visit the shop and discuss our findings over a nice lunch."

By now, Wendy and I were both laughing. "You know, ladies," I said, "soon we're going to need a new name for our enterprise. The Leta Parker Detective Agency just doesn't do it."

"Leave it to me," said Wendy. "I bet Mum and I can come with a clever literary reference a la Arthur Conan Doyle or Alexander McCall Smith. Too bad we can't steal 'The No. 1 Ladies' Detective Agency' for our name. That pretty much fits the bill."

Names started flitting through my head with words that went with ladies—literary, lovely, lucky, leading. "Given that you and I love to read and were once English teachers, perhaps Literary Ladies Detective Agency would work."

"I like to read too," said Belle. "That name could work, but let's not decide yet."

We agreed Wendy and Belle would bring dessert and set 6:30 pm as the time for dinner Monday evening. If anything major came up before then, we could always adjust.

I fixed a plate of fruit and cheese and pondered next steps. I'd planned to drop in unannounced to see Libby in the morning but thought better of it. On a typical Monday, the inn was all but empty, but if she had a full house, she might be too busy to chat.

I slipped Dickens a bite and rang the inn. Gavin answered

sounding a bit harried, odd for a Sunday evening, but this had been no ordinary Sunday. "Oh hi, Leta. If you're looking for Libby, she's resting."

"That's good. That scene this morning was awful, and she needs to take it easy. How are you and Jill holding up without Libby's help?"

"Pretty well. We've only one couple staying the night, and they plan to be up and out early. Don't want more than coffee and scones to go. Makes for an easy day, so easy in fact that I'm sitting in front of the fire taking a break," he said.

I could picture him in his favorite chair with his feet on the ottoman. Henry and I'd stayed at the inn on our trip to the Cotswolds, and then I'd stayed for a month when I was house-hunting. I'd spent many an evening relaxing in the sitting room with Gavin, Libby, and Paddington.

"In that case, is it okay if I come by early tomorrow to see Libby? I know what a shock she's had, and she'd likely benefit from some company."

Gavin sounded relieved. "Sure, I hardly know what to do or say beyond hugging her. Why don't you come for breakfast? You know we cook a big one even when it's just the two of us, so there'll be plenty. You bringing Dickens or his alter ego, Toto?"

"Of course. I go very few places without my boy. That's one of the things I love about England—dogs are welcome most everywhere."

He laughed and hesitated before he spoke again. "This is usually Libby's department, but she's not noticed yet. Something is off with Jill, and I don't want to intrude, but . . ."

"But you'd like me to see if I can find out what's bothering Jill?" I asked. She was probably upset about the dead body at the inn. Who wouldn't be? With coffee, a hug, and a few carefully phrased questions from me, she was sure to open up.

"Phew," he said. "Thanks for making that easy for me. See you in the morning."

I'd settled my morning sleuthing agenda, Wendy and Belle were going to Cheltenham, and Beatrix was scheduled for dinner. The plan was taking shape.

"Dickens, Christie, let's put another log on the fire and relax. I could do with a few hours of reading. I'm enjoying getting to know Tommy and Tuppence."

I propped my feet on the ottoman, grabbed my fleece throw, and invited Christie into my lap. After kneading my stomach a few times, she curled into a purring ball. Dickens lay on his dog bed in front of the fire.

I sighed and looked around my comfy sitting room, thinking how warm and inviting it was. This is what I'd envisioned when I first walked into the cottage with my real estate agent.

Built as a schoolhouse in the 1800s, the building had later been converted into a spacious home, its two downstairs classrooms turned into a sitting room and a large bedroom. I used the bedroom as my office and positioned my desk so I could gaze out the picture window at the garden.

The master and guest bedrooms were upstairs and the bathroom up there had a huge walk-in shower. My favorite touch was the school bell hanging to the left of the front door. Judging by how frequently my neighbor Timmy rang it, it was his favorite part too.

I scratched Christie's ears and reflected on my decision to retire to England. After I'd lost Henry, I'd returned to my corporate job and buried myself in work. Though my financial planner had made it plain I could comfortably take early retirement, I couldn't imagine myself not working. It wasn't until a year later that the seed she'd planted sprouted. One too many encounters with my witch of a boss did the trick.

Retiring to England had been a dream of mine, and here I was. I liked to think Henry was looking down on me, marveling at the leap I'd taken. More likely he was looking down wondering when I'd get the hang of driving on the *wrong* side of the road. Whichever it was, I hoped he was smiling.

Monday morning was damp but not yet rainy. More often this time of year in the Cotswolds, it was chilly, cloudy, and misty with rain in the offing. We'd lucked out with a sunny, mild day for the Fête.

I donned my hooded rain jacket and gloves, grabbed Dickens, his leash, and a few carrots, and set off for the inn. My plan was to feed Martha and Dylan on our return trip, but I gave in to their insistent braying and fed them on the way. I'm not sure how I'd become so attached to them, but the sight of the two donkeys never failed to make me smile.

I let Dickens off his leash when we turned into the gravel drive to the inn, and he dashed to the front door. Jill was bringing an armful of dirty sheets down the stairs as we stepped into the entry hall, Paddington trailing behind her. One of his favorite pastimes was diving in the pile of dirty linens in the upstairs hallway as the rooms were cleaned each day. Dickens had joined him in that game a time or two.

Dickens barked a greeting. "Hey Paddington, ready to romp?"

"You missed the fun," meowed Paddington. "Only one

room to change out this morning, so that's it for today. Let's check out the garden."

The two darted out the front door, and I followed Jill as she passed through the kitchen to the laundry room. I could smell an inviting breakfast casserole in the oven. "How's Libby this morning?" I asked.

"I haven't seen her yet. When I arrived, our Sunday night guests were driving away and Gavin was in the kitchen making a grocery list. He said the sedative the doctor gave Libby had knocked her out good, and she was just beginning to stir. This is the first time since I've been working here that she hasn't been in the kitchen first thing, going ninety to nothing."

She started a load of sheets and towels and picked up a cloth-lined basket. "Libby usually takes breakfast to Gemma, so I'll get it ready."

I watched as she wrapped scones in a napkin, set out small crocks of butter and jam, and prepared a bowl of berries. She placed everything in the basket and covered it with a tea towel. "There, ready to go," she said. "How 'bout you? Would you like some coffee and a warm scone while we wait on the main course?"

I was torn. Should I stay and talk to Jill, or should I offer to take the basket to the guest cottage in the hope I'd catch Gemma? I opted for Gemma. "Let me take the basket to Gemma, and then I'll have a cup of coffee. I'll be back in time for breakfast. Will you be here for a bit?"

"Oh yes. I've yet to clean the ashes from the fireplace and dust and vacuum. Not sure how many guests are coming in tonight, or whether Gavin will want me to prepare a tray of nibbles for their arrival."

I was in luck. As I walked across the courtyard, Gemma

sprinted up the driveway. She ran five miles most mornings. I hollered hello and met her at her front door.

"Mum not up yet?" she asked.

"Word is she's moving, but she hasn't put in an appearance downstairs. Leta's Delivery Service is pitching in."

She opened the door and motioned me inside. "I'm sure there's enough for two in that basket, and I've got a pot of coffee going. Want to join me?"

I looked around for Dickens, but he was nowhere to be seen. Hopefully, my boy was getting the scoop from Paddington, and I'd get the same from Gemma. "Thanks, some coffee would be great."

Gemma poured two cups, and we talked as she munched. "Guess you know how I spent yesterday. I hate death notifications."

"I bet. I thought it best for Trixie to have company until her mother could get there, so I popped in. I suppose I got much the same story you did. She was sniffly but calm when I got there."

I got the eye roll, but Gemma refrained from chastising me about my visit. "Surprisingly, Trixie was pretty calm, though she was appropriately shocked. Didn't give her many details, just that we'd found her husband dead and asked when she'd last seen him. Got the story about seeing the top hat in the truck and finding him by the river. Says he was lying there snoring when she left him. Nothing else."

I took a sip of coffee. "Do you believe her story?"

"Maybe. She knew her husband was bad news and she'd initiated divorce proceedings, but she didn't hate him—not sure why not—and I want to believe her story. I see her as a quiet mouse. But you know me: my second thought? She's maybe a little too good to be true.

"I need to find out about their finances. Can't imagine there's any joint property to speak of, but if there were, it would go to Trixie. So, that would give her another motive in addition to getting out of the marriage."

I thought about my few interactions with Trixie. "I don't know her well, other than seeing her at the bookshop and book club and then at the Fête, but my perception jibes with your first one—she's young, kind of naive. When I spoke with her yesterday, it sounded as though she'd been taken in by Max's good looks and his charming side."

Gemma choked on her coffee. "Charming? Not a word I'd use for that one."

"Me either. By the way, did the SOCOs find the top hat?"

"No. No sign of it or the cane. So I have to ask, why would someone take them?"

I looked out toward the river, thinking. "Good question. By the way, did you speak to Sparkle?"

"As a matter of fact, I sent Constable James to see her after hearing the apple bobbing story from Belle. Been trying to find opportunities for him to do more interviews, so I called him at the station. Told him to locate Sparkle and speak with her.

"He didn't learn much. You didn't come up with an excuse to interrogate Sparkle yourself, did you? As in you don't already know her story?"

I laughed but didn't take the bait. Gemma was being unusually forthcoming, and I didn't want to stem the flow of information by ticking her off. "I learned my lesson last time, and I'm trying to behave. I don't even know where to find Sparkle."

"She's at Summer's flat in Cheltenham and will be for at least a week because they have a fair in Burford this weekend and some luncheons lined up. Who knew there were ladies' groups looking for fairy hair? She may well be here longer than a week if her story doesn't check out."

"So, what was her story?" I prompted.

"According to Constable James, her shock and grief were about over the top, but I've learned everyone reacts differently. He let her settle down and then asked when she'd last seen Max. She said it was at the pub right before Phil told him to get lost.

"When he queried her about their relationship, she told him they'd dated off and on starting in late summer and that she was shocked to find out he wasn't yet divorced."

I pointed out that story lined up with what I'd heard Saturday afternoon at the Fête, that she never would have gone out with him if she'd known he was still married. "As for her reaction, maybe she was more upset because she was still in a relationship with him, unlike Trixie, who was trying to get rid of him."

"Good point," said Gemma, "but when he asked whether she'd seen Max's truck when she went to the inn to get her car —so he could get a fix on where Max was when— she hesitated, which made him suspicious. He's learning. So, he pressed her, and she admitted to seeing Max at the inn that night."

"Uh-oh. Where exactly at the inn? And why did she lie about seeing him? That doesn't give me a good feeling."

"People lie to the police for all kinds of reasons. Sometimes it's because talking to us is just plain scary. Other times it's because they have something to hide. Constable James went with the standard line, 'So, let's try this again: exactly when and where did you last see Max?'"

Just like in the movies, I thought. *Except this is real life, and it bothers me that she lied to the police.*

"Gave him a bit of a song and dance about seeing the truck and worrying about him. I have to tell you, it's unbelievable to me how concerned these girls were about the guy. Why did they care so much? Anyway, Sparkle finally said she'd seen Max maybe late that night. She knew she'd left the pub before closing but couldn't be precise about the time.

"Claimed she saw Paddington stalking something and followed him to the river. That cat's out hunting every night, so I could believe that part. Said Max looked fine lying there, so she turned around and went home."

The situation wasn't getting any clearer to me. "No mention of an apple in his mouth? So did yet another person go to the river after those two left? Sparkle's story jibes with what Trixie said about Max being passed out but fine otherwise. They both saw him at the river, and say he was okay when they left him. So how did the apple get in his mouth?"

Gemma rolled her eyes. I'd been waiting for her to do that, as it was one of her habits. When she rolled them at something I said, it aggravated the heck out of me, but that wasn't the case this time.

"I wish I knew what to think. I told Constable James not to mention the apple in the mouth. I didn't mention it to Trixie either. Not ready to give that away yet. We just asked each of them if they saw any apples. Both said they saw some scattered on the bank, but that was it.

"If Sparkle got there after Trixie, and if they're both telling the truth about him being alive when they left him . . . well, where does that leave us? I can't see it being anything but murder, but I won't know how until the medical examiner gets him on the table. Same for the SOCOs and their analysis of what they collected at the scene."

"What did Sparkle say about earlier Saturday? About the apple bobbing?"

Gemma grimaced. "Said he was acting the fool like he'd always done, that sometimes his playing around could be borderline mean."

I sipped my coffee and wondered whether Max had any redeeming qualities. "Well, hell. Does Sparkle's story at least let Trixie off the hook?"

"Off the hook? Not yet. My gut's hemming and hawing. If it was murder, then one of those girls could've done it and lied to us. They were both furious with him, but for different reasons. Maybe Trixie returned after Sparkle left. Or it could be someone else entirely."

I sighed. "I'm gonna go out on a limb and say it wasn't Trixie or Sparkle. You know, if you were Inspector Barnaby in *Midsomer Murders*, you'd soon find several more suspects and forget about the girls. Guess you'll be interviewing other folks today, corroborating statements, and running background checks."

"Oh sure," Gemma said, "our cases *always* work out like those on the telly. But you are right about the grunt work. I'll have Constable James doing that after he finishes following up on what's on the phone we found."

I perked up at the mention of the phone. "Anything interesting so far?"

"Lots of texts, but only a few contacts. The texts we could figure out were messages about festivals and his schedule at the magic shop. Plenty of others were more cryptic. Seemed to indicate meeting times and money. There were also lots of photos of him in his tails and top hat doing tricks at parties. Looked like he forwarded those pics to the shop. Also an unflattering shot of Sparkle looking sullen."

"Well," I said as I stood up, "your dad invited me for breakfast, and whatever's in the oven smelled scrumptious. Thanks for the coffee and the update."

I didn't want more coffee, but I needed a reason to sit down in the conservatory where Jill was dusting and straightening. Armed with a steaming mug, I made myself comfortable in an armchair. "So, Jill, how are you taking this whole Max thing?" I asked. "Just the idea that a dead body was found on the property must be disturbing."

She glanced at me and hesitated. "It's definitely not something you'd expect. Except for the Fête, it's peaceful here. Beautiful grounds, a quiet garden, the sounds of the river and the birds. Not the place for a dead body."

"I know. I'm so sorry Libby had to see it."

Dickens was a natural at sensing even mild discomfort, but the way he moved to Jill's side told me she was giving off high anxiety vibes. He rubbed against her legs and nudged the hand with the dustcloth.

She dropped into the chair opposite me and rubbed Dickens's head. "I'm scared, Leta. I shouldn't be, 'cause he's dead and I don't have to see him again, but I'm scared."

Huh. What was she talking about?

"I've never been afraid of the dark before. I've ridden my bicycle back and forth to town, the inn, the pub, and never thought a thing of it. Now, I'm not sure I can."

"Because a body was found at the river?" I prompted.

And that's when she told me the story. "Because I ran into

Max before he died. I mean he ran into me . . . oh, I don't want to talk about this."

Dickens whimpered and licked her hand, and I stood up and gave her an awkward hug. I wondered what Max had said to her. "It might help if you talk to someone, and I'm happy to listen. What did he say to you?"

"It's not what he said. It's what he did." She took a deep breath. "He . . . he groped me."

"What? What did he do?"

I listened, appalled, as the floodgates opened. "I was getting my bike from the garage, and I never hesitated about approaching him. I hadn't noticed him leaning against his truck until he called to me and asked for help. When I got close, I could tell he had a bloody nose, so I told him to wait while I fetched a wet rag from the kitchen. I tried to clean him, but it wasn't easy 'cause he was staggering drunk.

"He bowed politely and said thank you, and then caught me off guard when he tried to kiss me. And . . . before I knew it . . . his hands were all over me, and he pulled my blouse so hard, buttons popped off. "

"Tell me he didn't . . . hurt you?"

She was twisting the dustcloth in her hands. "Would've if I hadn't kneed him proper. He went down hard, and I scrambled to my bike and took off. But, Leta, what if he hadn't gone down? What if I couldn't have stopped him? How far would he have tried to go? What would've happened to me, here by myself? Might've been some guests inside, for all I know, but not Libby or Gavin."

Must have been Jill I saw on her bicycle Saturday night, I thought. I did my best to calm her. I was sure I was the only person she'd told, but I asked anyway. "Jill, did you tell Jenny or your parents?"

"No. I'm ashamed, and I feel stupid. Dad would say I shouldn't have gone over to him, I should've known better. But it's right to help someone, isn't it?"

"I think it's a natural reaction, Jill. We tend to take folks at face value and not think the worst—or at least I do. I don't think you were stupid, and certainly, you shouldn't be ashamed."

I glanced out the window and saw that Gemma's car was still here. "Jill, would you be comfortable sharing your story with Gemma? I hate for you to have to repeat your story, but I think she needs to know. Everything that happened here could be pertinent to her investigation."

Jill looked at me for a moment before nodding yes. "Okay, then," I said. "You stay here with Dickens, and I'll go get her."

I hurried to Gemma's cottage. When I told her she needed to speak with Jill and why, she didn't miss a beat. Still in her running clothes, she went straight to the inn. I walked to the garage, wondering whether Jill's buttons would be visible in the gravel. It had rained the day before, and guests had come and gone, but the buttons might be there.

I was hardly going to disturb the crime scene, given the luggage that had been loaded and unloaded and the cars that had pulled in and out since Saturday night, but I was careful anyway. I saw a speck of white and knelt down. I used a piece of gravel to dig a bit of dirt. Sure enough, it was a white button. I left it there so Gemma could retrieve it without my smudging any fingerprints. I wasn't sure fingerprints would help, but you never know.

Paddington was in the hall when I strode in the front door. "Glad you spoke to Jill, Leta. She needs taking care of. She hasn't sat still long enough for me to crawl in her lap to comfort her, but Dickens seems to be making her feel better."

I scratched his ears. "Paddington, didn't you tell Dickens you saw Max's top hat in his truck?"

"Sure did. Funny thing. It smelled musty. Didn't smell like a rabbit at all."

That made me laugh. "Trust me, Max never pulled a real rabbit out of that hat. And it was there in the truck after you saw Max at the river?"

Paddington assured me that was the case. I was thinking about that when I heard Gavin call me. He was in the kitchen. "What on earth is going on? When I walked into the conservatory, my daughter shooed me out. Does Gemma talking to Jill mean something else has happened? Something beyond Libby finding a dead body?"

Gavin had been right in his sense that something was wrong, but It wasn't my place to tell him Jill had been assaulted. Though her quick reaction had staved off the worst, she'd had a terrible experience.

I was spared having to come up with a reply to Gavin's question when Libby appeared in the kitchen. She looked better than she had the day before, but not much. "I feel as though a truck hit me. Coffee, I need coffee."

I poured her a cup and moved her to the kitchen table while Gavin pulled the breakfast casserole from the oven. After I poured three glasses of fresh-squeezed orange juice, we dug in. Well, Gavin and I dug in—Libby moved her food around her plate.

Gavin and I were on the same wavelength, wanting Libby to get some food down. Gavin thought eating would help her get back to her old self—the way she'd been before finding a dead body. I wanted her to be fortified and less shaky in case Jill chose to share her story, but it soon became apparent she wasn't going to eat.

Dickens wandering into the kitchen took the focus off Libby. When he sat and looked expectantly at her, she slipped him a chunk of the scone she'd crumbled in her plate. My boy was adept at picking out the softest touch. He tried the same approach on me, but I told him no way. He was putting the touch on Gavin when Jill and Gemma came into the kitchen.

"Mornin' Dad, Mum," said Gemma. "Oh good, you saved us some coffee."

She busied herself at the coffeepot, and Jill sat down next to Libby. "Okay, this is hard for me," she choked out. Gemma handing her a cup of coffee seemed to strengthen her resolve. "But I want you both to know what happened Saturday night before I left for home." With that, she repeated much the same story she'd told me.

Gavin and Libby were both speechless. With tears in her eyes, Libby put her arms around Jill and pulled her close, and I could see Jill's shoulders relax as Libby stroked her hair. They sat like that for a few moments until Gemma spoke up. "You're a strong girl, Jill."

Gavin shook himself and asked, "Don't you want to take some time off, Jill? I mean I don't know what's best in the circumstances, but being here can't be helping, can it?"

Jill frowned. "I'd rather keep working, if it's all the same to you. I feel comfortable and safe here with you and Libby, and staying busy helps."

Libby and Gavin quickly agreed, and Jill headed to the laundry room. As prone as Libby was to tears, I was surprised at her calm. She asked Gemma a few questions and shook her head, but she didn't break down. I suspected the pills the doctor had given her had numbed her to some extent. *She'll get through this*, I thought, *and so will Jill*.

As I finished clearing the table, I pulled Gemma aside and

told her about the button. She scowled. "Bloody hell, you didn't pick it up, did you?"

"I keep trying to tell you I've learned my lesson, Gemma. Give me some credit."

And then she did it. She rolled her eyes at me. "If you'd learned your lesson, you wouldn't have gone near the garage at all."

I snapped back at her. "You know good and well I couldn't disturb something so many people have already trampled. Repeat after me," I mimicked her. "Do not disturb the crime scene."

She muttered something like here we go again and left. It seemed a good time for Dickens and me to do the same.

Dickens pestered me to tell him what I'd learned from Gemma, but I wanted time to think. Walking home in silence would help me sort through both facts and impressions. Gemma had chided me in the past about relying too heavily on intuition, but it paid off as often as not. Who was I kidding? She hadn't chided me. She'd implied I was an idiot.

I don't know why I let her get under my skin. Well, really, I *did* know. I'd figured out long ago that I didn't take criticism well and any implication I was slow on the uptake got all over me. Not a fatal flaw, but a flaw nonetheless.

Something told me Gemma and I would be at loggerheads before long.

Chapter Five

I reminded myself that sleuthing wasn't the only thing on my to-do list for the day. I pulled out the ingredients for spanakopita so I could put it together ready to pop in the oven when my guests arrived. I'd thawed the phyllo dough and spinach overnight, so now all I had to do was chop the feta, onions, garlic, and dill, and put everything together.

Some people spread olive oil on the layers of phyllo instead of melted butter, to make the dish lighter, but to me, butter—lots of butter—made the recipe. Soon enough, the 9x12 casserole dish was filled, covered in foil, and placed in the fridge.

The salad I could throw together when I put the main dish in the oven. Wendy was bringing dessert, and I had several bottles of red wine on hand.

Next on the to-do list was adding details to my column about the Fête. I described the costumes, the fairy hair, and more, everything except Max the Magnificent's ugly behavior and the discovery of his body. My columns were upbeat and all about smiles, so mentioning a death at the Fête wouldn't do.

That done, I perused my topic ideas for the remainder of

October and asked Christie if she'd like to take over for Halloween. She'd long been vocal about the bad rap black cats had, and this would give her an opportunity to debunk the myth they were evil. My editor got a kick out of the occasional columns written by the dog and cat. He thought I had a real knack for imagining their voices and had no idea I simply typed what they dictated.

Christie looked up from her cozy spot in the file drawer. "That's a great idea, Leta. I know just what I want to say, so let's get started. People need to know we black cats are special because we're exceptionally intelligent, not because we're evil."

I chuckled at her indignation. "I know you're not evil, but this is the first I've heard that black cats as a group are highly intelligent. Don't get me wrong, I know *you* are, but all black cats?"

She purred. "You'll have to trust me on this, Leta."

And so it went. Christie meowed her thoughts, I typed, and Dickens snored gently beneath the desk. At least two of us had a productive afternoon.

I was preparing a plate of grapes, hummus, and pita chips when Beatrix knocked on the door. She looked harried, and I was quick to pour a glass of wine and sit her down at the kitchen table.

"How's Trixie doing today?" I asked.

"Probably better than you or I would be. The young are for sure more resilient. She sent her mother home after lunch and told her she'd busy herself working at the bookshop and be fine. Since she's been out two days, I'm behind on paperwork. Glad she's ready to come back.

"She had an asthma attack last night when her mum was here, but she's recovered well. I think telling the story over and over plus Gemma telling her not to leave town was too much for her. I don't know whether or not doctors think stress can trigger an asthma attack, but I think it does."

"Gee, Beatrix, I think I read somewhere there's a connection. Poor kid."

"Yes, her parents were probably overprotective of her because of her asthma. Could be why she fell hard for Max. First time really out on her own, you know."

We heard Wendy and Belle coming in. I hollered for them to make themselves comfortable in the sitting room and asked Beatrix to take the appetizer tray and join them. I followed behind her with the wine bottle and glasses.

I poured wine. Christie jumped in Belle's lap, and Dickens rolled over for a belly rub from Wendy. I hoped the relaxed setting would make our discussion easier.

Wendy pulled out her phone. "Let me show you the Fête photos I found on the *Astonbury Aha!* There are lots of great crowd shots and quite a few of our costumed gang. And, I did find a few of Max. Nothing particularly telling, though."

As we looked at the website, I had to admit that Max was a hit with the crowd. I could almost hear the children laughing as I swiped through shots of him doing tricks. I pulled up a photo of him with Sparkle. She was smiling as he placed his hat on her head. The next picture caught her grinning as she pulled flowers out of the hat. They looked happy together.

Beatrix looked thoughtful. "He seems so nice in these photos. I suppose he was once the same way with Trixie."

"I'm sure he was," said Belle. "Good-looking, charming, all the things young girls fall for."

I shook my head in wonder. "Well, on that note, shall we dive into what we've learned?"

Beatrix spoke up. "I've been busy at the bookshop and only know what Trixie's told me, so I'm eager to hear from you ladies. I'm sure you've plenty to share."

She was right, so I recapped what we knew from my visit to the scene on Sunday morning and from Trixie's story. I added the little bit Constable James had learned from Sparkle and the fact that she'd initially denied seeing Max after the pub encounter.

Hearing that Sparkle had lied elicited a gasp from Beatrix. "What else do we know about this Sparkle girl? Why would she lie?"

Before I could say anything else, Belle spoke up. "Don't know the answer to that, Beatrix, but Wendy and I did find out more about her today. We visited Summer at the soap shop. We arrived when it opened, and it was a slow day for the fairy hair business."

Wendy nodded and said, "Seems Summer and Sparkle have been business partners for about a year. Summer's been a fairy hair pro for several years and only met Sparkle last year in Totnes when there was a festival there."

Belle picked up the story. "Sparkle worked in a hair salon washing hair and thought doing fairy hair might be her ticket to a better job. It seemed a win-win for Summer to train her to do it in Totnes and at the same time gain a helper to join her at festivals where she always has more business than she can handle.

"Summer trained Sparkle at the soap shop in Cheltenham for a week and let her stay at her home. Sparkle was a natural and became a regular on the festival circuit with Summer. This was last year, and together they've done rather well."

"They've got a good thing going," said Wendy. "They get along well, split the travel expenses and entry fees for the events, and then split the weekend's take."

Beatrix seemed impatient. "Did you learn anything about Sparkle and Max?"

"Just that she's only recently started talking about him. She wasn't in a relationship when Summer first met her," replied Wendy.

I considered what I was hearing. "Did Summer say what time Sparkle got in on Saturday night?"

"Yes," said Belle. "Summer left soon after Trixie, a bit after 9. They often take two cars to events because Sparkle likes to party later than Summer does. Summer got home and followed her routine of straightening and storing her silk threads and hooks before going to bed. She thinks she heard Sparkle around midnight, which would be an early night for her. She said she can't be sure."

Wendy added, "Summer said they'd all three had more than enough to drink, and she's surprised she heard Sparkle at all. She's a sound sleeper, especially after a few too many pints."

Belle looked at me. "Is this it as far as news? It's past time for my dinner, girls."

Oops. I'd preheated the oven but forgotten to put the spanakopita in it. I told my guests I'd serve the salad, and it wouldn't be too long before the main course. It was nothing to throw together the salad and uncork another bottle of wine.

We moved to the dining room table, and I heard no objections to refills. I plated the salads and offered a toast to good friends before we dug in.

Belle took a few bites before exclaiming, "Goodness, how I love this salad. You're either going to have to invite me over more often or start a delivery service."

I thanked her and told the story of how Henry and I had participated in an annual Christmas dinner for twenty years with several couples. On a weekend night in December, we went to the same house every year and ate the same main course, beef tenderloin cooked on the grill. The rest of us brought appetizers, sides, and dessert.

I brought Greek salad all but one time. That year we'd decided to mix up our assignments. I arrived with the appetizer, Rosalynn Carter's Strawberry Cheese Ring, and someone else brought a different salad. Both were delicious, but my friends unanimously proclaimed my assignment would forever after be Greek salad. Boring for me, but darned easy.

While we waited for the main course to bake, I first swore the group to secrecy and then shared an abbreviated version of Jill's story. They didn't need to know the details, but his behavior with Jill was something we needed to consider as we tried to figure out who the murderer could be. The horrified reactions were no surprise.

"Oh no, poor Jill," exclaimed Wendy.

"Not something she'll soon get over," said Belle.

"I knew he was a rotter, but . . . but . . ." exclaimed Beatrix. "I wonder if he was abusive with Trixie. Is that why she was divorcing him? I still can't believe she married him in the first place."

Though I'd had all day to digest Jill's shocking disclosure, I was still reeling as I considered what it could mean. "It occurs to me that Jill may not be the first one. What if this is a pattern, but no one's ever reported him?"

Wendy's eyes widened. "It that's the case, there could be women lined up out there wanting to kill him. For that matter, there could be boyfriends, fathers, and husbands lined up too."

I pulled the spanakopita from the oven and cleared the

salad dishes. Once the main course was on the table, there was very little chatter.

"Oh my gosh, scrumptious," remarked Wendy. "I've eaten this before in Greek restaurants, but this is so much better."

"Please add this to my delivery order," said Belle between bites.

"Ditto and ditto," sighed Beatrix.

It was nice to hear the compliments. I'd made this dish any number of times, but mostly for girlfriends. Henry had a thing about cooked spinach and might tolerate a bite or two, but that was about it. Funny, neither of my brothers-in-law liked cooked spinach either. A spinach salad was fine, though.

Wendy and I shooed Beatrix and Belle back to the sitting room, and we cleared the table, brewed a pot of decaf, and sliced the carrot cake she'd picked up in a Cheltenham bakery. Soon dessert and coffee were served in front of the fireplace.

After I all but licked my plate, it was time to get back to business. "Now, ladies, where do we go from here?"

"To bed?" asked Beatrix.

"Right, but not quite yet," I responded.

"What she means, Beatrix," said Wendy, "is what are the next steps on our sleuthing agenda?"

Beatrix looked slightly aghast, and I realized she hadn't been as actively involved in the last investigation as we had. In truth, I'd briefly considered her a suspect. "You ladies aren't serious, are you?"

Belle looked at her. "Serious as a heart attack, dear. Considering your niece is high on Gemma's list of possible murderers, we need to expand the suspect list. Better yet, we need to identify the killer."

I'm not sure I'd have put it quite so baldly, but Belle was right. We had a vested interest in clearing Trixie. She was one of our own now. My intuition, despite Gemma's doubts, was telling me someone else had done the dastardly deed.

Wendy had been sitting with her feet tucked under her. I watched her slowly unwind herself and put her feet on the floor. She had an idea. I could tell.

"Let's go to Totnes."

"Totnes?" I asked.

"Yes, we can find out more about Max and what other trouble he's been in. You know he didn't turn into a different person because he came to Astonbury. There has to be a pattern. And we can nose around about Sparkle too. Consider it background. We're in need of background."

I thought she was on to something. "That's not a bad idea. And, Beatrix, wouldn't you love to know more about how Trixie came to marry Max? I was intrigued by the few details she shared with me, but there's bound to be more to it."

Beatrix was showing interest. "I'd love to know that story. She never had a serious boyfriend in school as far as I know. Then, bam, she meets Max and she's married."

The three members of Leta's Detective Agency, or whatever our name was, looked at each other, and it was the senior member who spoke first. "So, when do we leave? Have to get Peter to look after the animals."

We'd finally gotten Dickens's attention. "You're taking me, aren't you?"

I glanced up at my companions and said, "I think Dickens wants to go."

Neither of them realized I'd understood him, but Wendy said, "Sure, let's take him. Most of the B&Bs allow dogs."

Henry and I'd visited Dartmouth on one of our trips and taken the ferry to Totnes. We'd wandered up and down its steep High Street, and I remembered it being packed with small shops. I recalled reading that back in the day, Totnes had been known for its hippy population, and it still had a bit of that vibe with its mix of New Age crystal shops, organic markets, and vintage clothing shops.

Belle was in planning mode. "Shall we stay in Dartmouth or Totnes? I admit I have a fondness for Dartmouth as I vacationed there once many years ago, and I adore the ferry on the River Dart. May have to bundle up this time of year on the water."

"Maybe we should stay at the hotel at the Dart Marina because it has an elevator and patio rooms too," I said. "I love the charm of a B&B, but we can't have you going up and down the stairs, Belle. I'll check around both towns. I know we'll be working, but let's make an excursion of this, maybe visit Agatha Christie's Greenway while we're there."

Christie's ears perked up and she meowed. "You're going to Agatha Christie's home, and you're not taking me? You *cannot* be serious."

Wendy looked at my vocal cat. "Do you think she heard her name? What was that screech about?"

"Oh, she probably wants to go too," I said, "But there's not enough room in my taxi for three women, a dog, and a cat carrier. Good thing she likes Peter."

Christie reached up and patted Belle on the chin and meowed again. "I really like you. Tell them you want me to go."

We all laughed at her. Christie knew good and darned well only I could understand her. Her message was coming through loud and clear, but there was not a chance she was going with us.

"Shall we shoot for a Wednesday departure? By then, Gemma will have the medical examiner's report and if it wasn't murder, we can skip the sleuthing part. We can spend all our time shopping, eating out, and taking tours. What do you think?"

Wendy was full of ideas. "It's about a three-hour drive. If we leave by noon, we'll be there by mid-afternoon and have time to visit a few shops before dinner. Leta, do you want to book the hotel for three nights, and we can return home Saturday after breakfast?"

Beatrix looked as though she didn't know what to think about our expedition. "There's a part of me that wants to go with you, but I think I'm just happy to putter around my bookshop. Will you keep me posted along the way?"

"Sure thing," said Wendy. "And, Leta, I'll get with Peter about taking care of Tigger and Christie. Least I can do if you're making the lodging arrangements. Now, Mum, it's time we called it a night."

We all walked out together, and Beatrix drove off first. "Ladies," I said to Belle and Wendy, "Looks like, for now, our new name is Leta's *Traveling* Detective Agency."

Wendy helped her mum into the car and broke into song. "'On the road again' . . . And a theme song too! See you Wednesday."

Chapter Six

With no detective tasks on the schedule, Tuesday felt like a day off. I didn't have to rush out the door to check on anyone, and I could drink coffee and scan the online news still in my robe. Heck, I could make a morning yoga class at Rhiannon's studio. I let Dickens out, gave Christie her expected puddle of milk, and sipped my coffee.

Christie was being unusually sweet, not that she wasn't an affectionate cat, but I expected huffy behavior after last night's discussion of leaving her behind. She put her paws on my chair seat and jumped into my lap. "Okay, I get why I can't go, but I hate being left out. Will you bring me something from Agatha's place?"

"Agatha's place? Now you're on a first-name basis with Dame Agatha? Not sure what you'd like from a home that's a museum, but I'll see what I can do. Perhaps I'll find some special kitty treats in Totnes. Would organic treats suit you?"

The princess purred. "As long as they're tasty, that would be super. No kale."

Dickens barked at the door to be let in. As was his habit,

he lapped up the bit of milk Christie had left in her dish. Heaven forbid there be any trace of food or milk remaining. Only after Christie's dish was clean did he turn to his own bowl.

"So, boy, when I come back from yoga, shall we take a walk, maybe visit Martha and Dylan?"

"Oh yes, and we can discuss the case. I sure am looking forward to our road trip."

How nice that everyone was so agreeable this morning. As I changed into my yoga pants and headed to town, I wondered whether the backpack I'd ordered would be waiting by the door when I returned. That would be a nice treat for Christie . . . I hoped.

Today's session concentrated on inversions culminating with headstands. It was my least favorite of Rhiannon's classes. I had mastered headstands against the wall but didn't think I'd ever manage to do one in the middle of the room. Rhiannon continued to tell me it was my mind that was holding me back, not my body. She said my arms and shoulders were strong enough, and one day she'd get me up.

Rhiannon tidied up the room when class ended. "Ready for cup of coffee at Toby's?" she asked.

"Love one. Wonder if he'll have some pumpkin spice scones left after the early morning rush. That and a latte would make my day."

We were in luck. Jenny was taking a fresh batch of scones from the oven when we walked in, and we each ordered one to go with our drinks. Rhiannon was tuned into the village grapevine and knew about the body at the inn and Gemma interviewing Trixie. She'd checked on Libby this morning by phone and said she sounded near to her old self.

When I told her about our trip to Totnes, she broke into a grin. "Wish I could go, but I can't very well shut down the studio. I love the vibe in Totnes. You know they say New Age happened there before it hit most other places in the UK, and it's always been a magnet for artists, musicians, and pagans. I've been to a few yoga retreats there and would love to go back. Maybe you, Wendy, and I can sign up for one this winter when business is slow in Astonbury."

"I bet we'd enjoy that. I'll see what I can find out while we're there. Our focus this trip is finding out what we can about Max and Sparkle and whatever else, but I'm sure we'll find time for a bit of retail therapy. What better way to make inquiries than to visit the shops on High Street."

Rhiannon looked at me thoughtfully. "I think your trip sounds grand, but I'm curious. You've spoken with Trixie. Why not Sparkle? Seems to me she could give you another perspective on Max. And the poor girl could probably use someone to talk to. After all, she just lost her boyfriend."

She had a point. Why hadn't I spoken with Sparkle? At first, it was because I couldn't imagine she'd want to speak with me. I thought for a moment. When I heard Sparkle had lied to Constable James, had I subconsciously formed an unfavorable impression of her?

"Gee, Rhiannon, that's a good question. You just gave me a much-needed shake, and I feel bad that I haven't reached out to the girl. I think in my concern for Trixie, I lost sight of Sparkle's feelings, and that's not like me. At least, I hope it isn't."

Rhiannon shook her head. "How like you to feel guilty. I didn't mean to imply it's your job to comfort everyone who crosses your path. Sorry if it sounded that way. I had as much interaction with her as you did, and I haven't sought her out either."

"Thanks for that. Bet you didn't know how prone I am to second-guessing myself. Still, you make a good point. I bet Sparkle could use someone to talk to, and she could also provide a more recent perspective on Max. I'll text Summer for her number."

Summer replied to my request as I was driving home, and I was all set to ring Sparkle until I spied the Amazon box propped against my garage door. I knew it was the backpack. Dickens and Christie both looked at me, and Christie meowed loudly. The girl loved boxes.

When I pulled out the contents, Dickens barked. "Are you taking a backpack on our walk, or is that for the trip?"

"This is for Christie if she'll give it a try. Are you game, girl?"

Christie backed away. "Game for what, exactly?"

I explained my idea for taking her on walks with me and Dickens. She looked skeptical, but she wanted badly to be included. She moved closer to the backpack and sniffed it. Next, she stretched out a paw for a tentative touch, and finally, she stuck her head into the opening.

"Kind of like a box," she meowed. "Except it's cloth."

I left her in the kitchen to explore the backpack while I changed into warm clothes. Dickens's reaction to my gloves, jacket, and wool cap was to bark and stand by the door. He was ready for his leash, but first I wanted to place Christie in the backpack.

"You ready to give it a try?"

Her response was to crawl all the way in, turn around, and poke her head out. Maybe this would work after all. I attached a short, slim leash to her breakaway collar and connected it to a ring on the backpack. I couldn't chance her leaping out but also had to be sure she didn't choke herself if she tried. When I had my arms in the straps, she meowed but stayed put.

"Okay, gang, let's be on our way. The Parker family is going on its first walk together." Christie meowed, Dickens barked, and off we went. The chatter was nonstop.

Dickens pointed out everything as we walked. "See the bird on the fence. And look, you can see the sheep off in the distance. Just wait 'til you see the donkeys. They're awesome."

Christie rode with her paws at the base of my neck and occasionally gave me a lick. With a soft meow, she spoke up. "Look at the birds in the trees. And, oh, is that a squirrel? Leta, this is super cool."

She was beside herself when Martha and Dylan trotted to the fence. When I reached into the side pouch to retrieve the carrots, she meowed, "Oh, that's who the carrots are for. I always wondered why you and Dickens took carrots with you."

I leaned over the fence so she could sniff Dylan's nose. The donkeys took this new visitor in stride, and it was only when Dylan's nostrils flared that Christie screeched and jerked back.

"That's one big nose," she meowed.

My experiment was going well, so I asked my companions if they were up for a visit to the inn. Christie had never met Paddington, and I wondered how that would go.

Dickens thought it was a grand idea. "Christie, I'll intro-duce you. Paddington and I have great fun together."

I couldn't see Christie, but I imagined her rolling her eyes.

"Pfft, is that the cat who thinks he's Leta's special friend? I'll be happy to set him straight."

My girl could get on her high horse in a heartbeat. Ever since she'd learned Paddington had slept in my room when I stayed at the inn, she'd been miffed. It was past time for the two to get to know each other and become friends.

Dickens was having none of her attitude. "Christie, I've already told Paddington you're top cat, and he's cool with that. If we're lucky, we can all play in the dirty linens together."

As we walked up the drive, I explained to Christie that I'd let her out of the backpack and off the leash if she'd promise to stay inside the inn. Probably because she was unsure of her surroundings, she agreed without putting up a fuss.

Dickens took off to look for Paddington, and I found Gavin at his desk in the conservatory. He chuckled when he saw Christie peeking out of her backpack. "Now that's a sight. How did you get her to agree to that?"

I couldn't tell him that Christie frequently fussed at being left behind, so I fudged. "She seems so lonely when Dickens and I take our long walks; I thought she'd enjoy going with us. So far, I think she likes it. You should have seen her sniff Dylan's nose.

"If it's okay with you, I'll take her out of the backpack and let her explore. Hopefully, she and Paddington will get along."

Gavin grinned. "Paddington might enjoy having a four-legged visitor—in addition to Dickens, of course. I suspect he makes plenty of friends on his nightly rambles. I've just never met any of them. I'm not sure what he gets up to every night, but sometimes he comes back with burrs or muddy paws, not to mention the occasional *gift*. If he could talk, he'd have a tale for us."

I set my pack on the floor, unlatched Christie, and lifted

her out. She crouched by the pack and surveyed her surroundings before stretching out a tentative paw. In a flash, she leaped to Gavin's desk, scattering papers. She dipped her paws and her nose over the edge to the file drawer. I knew exactly what she was after.

"Christie, I don't think Gavin keeps cat treats in his desk drawer."

She looked up as though in shock. "He doesn't? Why not?"

"Gavin, I keep cat treats in my desk at home, so that's what she's looking for. Do you have any around? Point me in the right direction, and I'll get them."

Now, he was laughing. "Oh, Paddington's are kept in the laundry room. Jill's in there. She'll point them out for you."

I left Christie stretched out on the desk, getting her ears scratched by Gavin. Sure enough, Jill showed me the cat treats. We chatted for a moment about how she was faring after her encounter with Max.

"Gemma tells me he'd been reported to the police several times in Totnes for the same thing, but no one ever went as far as pressing charges. Guess he could turn on the charm when he was sober. Do you think he'd have been by here the next day to apologize and chat me up if he hadn't died?"

"Could have been his pattern, I suppose," I mused. "But being let off the hook doesn't make him any less of a jerk in my book. What else did Gemma find out?"

"Not much. He was brought up in foster care, and she didn't find any immediate family. She said he'd been hauled in for bar brawls, public drunkenness, and the like, but never spent more than a night locked up. I think it's odd. He was so good with the kids on Saturday and seemed to genuinely enjoy entertaining them, but I don't recall seeing him smile much any other time."

"Maybe he didn't have a particularly happy life. Trixie might have been the one bright spot, but he blew that."

I took some cat treats and carried them to the conservatory. I could hear Dickens barking, a cat howling, and Libby laughing as I approached.

"Leta, will you look at this?" cried Libby. "Paddington seems riled that Christie's on the desk. He's perched on the bookcase, doing his low-pitched howl, and I could swear your cat's looking at him as if to say, 'I'm in charge now.'"

Libby didn't realize how accurate she was. Gavin was quiet, Christie was taunting Paddington, and Dickens was trying to make peace between the two felines. I grabbed Christie and whispered in her ear. "Behave, missy, or there'll be no treats for you . . . and no more trips to the inn."

How could she look so innocent? How had she managed to create an uproar without lifting a paw? Attitude. It was all about attitude, and Christie had it in spades.

"Leta, I don't know what you're talking about," she meowed sweetly. "I've been resting on the desk minding my own business. It's Paddington who's being inhospitable."

Paddington chose that moment to hiss. "She waltzes in here like some kind of primadonna and demands treats—my treats—and she calls me *inhospitable*? Who does she think she is?"

That was it. Much to the dismay of Paddington, I carried Christie to the bookcase. "Okay, you two, you're my favorite felines. Christie, you're my princess, and Paddington, you're my prince. I, however, am the Queen, and I expect you two to knock it off. Are we clear?"

They both huffed and looked at me. Then Paddington leaped down and twined around my ankles, and I put Christie on the floor beside him. The two circled each other as we all watched.

Dickens dashed over. "About time, you two. Now, let's have some fun. Jill left a pile of dirty linens at the top of the stairs."

With that, they took off. The looks on Gavin and Libby's faces were priceless.

"What just happened?" asked Libby.

I laughed and told a half-truth. "Who knows? I've found if I use a certain tone with Christie, she responds, and it seems to work on Paddington too."

"I've heard of horse whisperers," said Gavin. "Maybe you're a cat whisperer."

It was time to change the subject. "Right. Let's not get carried away. So, Libby, how are you doing today?"

Libby seemed to be improving. She'd slept Monday night without the sedatives and felt almost back to normal. When she offered me a cup of tea, we left Gavin to his paperwork and continued our chat in the kitchen. She was interested in the plan to visit Totnes and suggested I stay for lunch because Gemma would be coming by for a bite.

"I think Gemma's gotten the autopsy results, and she's stopping by here before she goes to the caravan park in Bourton-on-the-Water."

I was eager to hear what the coroner had to say and surprised that Gemma was just now getting to the caravan. Though my sister Anna had jokingly said Astonbury was crime-ridden, that really wasn't the case, and I knew the delay in the caravan visit stemmed from lack of manpower at the Stow-on-the-Wold police station.

I knew Gemma had her work cut out for her. "Guess it's not like Oxford or London, where a team of police officers would've already descended on the caravan, maybe the magic shop in Totnes, and who knows where else. Other than someone to run background checks on the computer, it's pretty much down to Gemma and Constable James to do all the legwork."

"Yes, and it's down to Gemma's mum to see the girl gets a decent meal now and then," said Libby. "When she's anywhere near, I encourage her to grab lunch or tea or whatever."

While we waited, Libby filled me in on how much money we'd raised at the Fête and how the various booths and events had done. I was pleased to hear our two costumed groups had brought in a sizable chunk, as had the auction of the scarecrows.

"That reminds me, I need to find the best spot for my Raggedy Ann and Andy scarecrows. Want to help me with that?"

Of course I did, so we fetched them from the garage and wandered the garden and courtyard. We decided they looked best in the flowerbed to the left of the front door where they could greet the inn guests.

Gemma pulled up as we were standing back to admire our work. "Good choice, ladies. Those two are sure to make weary travelers smile."

"Hello, dear. I've invited Leta to join us for lunch. I hope you have more than a few minutes."

"I'm due to meet the manager of the caravan park in an hour, so I have exactly forty-five minutes, Mum."

We hustled inside, where Libby ladled vegetable soup into bowls and pulled plates of chicken salad from the fridge. Gemma and I dug in as Libby took a tray to Gavin at his desk. We'd almost finished our soup by the time she returned to serve herself.

"Your recipe or Gavin's?" I asked. "Delicious."

Libby laughed. "It's different every time, so it's hard to say. We start with ground beef or maybe a bone from a roast and add whatever vegetables are available at the farmer's market. If you show up next week, it won't be the same."

That description brought back fond memories of my grandmother, my mom, and my aunts cooking in Atlanta. Greek dishes were standard and rarely varied, but good old Southern soups could be all over the board.

I looked at Gemma. "Your mother thinks you may have gotten the autopsy report. Have you? Was it helpful?"

"You *do* realize your name is fitting, right? Leta *Nosy Parker?*"

I chuckled. No one had called me that before, but I had to admit she was probably right. "Hey, it's Leta Petkas Parker to you. But if the shoe fits . . ."

"Well, you saw the obvious things—the battered nose, the apple in the mouth, and his scarf 'round his neck. It turns out he was strangled with the scarf. Odd thing about that. Apparently, the scarf was pulled tight enough to strangle him and then loosened. Who does something like that?

"The bloody nose was fresh, and we know the mark on his cheek was from Trixie slapping him earlier on Saturday. His torso was bruised too, consistent with someone walloping him a day earlier, and he had plenty of older injuries—broken rib, for one. Not hard to believe someone would rough him up given what we know about him. What is it you say in the States? He was cruising for a bruising?"

She was right. It wasn't difficult to imagine him getting in a fight. "But I bet the bruises didn't have anything to do with his death. And neither did the bloody nose, right?"

It was Libby who piped up. "Maybe not, but it could mean he'd angered someone enough to go after him."

"Exactly, Mum. We know he'd infuriated both Trixie and Sparkle, but I doubt either one beat him up. So who did? Could be someone came back to finish the job with the scarf, since neither girl happened to own up to strangling him. Heck, even Jill has a motive."

"Gemma," Libby exclaimed, "Surely you don't consider Jill a suspect?"

"Not a serious suspect, Mum, but I can't officially rule her out yet."

I asked, "Is this the way it always is? The more you find out, the larger the suspect pool gets?"

"Ah, the amateur sleuth begins to see the light," she wise-cracked. "Same as last time, right?"

It was time to butter up my police resource. "Sure is. You had more suspects than you knew what to do with, but you narrowed down the list by getting alibis, and I ferreted out a few myself."

"Yes, you did, though you got a bit off track in the end, didn't you?"

That comment irritated me, but I managed to let it go. "Oh, let's not dwell on that. Back to this case. Was that it for the autopsy?"

"That was plenty, but we also got his bloodwork back. We knew he was inebriated based on what our witnesses told us, and the analysis bore that out, but he also had oxycodone in his bloodstream. That's not a good combination with alcohol, and he had enough in his bloodstream to incapacitate him. That would make it easy for someone to pull that scarf tight and not get much, if any, resistance from the victim. Probably took it to ease the pain from the battering he got Friday night."

"Isn't that a prescription drug? I wonder where he got it."

"Ha! The likes of him? Might have had a prescription, since his record indicates he was frequently in brawls. Still, with the proper connections, it's easy enough to come by. "

"That's what it seems like on all the TV shows I watch. Drugs everywhere. Jill mentioned you'd done a background check on him and discovered he had a record but no convictions."

"Yes, he was everything I thought he'd be, so there could be plenty of folks wanting to beat him up, but kill him? And most of his nasty behavior took place in Totnes, so why travel here to get at him? More digging to do. That's why I'm visiting the caravan today. I sent Constable James to check it out Sunday, but he'd barely gotten there before he was called to a break-in. All he had time to do was to padlock the door."

She took another bite of chicken salad and seemed to make a quick decision. "Want to meet me there? Like I said Sunday morning, there's no denying you're observant."

Wow. I didn't even have to ask. I could never predict how Gemma would treat me. She went from one extreme to another with little in between—she'd either seek me out and value my input or talk to me as though I were a flaming idiot. At the moment, I seemed to be in her good graces, except for her constant jibes. "Sure, glad to help, but I walked here with Dickens and Christie, so I'll have to get them home first."

Libby offered to save us some time by watching over my four-legged companions, and I suggested we take Dickens with us. Gemma gave me a look, but I knew she'd grown fond of Dickens during the last case. She threw up her hands and off we went.

Chapter Seven

I'd never visited a caravan park, or RV resort as we call them back home, but I knew folks who spent months traveling in their campers. Henry had made noises about doing that when we retired, but I was more of a rent-a-villa-in-France kind of gal. The only upside I could see to a camper was being able to take Dickens and Christie along.

The grounds at this site were well-kept, as you'd expect in the Cotswolds. The manager escorted us to Max's caravan and left us to it. From the outside, it looked to be in good shape, but the inside was a different story.

It had that unwashed smell you find in dorms or fraternity rooms. "That odor must be the same the world over. It reminds me of the house my college boyfriend shared with four guys. If they washed their linens quarterly, it was a miracle, and the ring in the tub seemed permanent."

Gemma grimaced. "That smell combined with the take-away containers on the counter and overflowing the garbage bin—disgusting. And I'm sure I'd be labeled sexist if I called this a male thing."

"You know you would, but I bet most women would agree. Maybe we should poll mothers to see what they'd say about the housekeeping habits of their sons."

Never one to miss an opportunity to eat, Dickens stuck his nose in a container, but I snatched it away before he could lick it. "What a waste," barked my boy. "You can tell he didn't have a dog to help with the scraps."

I cringed. "Dickens, don't even think about eating this food. No telling how long it's been here and what's crawling in it. This whole place is a health hazard."

Gemma, oblivious to my conversation with Dickens, handed me a pair of gloves. "Let's see what we find. Not likely to be anything obvious like a threatening note or an appointment book leading us to the killer, but maybe something's buried in this mess. I'll start in the back."

That left me the tiny kitchen area and couch. I went through the cabinets first. Most of the melamine plates and cups were in the sink or on the counter, so I made short work of that search. Two of the three small drawers contained only a jumble of utensils.

The third was a catchall for scraps of paper and takeaway menus. I found several check-cashing receipts from the Money Shop in Totnes and a late notice from the caravan park there. It appeared he was a month to month customer.

A paper clip held several scraps together. The best I could tell, they were scrawls about magic tricks. I wouldn't have thought of him as sentimental, but he'd held on to a coffee-stained birthday card from Trixie. And there was a wedding photo of the two tucked inside.

The fridge held only beer, and the freezer a half-empty bottle of Jagermeister. I remembered shots of the liqueur being all the rage among twenty-somethings years ago, but I'd never tried it. We Greeks stuck to ouzo if we wanted a licorice-flavored drink.

Beyond the takeaway containers on the counter, the only other item was a pottery sugar jar. It was an afterthought to pull the lid off, but it was a good thing I did. Stuck inside was a wad of £50 notes—twenty of them. Late on payments to his Totnes caravan park, but flush with cash?

I saved the most disgusting parts of the kitchen for last— the sink and the garbage. It was hard to tell the difference between the two. "Honestly, who lives like this?" I muttered.

Crumpled in the corner of the sink was the note from Trixie asking Max to meet her at the Fête to discuss the divorce papers. The tone was polite but firm.

"How's it going back there?" I hollered.

"It's disgusting and not very fruitful," she replied. "Unless you're looking to corner the market on condoms and porn."

Yuck. My opinion of Max was already pretty low, and it wasn't improving.

The couch was covered in dirty clothes. I shook out shirts and searched pants pockets but came up empty except for wadded up napkins and a lighter. There was no lingering smell of cigarettes, so I wondered what the lighter was for.

It wasn't until I'd moved the clothes around that I could see shallow drawers beneath the couch. Surprisingly neat, the first drawer held magic paraphernalia—a black cape, a wand, a silk blindfold, flyers for Max the Magnificent, several sealed packs of playing cards, and a red fringed scarf.

Dickens snuffled in the cape. "There's something here, Leta. Smells funny."

I reached in and pulled out a baggie of pot from beneath the cape. That explained the lighter. And there was a bottle of pills. Those I couldn't identify, but I wondered if they were oxycodone. The second drawer held neatly folded black satin sheets. Now that *was* a surprise. Apparently, he *did* know how to do laundry, despite all evidence to the contrary.

I felt the bottom of the drawers like the detectives do on TV, but there was no tell-tale clue pointing to the villain. Shoving clothes to the side, I laid out my finds on the couch and snapped photos. Christie would be eager to study those.

"Paydirt!" yelled Gemma. She came toward me holding a little red book and a laptop in her gloved hands.

Max didn't strike me as a guy who'd have a laptop.

Gemma was pleased with her find. "This could explain why there wasn't much on his phone. Maybe he did most things on this computer. If so, it could help us identify his friends and associates, but we won't know until we can analyze what's on this thing. And we need to check out what's in this little book. What did you find up here?"

I pointed to the arrangement on the couch. "A few interesting things. Pot and pills plus a wad of cash, yet he's behind on his bills."

Gemma studied the collection. "I wonder whether the drugs are for personal use or whether he's a small-time dealer. That's a fair number of pills, and the cash could point to dealing, but not in a big way. Remember I said his phone had texts about money and what appeared to be appointment times? At first glance, that's all I can see in this red book, except these notes have initials too. Maybe they're all clients, and *not* for his magic act."

Looking at the cash brought another question to mind. "What about this caravan and his truck? Does he owe much on them?" I asked.

"He owes more than they're worth, so we can strike money as a motive for Trixie. Based on what Constable James has uncovered, this cash is about all Max had to his name. This note from Trixie confirms what she said about wanting him to sign the divorce papers. The clock was ticking. That alone doesn't seem much of a motive for murder, but it's the only one we've uncovered so far."

Gemma looked around the living area. "And satin sheets? Not a clean spot in this lousy place. Bedding that should be burned, but carefully folded clean satin sheets? Go figure."

I had to agree the caravan was disgusting. "A filthy garbage-strewn living space, but two clean, organized drawers. I wonder how long it's been since he's had the opportunity to use his satin sheets."

"We need to know a lot more about him. I can ask the Totnes police to help, but they're as short on manpower as we are."

It was time to tell Gemma my Totnes plans. "I may be able to help with that. Belle, Wendy, and I are taking a trip to Dartmouth and Totnes this week. We thought we'd do a bit of shopping, eat fresh seafood, ride the ferry and the train, visit Greenway, and poke around and see what we can learn in Totnes."

That got an eye roll and a snort of laughter or anger. I wasn't sure which. "Here we go again. You expect me to believe you suddenly have an urge for seafood? And that nosing around Totnes is an afterthought? Why don't you have business cards printed—Miss Marple and Company?

"Do you really think those people on the coast will tell you three anything? Why would they? And more to the point, what makes you think I want your help?"

My mantra when dealing with Gemma was 'you catch more flies with honey,' but her snippy reactions made it difficult to listen to my internal voice. "Gemma, I realize the police are much better equipped to conduct a murder investigation, but you just said you're undermanned.

"And, as Belle likes to say, you'd be amazed at what folks will tell a sweet little old lady, especially one with a cane. She's our secret weapon."

"Bloody hell. I should know after last time, there's no stopping you. Just do me a favor and don't let the local constabulary know what you're up to, okay?"

I smiled sweetly. "No problem. We'll stay away from them, and if we unearth anything that might be helpful, we'll let you know."

That got me a huge eye roll, but no snide comment, so I was making progress. I waited by the car as Gemma fastened the padlock.

Dickens had been unusually quiet but chose this moment to pipe up. "Leta, has Gemma mentioned what they found in the wallet?"

Now, why hadn't I remembered one of the evidence bags had held a wallet? Dickens was no more a professional detective than I was, but he'd come up with a good question. When we climbed into the car, I asked Gemma.

"The SOCOs looked through it, but there wasn't much there. No credit cards, which isn't surprising. A bit of cash and a few fast food receipts. He *did* have one of those black and white picture strips from a photo booth—pics of him and Trixie. You know, those pictures and the wedding photo you found are the only truly personal things we've located. Could be he really did love the girl.

"We didn't turn up much in his truck either. The keys were on the floorboard, and the glovebox was crammed full of junk —gloves, paper napkins, chapstick, and the like. The metal storage container in the back held the stuff for his magic act, like stuffed animals, silk flowers, cards, his fold-up table, and tablecloth. Guess he sometimes set up a booth."

Almost as an afterthought, Gemma added, "But we did find one interesting thing—someone had written a message on the driver's side front fender."

"A message? What?"

"*Pig*. Actually, it was the word and a cute drawing of a pig. That's usually a reference to me and my lot, but in this case, I think it was intended differently. I can think of any number of people who might call Max a pig."

"Good grief. How on earth do you make sense of it? I mean is there some way to figure out who wrote it? Not like hand-writing analysis, is it?" I said.

"You're right. The best I can do is consider who might have reason to use that insult. I'm sure it was a reference to his behavior, but anyone who's seen his caravan would also call him a pig. Like I said, there could be a long list."

I considered what I'd seen and heard so far. "Hell's bells. More clues, more suspects, and yet no nearer to the answer. I wonder if there's anything revealing on this laptop. If it's not password protected, maybe I can fire it up while you drive, see what's there."

Dickens barked and peered over my shoulder, something he never got to do in my London taxi because he was always strapped in. "Great idea. I want to see."

Gemma glanced at me and laughed. "What's got him so excited all of a sudden? Go ahead and check it out."

We were in luck. Max didn't use a password, and when I hit enter, the screen displayed another wedding photo, this one of Trixie alone. I tilted it toward Gemma.

"Too lazy to change it or carrying a torch?" she asked.

"Let me open his pictures folder," I said. "Wow, this tells

quite a story. Not just wedding shots. They're all of him and Trixie and plenty of Trixie alone. Several from Christmas and a few winter shots. It makes sense there aren't any recent one because she filed for divorce about six months ago. And, just think, he took the time to load them from his phone to his laptop.

"Gemma, I think you're right about him being stuck on Trixie. Her photos are the only personal ones here. It'll be interesting to see whether his emails tell you anything more."

She sighed. "I'll put Constable James on that as soon as I get back to the station. That is, if he's not tied up with our usual assortment of crimes like petty theft and vandalism. Not enough hands to go around for something this serious, but we've got to figure it out soon."

Libby must have heard us pull up because she came outside with Christie in the backpack. "She and Paddington had a big time, and it wasn't long before she curled up in her pack for a snooze. I think she's ready to go home."

Even Gemma chuckled at that. Dickens and I hopped out. Before Gemma pulled off, I leaned in the window. "Gemma, you're willing to share and share alike on this case, kind of like we did last time, right? Other than my inadvertent foray to one of the crime scenes, I think I turned up useful information . . . don't you?"

She sighed and gave me a sidelong glance. "What I want to say is 'hell no,' but that'd be cutting off my nose to spite my face. If you think your trio of little old ladies can turn up something useful in Totnes, go for it. And in return, I'll let you know what, if anything, we find on the computer and in that little red book."

Now I was ready to choke her. "Little old ladies?" I spluttered. "You're calling me and Wendy old?!"

She smirked and didn't reply. I ground my teeth and repeated my honey mantra. Now was not the time to rile her, given she'd agreed to pass me information.

"But seriously, I wish you well," she said sweetly. Part of her infuriating pattern was to follow a snide comment with sugar.

I put my backpack on and waved bye to Libby. Christie slept all the way home. I had visions of the two cats running nonstop up and down the stairs, under and over beds in every room, and finally collapsing.

Dickens and I had expected to be regaled with stories about playtime with Paddington, but Christie hardly stirred when I placed her on the dog bed in front of the fireplace. Though she had several cat beds, she preferred her brother's beds. I was lighting the fire when I remembered I hadn't called Sparkle. *So much for a leisurely day,* I thought, as I wondered whether I could squeeze in a late tea or possibly dinner with the girl.

My call clicked over to voicemail and I left a message. "Just checking in to see how you're doing. This has to be an awful time for you, and I wanted you to know I'm here if you need someone to talk to."

I'd barely hung up when she called me back. "Hi, Leta, how good to hear from you. To be honest, I'm not doing all that well. It's hard being here and not in Totnes with my friends."

"I have some idea of how you feel. I lost my husband a couple of years ago, and I don't know what I would have done without my friends to lean on. Would it help to visit over coffee in the morning? It won't be the same as sitting down with a good friend, but it may help to talk about it."

"Gosh, Leta. I'm sorry to hear about your husband. How awful for you. Yes, I'd love to get together. Summer's lined up several mother-daughter duos for fairy hair for Wednesday afternoon, but I'm free until then. Do you want to meet in Cheltenham?"

I thought for a moment. The Ladies Detective Agency needed to be on the road by eleven at the latest, and I could more easily make that if Sparkle would come to Astonbury instead. She was fine with that, and we agreed to meet at Toby's at 9 am.

I was putting the kettle on when someone knocked on the door. It was a nice surprise to see Timmy and Deborah from next door.

"Hi there," I said. "You're just in time for a cup of tea."

Timmy darted in the door and ran to the sitting room, and Deborah nodded. "That would be lovely. I wanted to show you the photos I took Saturday at the Fête. You all were so cute. I'm going to frame one of the Peter Pan group to hang in John's dental office."

Timmy ran back in followed by Dickens. "What's wrong with Christie? I made sure not to ring the bell, you know. She rolled over when I touched her, but she didn't get up. Is she okay?"

That assessment made me laugh. Timmy had learned not to use the bell on the front of my schoolhouse if he wanted to see Christie. When he rang it, she bolted and wouldn't come out until long after he'd left.

"Timmy, she's tuckered out because she visited Paddington today."

That led to his examining the backpack and turning it every which way. He looked at me and grinned. "Leta, if I put Christie in the backpack, could I take her for show and tell one day?"

Deborah jumped in before I could. "Timmy, Christie can't go out without Leta. Besides, I think she might be scared of the kids in your playgroup. You know she doesn't much care for noise."

Timmy was undaunted. "Okay, can I wear my Michael footy pajamas instead and carry the teddy bear?"

I'd never been in the UK on Halloween, and I wondered what the protocol was. Did kids wear costumes to playgroup or school on Halloween day or wait until the evening when they went out to trick or treat? In the States, I thought it was a mix of the two.

"Timmy," said Deborah, "you can wear your outfit on Halloween day and then again when we take you around the neighborhood that afternoon. Not before then. And that's still a few weeks away."

I couldn't tell whether Timmy had given up or was distracted, but he turned to Dickens and said, "Let's get a book," and dashed into my office. Deborah and I chuckled at the sound of Timmy asking Dickens which book he wanted to read and Dickens barking in response. Before long, we heard Timmy reading aloud from *The Cat in the Hat*, one of his favorites.

Their departure gave us a few minutes to sip our tea and peruse the photos. Deborah was right—they were great. I asked her to send them to me so I could share a few with my sisters and Dave and possibly send one to my editor.

I spent the remainder of the afternoon thinking through what Gemma'd told me about the autopsy, the wallet, and the truck. Then I pondered what we'd discovered at the caravan. A fair number of clues, but none that combined to shine a light on a single killer. I was feeling at a loss when Peter called. "Hi, Leta, fancy dinner at the Ploughman tonight?"

"Now Peter, are you inviting me because you want company or because you've not yet spoken with Phil?" I asked.

"Couldn't it be both?"

He had me there. "Guess it could be. The answer is yes, then. What time will you finish up at the garage?"

"It's been a slow day, so I should be able to make it by seven. Does that suit you and Dickens?"

"I'll have to check my boy's calendar but I believe he's available. Too bad I can't bring Christie in her new backpack. I'll tell you about that over a pint."

I drove to the pub. In the daylight, Dickens and I might have walked the three miles there, but not in the dark. The parking lot wasn't too crowded, and we had our choice of tables inside. Dickens didn't hesitate. He trotted to the dog bed closest to the fireplace, turned around several times, and stretched out. I had to settle for a table.

Peter wasn't far behind us. He gave me a peck on the cheek

as he shrugged off his coat. "Your usual cider or a glass of wine?" he asked.

I chose red wine. Funny how Peter and I'd grown to be close friends in the last month. He'd been helpful and neighborly before, but shy. These small displays of affection were new and warmed my heart. It was nice to have a male friend with no strings attached.

I studied the menu, which changed nightly at the Ploughman, and I noticed Peter was taking his time at the bar. Hopefully, he was getting the scoop about Max the Magnificent. I couldn't help but smile as I thought of Peter doing detective work. Would he get as big a kick from it as his mother did?

Phil gestured toward me with a bottle of red and grinned. Leaving his pint on the bar, Peter brought my glass over and explained that Phil had a treat for Dickens. Was this part of his sleuthing technique?

I sipped my wine as I watched the scene. "Dickens, Peter's taking his time. Maybe that means he's getting good information about Saturday night. Either that or they're talking sports."

Dickens looked up groggily. "Huh? I'd almost dozed off. Can this wait until the drive home?"

My boy was never one to miss a walk, a snack, or a snooze. He'd have a tough choice to make when Peter came back, but I knew he'd rouse himself long enough to grab a treat.

My phone rang and I was tickled to see it was Dave. "Hi there," I answered.

"How's my favorite detective doing?" he asked. "I can't wait to hear why I had to get the news about another murder in the village from Belle rather than you."

"Um, Belle called you?"

"No, I called her to let her know I'd finished the Peter Pan article, since she figures in it so prominently. I wanted her to be prepared in case the paparazzi showed up on her doorstep in Astonbury."

"You're joking about the paparazzi, right?"

"I think so, but you never know. The fact that she and her mother knew J.M. Barrie might bring out a few of 'em. So, tell me what's going on. Belle was talking so fast about magic and murder, I couldn't make sense of it."

I could imagine Belle's excitement making it difficult for Dave to understand her and keep up. I was giving him an abbreviated version of the tale as Peter returned to the table and nudged Dickens with a treat. When I mouthed that it was Dave, Peter reached for the phone.

"Hi, mate," he said. "Not trying to steal my dinner date, are you? Uh-huh, the Ploughman, where else? I'll let you have her back; just wanted to say hello."

Dave had become acquainted with most of my friends when he was here but was especially fond of the Davies family. When Peter handed me the phone, I assured Dave I wouldn't leave him hanging and would get back to him with the rest of the story before I went to bed.

Peter looked amused. "Boy, do I have some juicy tidbits for you."

"For a man who was hesitant to get involved, you sure are enjoying yourself. And let's not forget you were aghast at the idea of me, your mother, and your sister asking questions."

"Yeah, but that was before I knew how exciting it could be to discover clues. What Phil has to say muddies the waters."

"How so?"

"For starters, Max was in here causing trouble Friday night before the Fête. Seems Barb met him in Totnes this summer."

"Barb? I was wondering how she knew him. What was she doing there?"

"It was a holiday on the coast with her flatmates. Met him at the magic shop when they were shopping on High Street. He suggested they meet at the pub, and well, you know what happens on holiday, right?"

"Is this like 'girls just wanna have fun' or something similar? Like what happens in Totnes stays in Totnes?"

"Pretty much. Anyway, he spoke to her Friday when she was setting up scarecrows and then he came here Friday night. He suggested more of the same and wasn't taking no for an answer. Followed her outside on her break and tried to *persuade* her, I guess you'd say."

"No, if he tried to force himself on her, I'd say something much worse than that. Did he?"

Peter smiled a satisfied smile. "Looked like it, but he didn't get anywhere because Barb surprised him with her karate moves. According to Phil, Barb walloped him good."

"What time was this?"

"Hold on, I'll ask."

Dickens had perked up as Peter and I talked. I was discovering that my boy loved playing Detective Dickens. "So someone beat him up? I told you there was something off about that guy."

I nodded yes as I thought about what I'd heard so far. He'd asked Sparkle to dinner and he'd visited the pub the same night. Max sure got around. Good grief. I had more and more questions.

Peter came back, looking proud of himself. "It was late, after nine. But you interrupted my story. There's more. You saw Max Saturday night when Phil grabbed him at the bar, right? What set Phil off was the git saying something rude about having a threesome with Trixie and Sparkle. He told Max the Magnificent to get lost and stay lost."

"I figured he'd said something disgusting. I never thought to ask Trixie what it was, though. Good for Phil for setting him straight."

Peter wasn't done, though. "I've got one last bit you'll find interesting. You found out Trixie left first Saturday evening and Sparkle stayed on. Well, before either of 'em left, Phil went outside for a smoke and saw Max coming down the path from the inn. Says he smelled like he'd been drinking, acted like it too. Told Phil he wanted to see his girls.

"That was the last straw for Phil. He told him no way, grabbed him by the collar and tossed him on the path. The idiot got up and took a swing at Phil. That's when Phil punched him in the nose."

Well, that explained the bloody nose. And Barb fending him off with whatever kind of karate move Friday night accounted for the bruising on his ribs. *Wonder if she kicked him?* Imagining her kicking him in the ribs made me smile. Was there no end to the guy's stupidity?

"Peter, let's lay out the Saturday night timeline. Phil gives him a bloody nose, and after that Max grabs Jill in the inn parking lot. Jill knees him and maybe he stumbles to the river, where Trixie finds him hanging over the bank and a bottle by his side. So he must have gotten a bottle from his truck if he didn't get a drink from Phil."

"He was hanging over the riverbank? I thought Libby found him lying on his back Sunday morning."

I paused. I'd forgotten Peter wasn't privy to the information Gemma and I had uncovered. I gave him the highlights.

Peter put his chin in his hand. "Those poor girls."

"Anyway, where was I? Oh, the timeline. The bottle of

whiskey. Maybe he was drowning his sorrows. Then, Sparkle finds him in the same spot. She says he was still passed out when she left him. Who saw him next? We don't know, but our list of people who had reason to want him gone or dead keeps growing. That's good news for Trixie, but I don't envy Gemma trying to fit these puzzle pieces together to figure out who the heck killed him."

Peter groaned. "Is this how it goes? You get information, which is kinda fun, but then it doesn't get you any closer to identifying the killer? And what happens if you've been talking to the killer? What happens next?"

"Well, last time we had a body in Astonbury, I talked to the killer. And you know how that turned out."

"Bloody hell, I do. And you were lucky to get out alive. I knew there was a reason I didn't want my three favorite ladies investigating this murder. You and Mum and Wendy have to be careful. Who's gonna look out for you when you start asking questions in Totnes?"

I smiled sheepishly. "Dickens?"

"Not funny, Leta. Can I at least get you or Wendy to check in with me nightly so I know you're okay?"

It was time to stop joking. "Yes, we'll do that, Peter. And if you don't hear from us, which is highly unlikely, but if you don't, then you can go to Gemma and tell her what you heard last. Well, after you at least try to reach us yourself. Now, I'll get the next round and we can order dinner. I'm starved."

I couldn't help myself when I got to the bar. I wanted to be sure we'd gotten all we could from Phil. "Phil, I appreciate the information you shared with Peter. You know, the police are looking at Trixie as a prime suspect for Max's murder, and any little piece of information we can give them could help her. I mean, can you picture Trixie killing her husband, even if he was a rotter?"

Phil snorted. "No way. Unless she's a hell of an actress, I can't see her harming a fly. I'd be a better bet as a suspect if I were one to hold a grudge, but in this business, you can't let plonkers like Max get to you. You handle 'em and pour the next drink."

"What about Barb? Is she as nonchalant about men like Max as you are? Sounds like he was pretty nasty."

"Yeah, he was, but our Barb can take care of herself. It was her dad made her take karate lessons before he'd let her work in a pub. Smart guy, though she's never had to use her skills here—until Max, that is. Have you heard the story of how she got back at one of our drunk customers who smacked her on the backside?"

"No, but I bet it's a good one."

"She brought him a shot on the house—spiked with tabasco sauce. You should have seen him when he tossed it back. She offered him a glass of water after that, but he wouldn't touch it. Our Barb has her ways."

Phil poured a pint for another customer and turned back to me. "If you ask me, Leta, based on two nights of dealing with the guy, there could be any number of people who had it in for him. But, even with the Fête on Saturday, there weren't many strangers in here over the weekend—mostly the couples staying at The Olde Mill Inn. Not likely any of them knew Max the Magnificent."

"Well in the interest of jogging people's memories, do you think Barb would talk to me? Could be she recalls Max bothering another girl or saw someone else outside when she was defending herself."

"She might. I don't keep up with her schedule, but she's here most nights."

"Thanks, Phil. I mean it. I have to believe that piecing all this together will lead us to the real killer. Now, if I can have another round for Peter and me, I'll get out of your hair."

The Tuesday menu at the Ploughman was all about fall flavors. For me, it turned out to be a butternut squash night, beginning with spiced butternut squash soup followed by lamb with lentils, butternut squash, chestnut mushrooms, and red wine jus. Peter went for the sirloin steak, and we split a serving of sticky date pudding.

Dickens was a happy boy when Peter and I each slipped him a chunk of meat. And I wondered why he tended to put on weight despite his regular walks. As the table was being cleared, he looked up expectantly.

"No way, Dickens," I chided. "You've had your taste and you don't get to lick the plates here."

As I drove home, bits and pieces of information from the day swirled through my brain. Good thing I'd have Wendy and Belle to help me sort everything out on our drive in the morning. Soon, we'd need to get things down on paper to keep it all straight.

In the kitchen, I fed Dickens a small amount of dog food and gave Christie her dab of wet food. Amazingly, Christie cleaned her dish. Usually, she took a tiny bite and walked away. By the time she returned, as often as not, Dickens would have cleaned her dish.

Christie looked at me. "Have you gotten any more

pictures? Anything I can look at to help push this investigation along?"

I pulled out my phone. "Sure have, little girl. Let me upload these to the computer, and you can look them over."

Christie sat in my lap, front paws on the desk, while I loaded the photos. She meowed her approval once the slideshow started. Only then did I call Dave.

He was all ears, and he was concerned. "I'm so sorry Libby had to go through this. Like you said, at least it wasn't someone she knew from the village. And judging by what you've said about his behavior with Trixie and then at the bar, dare I say he may have had it coming?"

"Maybe. Though I don't suppose being a jerk means you *deserve* to be killed. Still, it's a never-ending story. Bad news keeps cropping up about this guy. Oh wow, an image just came to mind. Remember the character Pig Pen in the Charlie Brown comics? With that dirty cloud surrounding him? I picture Max with a nasty aura like that. He seemed to spread insult and injury wherever he went."

Dickens chose this moment to complain about his rations. "Leta, don't you think I need another serving? I mean, we have a big day tomorrow, and I need to be well fortified."

"What he's barking about?" asked Dave. "Does he know it's me on the phone? Does he want a long-distance belly rub?"

"No, he appears to be demanding more food, but he's not getting any. It's not like I'm sending him to bed hungry. And speaking of bed, you know I'm about to turn into a pumpkin, and I still need to pack. I'll try to give you a call from Totnes, okay?"

We ended our call, and Christie told me what she thought about the photos. "Did this Max fellow really live in that place? It's disgusting."

"I agree with you. And these pictures aren't very useful, are they?" I asked.

"No, not a bit, not like the photos from your last case. I think from now on, I need to go everywhere with you and Dickens, so I can see everything firsthand."

The reference to my last case gave me pause. *How is it there have been two murders in Astonbury in a month?* I thought. *And more to the point, how is it I've gotten myself involved yet again?* I couldn't answer the first question and chose not to dwell on the second.

Dickens had been thinking about Christie's suggestion—or demand. "You know, Christie, they don't let cats in pubs, right? And I'm not sure they let them in inns either."

My four-legged friends debated the different rules for dogs and cats as they followed me upstairs. After years of business travel, my packing routine was well-honed and took no time at all. In bed, I picked up my Tommy and Tuppence book, but I kept reading the same paragraph over and over.

Knowing I wasn't going to be able to read until I mapped out what we needed to accomplish on our trip, I reached over to my bedside table for a pad and pencil. Soon, I had a game plan for my "trio of little old ladies." *Totnes, here we come.*

Chapter Eight

The next morning, I stowed my bag in the trunk, fastened Dickens in the back seat, and made it to Toby's Tearoom by 8:45. If time allowed, I'd stop by my cottage before picking up Belle and Wendy, but if not, I wanted to be ready to hit the road.

I almost didn't recognize Sparkle when she walked in the door. Her dark hair in a ponytail, she wore sweatpants and no makeup. She looked exhausted and frazzled. Grief will do that to you. I know.

I waved her over before she had a chance to go to the counter. "Sit. Let me get you something. Do you prefer coffee or tea? How about a muffin or scone?"

She asked for a large black coffee and a gingerbread muffin. I left Dickens with her and placed our order with Jenny. When I returned to our table near the back of the shop, Dickens was nudging Sparkle's hand. Today, her name didn't fit. Her eyes looked dull and her skin ashen.

Patting Dickens on the head, she looked at me. "Leta, you're so kind to invite me out. I'm not handling this very well.

I mean, I wasn't married to Max, but I did love him. I can't believe he's gone."

"I don't think you have to be married to a man to mourn him," I said. "And I don't think there's any rule about how long you have to be with someone before you can love him deeply. It's understandable you're grieving. It's bad enough he died. The circumstances make it even worse."

She nodded and teared up. "We'd known each other for years, didn't always date, but were friends. Just began dating again this summer . . . after Trixie. After his marriage ended."

I was taken by surprise when her demeanor suddenly changed. Her face turned red, and she looked angry. "I can't believe he was trying to get Trixie to come back to him. I thought he was done with her. I thought he loved me."

Dickens barked, "Is she angry with you?"

I touched Dickens to let him know I was okay. I wasn't sure how to respond to Sparkle's outburst, so I danced around it and replied in a soothing voice. "How sad to have begun again and then to lose him like this. Were you dating when he met Trixie?"

"Yes. No. I mean, he met her during one of our spats. We'd sometimes break up for as much as a month but always get back together. Maybe because we were both foster kids, we had a special bond. It's hard for people who had a regular mum and dad to understand."

"Oh gosh, Sparkle. So you don't have any close family?"

"No, I've got my flatmates in Totnes, but no family."

"You're fortunate to have them. When you go home, I think you'll find that reminiscing with them about Max will help you. I've found that sharing stories about my husband helps me to cope with losing him. It can be bittersweet, but I feel like he'll always be with me as long as I can talk about our time together."

Sparkle wiped her tears away. "Would you . . . would you like to hear more about Max?" she asked.

"Yes. Tell me how you met him, why don't you?"

"Meeting is ancient history. It was in school. He was a few years ahead of me, but we ran with the same crowd—the rough one. We were the kids who skipped school and had bad grades. Max treated me like his pesky little sister back then, but he looked out for me.

"Didn't see him for a year or two after he left school. But then I ran him into him at the pub one night, and we picked right back up. Told me about his magic act and how he was hoping to make a go of it and leave the shop behind.

"I was impressed. There I was washing hair at the Blue Hair Studio, and he was a magician. He had ambitions. I think it was his working to make something of himself that gave me the confidence to approach Summer about learning how to do fairy hair."

"See? That's a memory you'll always treasure. And fairy hair is so popular. Do you do it in Totnes too?"

The fairy hair conversation brought a small smile to her face. "Yes, it's wonderful. The studio set me up a spot for that. I still wash hair when I don't have fairy hair appointments, so it's a wonderful arrangement. And I get to travel with Summer for festivals."

"Sparkle, it just so happens I'm going to Dartmouth today with Belle and Wendy for a mini-vacation. Do you remember them?"

She thought for a moment. "Oh, you mean Peter Pan and her mum? Yes, I got a kick out of putting blue strands in that white hair."

"Well, we plan to tour Dartmouth and Greenway—we're Agatha Christie fans. And we thought we'd spend a day in Totnes. I'd love to set Belle up for a wash and set while we're there. Could you recommend someone at the Blue Hair Studio?"

"Oh yes, try to get Priscilla if she's not booked. Best shoot for Thursday as she's usually slammed Friday and Saturday."

I jotted down the name. "Thanks. Belle tires quickly when we're shopping, so having a sit-down appointment will give her a chance to rest."

"Gosh, Leta. You're right about memories easing the pain. I just had a flash of Max walking in the door of the studio with a bouquet of flowers for me. He only did it once, but he looked so dashing dressed in his tails and top hat, that red scarf around his neck. He *was* handsome, wasn't he?"

Dickens barked. "But clothes don't make the man, do they, Leta?"

I rubbed Dickens's head to quiet him. "That he was. He must have had a way about him, too. When I saw you together on Friday, I wasn't sure whether you were only friends or were dating. But what happened Saturday? I gather he dunked you in the apple-bobbing bucket."

I looked at her inquiringly. That was all it took.

"Typical," she spat. "He could be a fairytale prince one moment and a lout the next. He claimed he was just playing around when he pushed my face in the water. He had a bad habit of taking things too far—like he'd never grown up. Sometimes he could be a bully."

I could tell the change in her tone had disturbed Dickens because he stood up and licked her hand.

So that explained the encounter Saturday. A prince? An evil prince maybe.

"But no matter how angry you were with him, you cared enough to go looking for him Saturday night. You cared enough to worry about him and to want to be sure he was okay. Sounds like he didn't deserve you, Sparkle."

She sniffled and the tears started to flow again. "You're probably right, but like you said, he had a way about him. You know he was teaching me magic tricks. He said I was awfully good and we could be a team and go on the road together. Guess that's another dream gone."

It struck me that she'd known Max longer than Trixie had. "Sparkle, can you think of anyone who had it in for Max? Someone who would kill him?"

She hesitated. "The thing is," she said, "he's always had a way with women. They couldn't resist him. Guess that's why I overlooked his messing about. We'd have a row, and I'd hear he'd slept with someone else, but he always came back to me. Found out Saturday that Barb was one of those women. If I'm honest with myself, it's a long list."

"Are you saying someone he slept with might have had it in for him?"

"No. It was men he didn't get on with. He could be a bit of a braggart, and he could wind someone up in a heartbeat. I can't tell you how many times I drug him out of the pub to stop him getting in a brawl. If someone killed him, I'm thinking it could have been someone from Totnes."

Interesting, I thought. *Would someone follow him from Totnes to kill him? Because he was an insulting, arrogant, idiot? Why not kill him closer to home?*

"Wow. That would mean someone hated him enough to come all the way to Astonbury."

Sparkle thought for a moment. "Funny, I did see Max having an argument with someone at the Fête. I saw Max take a step back when the man poked him in the chest with his finger. I didn't get a good look at the guy, but he didn't look familiar. Could have been from Totnes. Could have been someone local."

"Can you describe him?"

She closed her eyes as though she was trying to picture him. "Tall, taller than Max. Burly, not slim like Max. Brownish hair. I mostly saw him from the back, and I think he had on one of those brown canvas jackets. You know, the ones with corduroy collars?"

Sparkle's phone buzzed. "That's Summer. Just a sec."

I gathered from the side of the conversation I could hear that Summer was calling to see how Sparkle was holding up.

When the conversation ended, Sparkle said, "I'm lucky to have Summer. She's been a trooper these past few days, checking on me while she's working and making me eat. It's time for me to get back to her place to shower and dress for our afternoon appointments. We've got several luncheon jobs lined up, so they'll be a good distraction for me. And then we've got the Fair in Burford this weekend."

She stood up and gave me a hug. "I can't thank you enough for reaching out to me. I still can't stop crying, but I feel just a tiny bit better after our talk. I'll keep in mind what you said about memories and about talking about the good times. That will help."

Dickens couldn't wait to share his thoughts as we got in the car. "Gosh, Leta. That was a strange conversation. She'd be sad one minute and angry the next."

"I know. But when I think about it, she's had several

shocks these past few days. She finds out Max lied to her about his divorce. She meets his wife. She meets Barb, one of his flings. And then she finds out the man she loves has been murdered. No wonder her emotions are all over the board."

"Maybe you're right, Leta. But tell me something. Why did these two nice girls like that Max guy? I'm sorry they lost someone they cared about, but I don't understand how they could've loved him in the first place."

"Well, Dickens, the heart's a funny thing. Before I met Henry, I didn't have very good luck with men, and I certainly dated my share of losers. Men who charmed me only to show their true colors later. That could be what happened here."

"What did you think about the guy in the brown jacket? Do we know him?"

"You know, he doesn't sound familiar to me, but I don't know everyone in Astonbury. He could be from here or a neighboring village . . . or from Totnes. I don't know."

I made it to the Davies home in plenty of time, and by 10:30 am, we were on the road--Wendy in the back seat with Dickens, and Belle riding shotgun. I'd booked us into the Dart Marina Hotel, and I was looking forward to one of their seafood dinners. When Henry and I'd stayed there, we'd dined at several highly recommended local restaurants, and rated the dinners at the Marina the best.

"Ladies, I've simmered down, but let me tell you what Gemma said yesterday. She referred to us as little old ladies—all three of us!"

I saw Wendy's indignant look in my rearview mirror. "Are you kidding? I mean, Mum's near ninety, but the two of us?"

Belle was chuckling. "She can call me whatever she likes. I'm proud to be little and old and still kicking. I think the excitement you two stir up has taken years off my life. Heck, maybe we should incorporate the phrase 'little old ladies' into whatever name we come up with. Wendy and I still haven't hit on the right one."

She had me laughing too. "We need a name, and we need T-shirts. I saw some on the internet, something to the effect of 'Thinking I'm just an old lady was your first mistake.' I bet we can come up with just the right slogan—once we hit on our name, that is."

Even Dickens chimed in. "You know I don't like being called little, but I still want to be part of the team."

Wendy tickled his chin. "What got him all fired up?" she asked.

He barked again and licked her hand. "Tell her, Leta. Detective Dickens is on the job."

We were all laughing by then, even though Belle and Wendy had no clue what Dickens was going on about. We had lots to discuss, so it was good we had a three-hour drive ahead of us. I started with a review of what I'd discovered with Gemma and Peter.

Belle shook her head as I told them about the photos on the laptop. "How sad. Do you think he ever really loved Trixie? Or was he in love with the idea of her? Whatever it was, I can't help feeling a little sorry for him."

"Sorry, Mum, I can't see it. He may have suffered from a broken heart, but from what we witnessed, he deserved it."

I glanced in the rearview mirror and caught Wendy's eye. "Wait until I tell you about my conversation with Sparkle this morning. Another interesting perspective. But you know me, I like to take things in order, so first let's talk about your brother at the pub."

The story of Peter playing detective cracked Wendy up. "Leta, I'm telling you, Peter's a changed man since he's gotten to know you. I'm glad you thought to ask him to help us out, but I certainly never would have imagined he'd take to it like he has! The way you're describing his conversation with Phil, it sounds as though my brother's a quick study."

"That he is," I said. "It's not as though I coached him. I bet he and Phil talk about cars and sports all the time, so Phil thought nothing of sharing what he knew about Max."

By the time I finished the tale of Barb's fling with Max, her altercation with him Friday night, and the bloody nose from Phil late Saturday, we were all shaking our heads.

"Okay," said Belle. "Let's hear about your morning with Sparkle."

"You know, I have to credit Rhiannon with setting me straight—in a nice way, of course. I'm afraid I was quick to form a negative impression of Sparkle based on very little information. I'm glad I sat down to talk with her—not only because I learned a few things, but also because I think I helped her to feel better."

I explained it was my sense she genuinely loved Max. And, it occurred to me, the two may have been better suited for each other than Max and Trixie were. They had similar backgrounds, while Trixie had been a sheltered only child.

"I think the fact they were both foster kids explains a lot about their mutual attraction. Except that they seemed unable to be together very long without breaking up and making up. Sounded like a volatile relationship."

Wendy started to speak and hesitated. "I'm having a hard time figuring out how to say this. He was flamboyant. He was a performer. He was arrogant He was ambitious. Do you think he got caught up in the fantasy of marrying the fairy princess? I mean, Trixie *looks* like a princess. She's the complete opposite of Sparkle in looks and probably in personality. Was that the attraction?"

Belle snorted. "Okay ladies, we're drifting into psychology here. It's enough I've become an amateur sleuth without dabbling in psychology too. Let's focus on what this tells us about who might have killed Max."

"Right," I said. "I'm not sure it tells us anything other than she didn't have any more reason to kill him than Trixie did. I mean, Sparkle was angry with him because he lied to her about Trixie, but Trixie was angry with him about not signing the divorce papers. So far, Trixie's the only one I see gaining anything from his death. She no longer has to wait on a divorce—she's free."

Wendy quickly shifted gears. "I say we think more about other suspects and see where that takes us."

That's when I remembered the other bit of information from Sparkle. "I almost forgot. Sparkle says she saw Max and some guy arguing on Saturday. The other fellow was punching his finger in Max's chest. Of course, we don't know who it was."

"All the more reason to consider other suspects—from wherever," Belle said.

We went back and forth discussing how to do that, what we'd learned so far, and what bearing the various clues might have on our Totnes plans.

I asked Wendy to reach in my handbag for the plan I'd sketched out, and we talked it through with Wendy making notes. The first thing she added was to be on the lookout for a tall, burly guy with brown hair. *Right*, I thought, *like that's going to be easy*.

We'd adjust our sleuthing plan as we went along but agreed we had to visit the magic shop where Max had worked, the

Totnes Bookshop where Trixie'd worked, the salon where
Sparkle did fairy hair, and possibly the pub Max frequented if
we could figure out which one it was.

Wendy looked thoughtful. "I bet we could get a good sense
of how Trixie and Max's relationship developed if we spoke
with the family she rented the flat from before she got
married. But we need a reason to speak to them, don't you
think? I mean, we can't just show up on the doorstep and start
asking questions."

"Why not involve Trixie?" Belle suggested. "I see clearing
Trixie as our number one job, and if we solve the murder too,
that's a bonus. If we kill two birds with one stone . . . uh-oh,
poor choice of words . . . but if we do, all the better. So, let's
put Trixie in the picture and have her call her landlady. Heck,
she can contact her old employer at the bookshop too."

I liked the landlady idea but wasn't sure about the bookshop. "Let's take it a step at a time. Pursue the landlady angle
with Trixie, but approach the bookshop without an introduc-
tion. We're more likely to get an unfiltered opinion from Trixie's employer if she doesn't know what we're up to. We can
spend all kinds of time in a bookshop and chat up the folks
who work there. We might even mention we're from Astonbury and see if anyone makes the connection to Trixie moving
there."

"I love it when a plan comes together," said Wendy. "As for
the magic shop, we can wander in and tell them we got their
name from Max before his unfortunate demise. Mum, do you
think you can spin a yarn about wanting to get your great-
grandson a starter magic kit?"

"As in my fictional great-grandson, dear?" said Belle. "Since
neither of my children has seen fit to bless me with grandchildren, I can't very well have a great-grandson."

"You know, as soon as those words were out of my mouth, I knew it was a mistake," Wendy said with a sigh. "Since I'm now a *little old lady*, I think I'm in the clear. As for my twin, unless he suddenly develops a way with the ladies and marries someone much younger, fictional offspring are all we've got."

I tried not to laugh. If my mother were listening, she'd be chiming in with, "I feel your pain; I never got any grandchildren, and I had *three* daughters." I don't think she'd ever forgiven me and my sisters for that omission. We'd provided her with plenty of four-legged grandchildren but none of the two-legged variety. Heck, my sister Anna never failed to have a houseful of five to six cats plus a dog or two.

"Enough of this, ladies. Are we good with the magic shop plan? What about the hair salon where Sparkle does fairy hair? I don't know what excuse to use for talking to them. We don't need fairy hair, and I'm not trusting my hair to a different hairdresser for a trim."

"Me either," said Wendy. "Mum, how 'bout I treat you to a wash and set? That's not too risky, and I'm sure you'd enjoy it. Think of all the gossip you'd pick up. Should be pretty easy to steer the conversation to Max's death and to Sparkle. Those ladies would eat it up."

Belle rubbed her hands together in glee. "Oh, you're so right, dear. I can tell them Sparkle did my hair and more. This will be fun."

Little old ladies, indeed! We amateur sleuths were on a roll. "I think it will be, Belle. And maybe someone at the magic shop can tell us which pub Max frequented. Who knows what else we'll uncover? And, oh, we can stop by the Totnes caravan park and figure out a reason to chat them up."

As we tossed ideas back and forth, I realized I hadn't gotten around to sharing any of Phil's information with

Gemma. It had been too late for me to get into it with her last night, and I hadn't thought of it again until just now. I grabbed my phone and found Gemma's number.

What did it say about me that I had a Detective Sergeant's number programmed into my phone? How my life had changed since I'd left Atlanta.

As I waited for Gemma to pick up, I said, "Hope you ladies don't mind hearing this story again, but I promised to keep Gemma in the loop, and now I have the information Peter gathered plus what I heard from Sparkle."

When I got her voicemail, I explained I was on the road but had new information about Max that I thought she'd find useful. Hopefully, she'd call back soon.

This spur-of-the-moment trip may have sprung from a need to support Trixie, but we didn't intend to spend the whole time working. We decided the afternoon in Dartmouth would be playtime. Belle wanted to rest once we checked in. Wendy, Dickens, and I would check out the Dartmouth shops and see about tickets for the ferry to Agatha Christie's summer home for later in the week.

Belle's face lit up when she saw the view from her room. "Oh my. I can't believe the sun sparkling on the river. Almost makes me want to skip my nap so I can enjoy the scenery. We don't often get days like this in October."

Wendy and I left her in the room with a pot of tea and knew she'd soon be napping. It may have been sunny, but it was still chilly along the river, so we bundled up for our walk to town. I was glad I'd brought along my red wool beret and a warm scarf, and Dickens was in heaven with the brisk breeze ruffling his heavy coat.

Dogs and their owners filled the brick-paved walkway, and we exchanged greetings with pet parents as we strolled. Wherever I took Dickens, I could count on hearing "How cute! What kind of dog is he?" Most folks recognized him as a Great Pyrenees, but his diminutive size threw them. I explained he was a dwarf Pyr and that in the not so distant past, breeders had culled or hidden these small dogs, seeing them as imperfect.

People like me, however, were happy to have a forty to sixty-pound version of the gentle giants who often weighed as much as 140 pounds. Dickens had the personality and temperament of his larger brethren. He was just relatively tiny.

Our first stop was the Dartmouth Community Bookshop on Higher Street. It had replaced the famous Harbour Bookshop started by Christopher Robin Milne in the fifties. When his shop closed in 2011, the town rallied to keep it going in a new location as a community co-operative.

"Wendy," I said, "can you imagine meeting the real Christopher Robin? That would have been a treat."

She nodded in agreement as she explored the section of the shop labeled Pooh Corner.

Dickens was enchanted with the stuffed animals there. "Oh, that bear is just the right size for me, Leta. Let's take him home."

I grabbed him just before he picked up the bear in his mouth. "Uh-uh. You have plenty of toys at home, young man."

The shopkeeper laughed. "Like having a two-legged child, isn't it? Are you sure you don't want the Pooh bear?"

"It's beautiful," I replied, "but too nice for Dickens to carry around and drool on. Our next stop will be the pub across the street, and we'll get him a treat there."

Wendy looked out the window. "You mean we're visiting the Cherub Inn, the pub you told me about? Surely, it's almost time for a pint."

"Just about. You're going to adore this place. It dates from 1380 and is the oldest building in Dartmouth. It still has several old ship's timbers from when it was built as a merchant's house. Have you read any books by Kate Ellis? They're set in a fictionalized version of Dartmouth, and she features the pub but with a different name."

Wendy turned to the woman behind the counter. "Do you have her books? I'd like to start with the first one if you have it."

The clerk was happy to oblige and added *The Merchant's House* to Wendy's stack of books. I'd discovered the author on my first visit to Dartmouth and was working my way through her mystery series.

My sister Sophia was a Pooh fan, so much so she'd named her North Carolina mountain cottage "Winnie's Place," and I'd already selected some Pooh prints and postcards to send her when I noticed *The Natural World of Winnie the Pooh: A walk through the forest that inspired the Hundred Acre Wood*. When I read the mention of Poohsticks Bridge on the back cover, I knew I had to get it for her. I was simply incapable of walking out of a bookshop empty-handed.

We forced ourselves to leave, knowing full well we didn't have time to spend hours browsing. In moments, we were at the door to the Cherub Inn, where we took two steps down to another world. The bookshop had been light and bright. The pub was dark with a fire in the wood-burning stove. We found seats against the wall beneath the window, and Wendy went to the bar for two pints.

As she was bringing our drinks to the table, the bartender called to me, "Would the pup like a snack?"

Dickens barked and darted to the bar. "How'd you know? I'm famished."

"Blimey, I think he understood me," said the bartender.

I chuckled and joked. "I'm sure you understood his response. Please give him one. He never turns down a snack."

We girls sipped our cider and chatted about books. "Wendy, you know there's another bookshop in town, but I'm afraid if we wander in there, we won't see anything else this afternoon."

Wendy grinned. "You know that's a good bet. Let's meander and see what else strikes our fancy, and we need to investigate the ferry to Greenway. Maybe for Friday?"

"Good idea. And before we head to the hotel, let's stop in at least one fudge shop. You know how your mother likes fudge."

We finished our pints and started up Higher Street. The mix of shops and homes along the way all looked down on the harbor. We mused about which ones we'd live in if we moved to the coast. Some had doors opening directly onto the sidewalk; others had iron gates with small gardens beyond and the homes set farther back from the street.

As it began to get dark, we made a quick stop in a fudge shop and then returned to the quay for ferry information. Finding we could easily get tickets on the day of our excursion, we decided to wait. By now, the trees along the river were lit with white lights, making for an enchanting stroll to our hotel for our dinner reservations.

We grabbed mugs of hot cocoa in the lobby and agreed to

meet in the dining room at seven. The walk and the sea air had relaxed me to the point where a short nap seemed in order. It was possible the midafternoon pint at the Cherub had also been a contributing factor. Pulling the down comforter to my chin, I closed my eyes and was asleep in an instant.

It was a good thing the phone rang around six or I might have slept through dinner. It was Gemma.

"Hi there, Detective Parker. Have you cracked the case for me?"

I couldn't tell from her tone whether she was being humorous or sarcastic, so I took the high road. "Not quite, but I have some new information. Peter and I had dinner at the Ploughman last night and heard some interesting things about Max's visit there on Friday and more about Saturday night too. I think your suspect list may be growing."

I shared Barb's story—the Totnes fling and the Friday night encounter with Max. Gemma didn't know anything about that, nor did she know about Max's attempted return to the pub later on Saturday. My assumption was since she'd witnessed Max's abrupt departure herself, she hadn't thought to look beyond that.

"And I don't know why I keep forgetting this, but Sparkle saw something interesting at the Fête," I said.

Gemma laughed. "Aha. So you did speak to Sparkle."

"Yes, at Toby's this morning. Heard about how she and Max met in school. Not much news except she saw a man in a brown jacket poking his finger in Max's chest, like they were arguing. As you'd expect, she had no idea who he was. She described him as taller than Max and more sturdily built, brown hair, and wearing what sounded like one of those Barbour jackets."

"A Barbour jacket like half the men in Astonbury wear?" she asked.

"That thought did cross my mind. Those jackets are like a uniform over here."

"Gee, guess I'll have dinner at the Ploughman tonight, talk to Phil and maybe Barb, and assess every man in a brown jacket while I'm at it," she said. "Much as I hate to admit it, Leta, you have an amazing ability to dig up information."

"Yup, we little old ladies have our ways, except, in this case, you could say it was a little old man who dug up most of the info, since it was Peter who had the conversation with Phil."

Gemma laughed. "I got under your skin with that comment, didn't I? It's so easy to get you going, Leta. You've got to learn to take a joke. Didn't people ever tease you in the States?"

She'd nailed it. I'd been overly sensitive my entire life and had never taken teasing well. I wondered if I was too old to adjust. Food for thought. But not tonight.

In the River Restaurant that evening, we started with a bottle of white wine. Dinner was heavenly. I'd never tasted hake until I'd visited Dartmouth with Henry. This evening, the tasty white fish was pan-fried and served with buttered new potatoes. Wendy had the sole and Belle the seafood bouillabaisse.

I sighed with contentment as I contemplated the lights on the river and watched the ferry go to and fro on its five-minute journey from Dartmouth to Kingswear on the opposite shore, sometimes with only one car aboard. I explained to Wendy and Belle that this small ferry was also called a floating bridge and was pulled across the river by cables. It was amazing the bits of trivia I'd retained from my previous visit.

Belle brought our evening to an end by raising her glass. "Ladies, here's to a successful day of sleuthing in Totnes. May the little old ladies rock."

I laughed so hard I nearly choked on my wine. "Belle, where on earth did you get that expression?"

"Leta, I may be little, and I may be old, but I can still pick up new things from the telly."

I loved Belle's enthusiasm. We agreed to meet at eight thirty for breakfast, and I fetched Dickens from my room for a quick walk to the ferry and back.

"Don't forget to call Peter," barked Dickens as we approached the hotel entrance.

"What a good boy you are. I'd completely forgotten."

I texted Peter that we were fine and our investigation would begin in earnest in Totnes on Thursday. By the time I readied myself for bed and read a few pages, I was once again fading, and it was lights out by ten. *Leads, we need leads*, I thought as I drifted off.

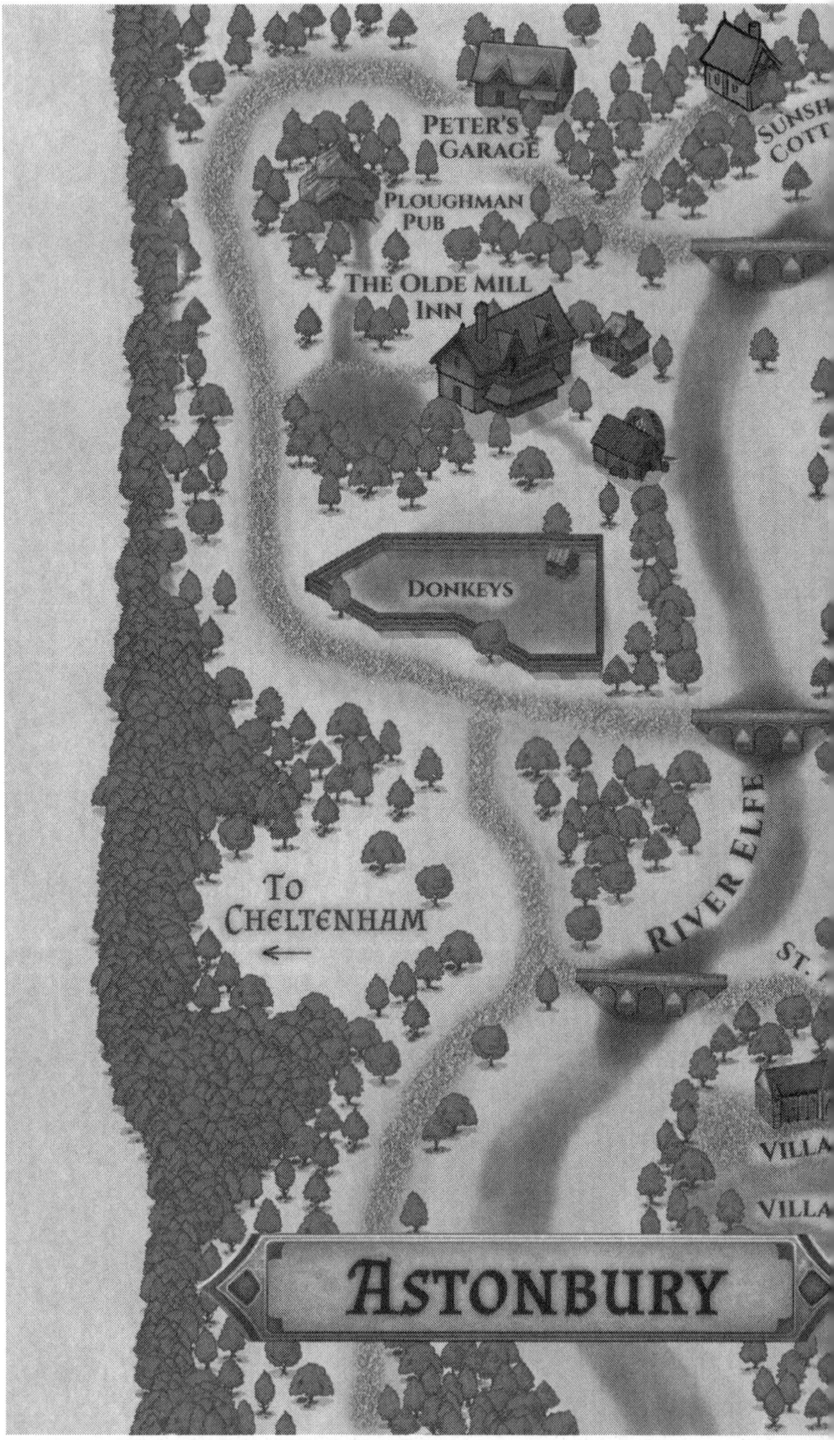
PETER'S GARAGE
PLOUGHMAN PUB
THE OLDE MILL INN
DONKEYS
RIVER ELFE
TO CHELTENHAM
ASTONBURY

To BOURTON-ON-THE-WATER
& STOW-ON-THE-WOLD →

ASTONBURY
MANOR

HOUSE LANE

WATSONS

LETA

CHURCH

HIGH STREET

LET IT BE
YOGA

A TOBY'S
TEA ROOM

BOOK
NOOK

Chapter Nine

Trixie called as I was headed to breakfast, and she seemed to be in good spirits, considering. "Leta, Sparkle and Summer invited me to join them at their fairy hair luncheons this week and next. I'm trying to work out my schedule with Aunt Beatrix so I can make at least one. Tomorrow it's the Knitwits of Chipping Camden. They knit blankets and caps for newborns at the hospital in Cheltenham. Sparkle says they're mostly bluehairs, but you'd be surprised how much they like fairy hair. Who knew?"

"Well, Belle likes her new do, and she's close to ninety. Guess it livens things up for them."

"Next week, it's the Twitchy Stitchers in Northleach. They're cross-stitchers who meet at the church. What a hoot."

Interesting that Sparkle, Summer, and Trixie were spending time together. I wasn't sure what to think about that, but I was glad to hear Trixie had some fun activities lined up, and I promised to give her a call when I was back in Astonbury.

Before hanging up, I asked Trixie about stopping by to see

her former landlady. She was appreciative and said she'd ring her right away to let her know we'd be in touch.

Thursday was a typically dreary October day, so we chose to drive to Totnes rather than take the ferry. Knowing that working our way uphill on High Street wouldn't work for Belle, I dropped her and Wendy halfway up the street at the White Rabbit and went in search of parking. I finally found a car park about fifteen minutes later and hustled to meet up with mother and daughter.

Arriving at the magic shop, I peered in the window to see Belle sitting in a chair chatting with the clerk, her cane propped against the counter, and Wendy browsing. I was greeted effusively when Dickens and I entered to the tinkling of the shop bell.

"This must be the dog you told me about," said the petite brunette clerk, who was dressed in a colorful velvet jester's costume. "I think you're right, and he'd look grand in a top hat."

"A top hat?" I said. "He already has a bowtie and a satin vest—or waistcoat, as you Brits call it."

"That's what we're thinking," said Belle. "He needs a top hat to complete his ensemble for the upcoming holidays."

"Next, you'll tell me my boy's going to learn magic tricks."

The clerk laughed. "Not sure about that," she said. "I *do* teach tricks to humans, but I haven't yet had a canine client. By the way, my name is Chrystal, Chrys for short."

"Chrys has been showing Mum magic sets suitable for Peter's youngest grandson Michael," said Wendy.

Right, I'd need to keep that story straight. "How nice. Do

the sets come with a hat and wand too? With some kind of false bottom for hiding scarves and rabbits?"

Chrys smiled. "Ye of little faith. False bottom indeed."

Wendy became appropriately somber before uttering her next line. "Leta, we told Chrys we'd met Max and how much the crowd enjoyed his show Saturday. We were all so shocked by his death."

"Yes," added Belle. "Chrys told us she actually taught Max many of his tricks."

"Really?" I said. "Was he still in training?"

"Oh, Max was good; don't get me wrong. He'd mastered the basic hocus pocus, but Dad and I'd been trying to teach him some new things to add to his act. Dad owns the shop, you see, and he's awfully good."

"Wow, it'd be a treat to see him," I said. "So, are you the sorcerer's apprentice or are you as good as your dad?"

Chrys grinned. "Dad would be the first to say I've long since graduated from apprentice to sorcerer. Not to brag, but I'm topnotch. That's why I'm always the first invited to perform at the theater and at black-tie affairs. It irked Max no end that he was second choice around here. Bet that's why he jumped at the chance to work the Astonbury Fête."

"Jealous, was he?" asked Wendy.

"Not to speak ill of the dead, but that he was. And he could be nasty about it."

Belle looked appropriately horrified. "Nasty? How so?"

"He thought I didn't know, but this is a small town. When he worked a party I couldn't make, he'd tell the client he'd taught me, not the other way around. He even implied that I'd stolen some of his tricks."

"But he still got to work here at the shop?" asked Belle.

"Dad knew I could take care of myself, and Max was good

with the shop customers. It's not easy to find a clerk who can do a few magic tricks. Pulling a bouquet from your sleeve or a coin from behind a child's ear is a great way to make merchandise fly off the shelves. And he was awfully good with children. He was a big hit at birthday parties and school events."

"I see," I said. "Do you also know his wife Trixie?"

"For sure," said Chrys. "I met her at Sharpham Hall. I was teaching weekly magic classes, and she was taking that paper-making course. It was me who introduced her to Max. Big mistake that was."

This was the easy part of sleuthing. An inquiring look, a tilt of the head, and a pregnant pause worked wonders for getting folks to talk.

"Trixie was a sweetheart, and I think Max saw her as a challenge. Not his usual kind of girl. He flat-out wooed her, and in the end, he fell hard for her. Don't think he expected that. And she for him, until it was too late."

"Huh?" asked Wendy. "Too late?"

"Well, yes," Chrys explained. "He kept up a good façade as Mr. Charming. No yelling, no cursing, even cut way back on his drinking. He spent every dime he had, which wasn't much, taking her up and down the river on picnics and visits to castles here and there. Heck, he even tried to read the few books she recommended to him. That was a stretch."

Wendy worked the pregnant pause. "And . . ."

"Well, once they married, it wasn't long before his true colors surfaced, was it? Beats me how he thought she'd stay 'in love' with him when he went back to his old ways. Can't tell you how many times she called me crying, and with good reason."

I blanched. It was an awful story, and I hadn't yet heard any details. "How bad were his old ways, Chrys?"

"Out all night drinking, sleeping around, bar brawls, dragging Trixie out of the bookshop to yell at her. Guess he thought he was being good not to yell right in the middle of the shop. But you've got to give Trixie credit. She wised up pretty quick. Waited the twelve months needed to file for divorce and did it the next day."

"Trixie told me she thought he cheated on her when he traveled, but did he do it here in Totnes too?" I asked.

"Not while Trixie was still living with him. Before that, he was notorious for one-night stands. With his good looks, he seemed to have his pick of the locals and young female tourists. Had one local girl he always went back to until he met Trixie. Then, when Trixie filed for divorce, he started up with that one again. Don't know why she'd take him back after he dumped her. I mean, he didn't treat her that well even before he fell for Trixie."

"What a piece of work," said Wendy.

"Chrys," I said. "Back in Astonbury, the police are looking at Trixie, since they always look at the spouse first in a murder. Anything you can tell us about Max or Trixie that might help her out?"

"Huh? How could they even consider her a suspect? Most of us here think of her as an angel. Sweet as they come. Book-smart, but not too savvy about men or life. If it had happened in Totnes, the police'd have a whole list of suspects—every girl he's mistreated, their brothers and boyfriends, and all the men from his bar fights. There are girls he *didn't* sleep with but said he did. A total git he was."

Wendy looked at Chrys. "Who's the girl who stuck with him through all that and then took him back again? Talk about not bright about men!"

"Name's Prudence, lives around—"

A deep voice boomed from the back of the shop. "Chrystal! Need your help, girl."

"Oi, that's my dad. He'll soon be telling me I've spent too long gossiping. May I ring up the magic kit for you? And the top hat too?"

I wasn't sure Dickens needed a top hat, but I bought it anyway. "By the way," I said as Chrys rang me up, "Which pub did Max hang out in? Could be good for some local color."

"Um, it's the Whistling Pig. A little off the beaten path, but not too far."

Belle bought the magic kit, and we agreed we could give it to Timmy. We'd gleaned a bit of new information, but nothing earth-shattering, except the name Prudence. It'd probably be easy to follow that lead at the bookshop or the pub. Still, no matter the enemies he'd made in Totnes, I couldn't see why someone would follow Max to Astonbury to do him in. On the other hand, a smart killer could have realized that doing the deed out of town would throw the authorities off the scent.

Our next stop was the Totnes Bookshop. We were walking downhill on High Street, but the incline was steep, so Wendy kept tight hold of Belle's elbow.

When Belle saw the display in the bookshop window, she lit up. "Goodness, girls, there'll be no getting us out of here. Look at the cats."

She was right. The display was all about cats. Not only were there two plump cats dozing with their paws in the air, but there were also cat *books*. Centered in the window was a poster for the play *Cats* with T. S. Eliot's *Old Possum's Book of Practical Cats* in front of it. I spied Cleveland Amory's *The Cat Who Came for Christmas* next to an Edward Gorey calendar with the image of *Seventeen Cats on the Front Steps of 82 Maple Street* as the cover.

At least we had no problem breaking the ice. We oohed and aahed over the cat treasures. Then we found Trixie's cards. There were bundles of six in the notecard section and more elaborate individual cards for sale on the counter near the register. She was just beginning to build a similar collection at Beatrix's shop, and the selection here in Totnes was much larger. That was our entrée.

"Oh my, these look like the cards we saw in Astonbury," I exclaimed.

Immediately, the clerk broke into a smile. "That's where the artist moved. Did you see them in the Book Nook there?"

"Yes, but only the single cards. I wonder whether we'll get the notecards too?"

"Those take a bit of time to produce, and the artist committed to keeping us well-stocked for the upcoming holidays. Could be a while before she can keep up with the demand in both shops," replied the clerk.

It was time for my fellow sleuths to pick up the conversation. "Oh, Leta, this is Trixie's work. You know, Beatrix's niece?" said Wendy.

In a somber tone, Belle interjected, "Oh, the poor girl whose husband turned up dead after the Fête in Astonbury? How awful."

"We were all so sorry to hear about that," said the clerk. "I'm Suzanne, the manager here. Trixie used to work for me in addition to supplying me with her beautiful cards. We hated to see her go, and we miss her, but I know it was best for her to leave."

"Really?" I said.

Suzanne hesitated. "Not to speak ill of the dead, but the husband was why she left. She was trying to divorce him, and he wouldn't accept it. I'm sure she was better off far away from him. It's strange that he died in the town where she moved."

The expression "not to speak ill of the dead" seemed a common refrain in reference to Max, and I was beginning to think this wouldn't be the last time we'd hear it. At the other extreme, we hadn't yet heard anything negative about Trixie. The story was a bit like *Beauty and the Beast*, except this beast *stayed* a beast.

None of this was especially good news for Trixie. The more we heard about what a caveman Max had been and how he'd mistreated his wife, the more the police would believe she had good reason to kill him. Admittedly, my limited knowledge of police investigations came from books and TV where the spouse or significant other was always the primary suspect. Unless Gemma deviated from that pattern, Trixie would remain at the top of the list.

I continued to browse while Wendy chatted with Suzanne. She told much the same story we'd gotten from Chrystal. Max belittled Trixie, and he berated her in public. And Trixie was a saint and a talented artist.

I thought we'd picked up as much information as we could, so I took my two items to the counter. The Edward Gorey calendar was a must-have, and I'd spied a book titled *This Cat Does Not Love You*. It was billed as a cat's-eye view of the world that would reveal the meaning of your cat's "looks, twitches, and loving gestures." It looked to be a hilarious read Christie and I could enjoy together. Knowing my girl, she'd want to write the authors to let them know what cats *really* thought.

After Belle and Wendy made their purchases, we asked Suzanne to suggest a place for lunch, and she recommended Pie Street. We'd passed the café on our way to her shop, so we retraced our steps and sat down to savory pies. Belle went for the steak and ale pie, and Wendy and I tried the chicken with ham and leeks. It was a satisfying lunch for a chilly day.

A tiny space with tables packed close together, the restaurant wasn't conducive to strategizing next steps. Instead, we played the tourist card and asked for suggestions. First, we inquired as to which pub the locals frequented. That elicited two votes for The Whistling Pig, so not only was it Max's hangout, but we could likely find regulars there who knew him.

Next, I went to the counter to pay for our lunch and asked the grey-haired woman at the register if she knew anything about the Blue Hair Studio. There couldn't be that many hair salons in Totnes, and I could tell from her hairstyle she visited somewhere weekly for a wash and set. I couldn't believe my luck when she said the Blue Hair Studio was where she went and that Priscilla, the girl Sparkle had recommended, was her hairdresser too.

We huddled outside the shop to discuss how best to spend the afternoon. Wendy and I were sure Belle would want a nap, so we offered to schedule her appointment for the next day, take her to the hotel to rest, and then drive back to Totnes.

Belle surprised us. "Time's a-wastin', girls, and I can nap at home. Let's see if I can get an appointment at the Blue Hair for today."

Wendy grinned at her mum and pulled out her phone. In no time, she had Belle set up for a wash and set. I left them outside Pie Street and came back with the car.

On the short drive, Belle explained her game plan. "No worries, girls. I'll use my fairy hair as an opening to inquire about Sparkle, and I'll get the scoop. You know how women love to gossip."

I could hardly keep a straight face when I saw the exterior of the salon. In my mind, something called the Blue Hair had to be an old-fashioned beauty parlor that catered to . . . well, blue hairs. Was I ever wrong.

It was a modern shop decorated in shades of blue and silver. A few of the hairdressers *had* blue hair, but not what I'd envisioned. Several had short spiky hair, much like Wendy's style, but with blue streaks. One hairdresser had dyed all his hair blue.

I giggled as I whispered to Wendy. "Do you think the blue hair is a marketing concept?"

"Not sure," she replied, "but let's hope Mum doesn't go for color. I think the fairy hair she got on Saturday is enough for now."

The receptionist inquired as to whether Belle might want a manicure too. We knew that would give us more time at the pub, so we encouraged her to go for it. And the salon also offered wine and bubbly.

Before she left us to put on her smock, Belle turned to Wendy. "Dear, you and Leta enjoy yourselves. Since my salon visit is your treat to me, I'm going to make the most of it. You never know; I may even get a pedicure."

We both laughed and gave her a hug.

"In the States," I said to Wendy, "we'd call your mum a pistol."

"That she is. You know she meant it when she said we'd energized her. She didn't get out all that much until I moved back from North Carolina, and now with you around, she's having even more fun. She gets quite the kick from accessing her inner Miss Marple. Let's hope her innocent little old lady act pays off today."

We were still laughing as we entered the address of the Whistling Pig into my GPS. "Now, don't let me drink more than a pint, Wendy. I need to be fit to drive, and there's something about drinking during the day. It seems to get to me more. You, on the other hand, can drink to your heart's content."

"You mean it's my job to drink? It will be a burden, but I'm willing to take one for the team."

That's what I loved about hanging out with Wendy. We were always laughing. It had been a huge leap of faith for me to move to Astonbury and leave my sisters and friends behind, and I felt fortunate to have found a new best friend.

The GPS directions took us straight to the Whistling Pig without any sudden detours onto narrow dirt lanes. It was those unwelcome surprises that made me distrust GPS, and England seemed to have an abundance of narrow bumpy lanes lined with tall hedgerows.

Midafternoon, the pub was quiet with only a few patrons scattered at tables. I took a seat at a scarred wooden table by the window and Dickens found a sunny spot to lie in, while Wendy went to the bar for two pints. Her order was filled quickly, but she sipped her beer and chatted with the bartender for a bit before coming to our table. I considered that a good sign.

She was grinning. "I'm getting good at this sleuthing thing. Told him I'd met someone from Totnes at our Fête and gotten the name of this place. Naturally, he asked who that someone was. I said, 'That's the sad bit. It was Max the Magnificent, and he had some kind of accident that weekend.' He'd heard folks saying Max had died and asked if I knew anything more about it."

I took a small sip, knowing I had to make my pint last. "And what did you tell him?"

"Oh, I told him he seemed a nice enough guy when he was doing his magic act, but he'd gotten out of hand several times that day, that he'd accosted his wife, and been booted from our local pub. That didn't surprise him. Said Max was regularly booted from this one."

"My, my. Do continue."

"Our bartender's a chatty guy. Do you think most bartenders are? Anyway, I've adopted your nod and smile technique, and it paid off. He was full of information. Max drank too much and was mouthy and aggressive. It was a rare week he didn't tick someone off, either coming on too strong with a girl or getting in another guy's face. Most of the regulars ignored his behavior but a few put him in his place —physically."

"I think we saw all of that in Astonbury. Does 'physically' mean someone punched him?"

"That or strong-armed him out the door. Apparently, the bar patrons know better than to start a fight inside, though one of the barmaids slapped him a time or two when he fondled her. He seemed to take the slaps in stride, almost as though it was part of the game."

"Good grief. Did this guy have any redeeming characteristics at all?"

"Not that I can tell. The barmaid's boyfriend beat Max up proper the last time he got handsy with her. That was about a month ago. Next, I'm going to ask if he ever came in with Trixie or Sparkle. Fancy a bag of crisps?"

I laughed as Wendy went to the bar. We didn't need anything to eat after our pies, but sacrifices had to be made.

Getting the crisps took ten minutes, and I was anticipating plenty more gossip.

Wendy flounced back to our table. "Oh, this gets better all the time," she said. "Turns out he never brought Trixie in, but he did meet up with a girl named Prudence—been meeting up with her off and on for a few years. Seems the two had a volatile relationship. They had a few loud rows in here, but always made up."

"A few years?!"

"Yep. When I told him I knew Trixie's aunt and thought they'd been married for eighteen months or so, he laughed. I could tell he was having fun educating me on the history of Max the Magnificent. He gave me a timeline. Max and Prudence were an item—if you can call it that—for a year or more, though Max never gave up his one-night stands with the tourists. Word was that when Trixie came along, he dumped Prudence but picked back up with her as soon as Trixie left him. They've been at it ever since."

"Oh, for goodness sake. I need a new word. 'Jerk' doesn't do it anymore."

That comment cracked Wendy up. "We have plenty of words that will work–git, prat, rotter, pillock, plonker, tosser. Try one. You'll feel better."

She was right. I needed to up my language game. I'd learned to refer to a sweater as a jumper and a vest as a waistcoat, but not much beyond that. Learning insults would be way more fun.

"Okay," I said, "the *tosser* left a trail of aggrieved women wherever he went. How's that? Am I getting the hang of the insults?"

"Yup, that's a good start."

"And, now we know he *dated*, if you can call it that, not

only Sparkle but some girl named Prudence. I wonder if our bartender will be as chatty with me, 'cause we need to get more info about this Prudence girl. Are you ready for another round?"

Wendy reminded me it was her job to drink, so I went to the bar and asked for a second pint for her and diet coke for myself. That earned me a smirk from the bartender. Fortunately, my choice of drink didn't lessen his willingness to tell me more about Max's girlfriend.

"Prudence?" he asked. "Name's Prudence Potter. She lives near the Blue Hair Studio where she works."

Now, that was interesting. She worked at the same place as Sparkle. It seemed that Totnes was not only a tourist town but also a small town like Astonbury where the locals knew everything about everyone. When I asked about Sparkle, though, my theory was blown. He'd never heard of her. So, where did Sparkle and Max hang out when they were together, if not The Whistling Pig? Was Max smart enough to take his regular girls to two different places?

Wendy and I puzzled over that while she enjoyed her drink. Dickens stretched and rolled over to expose his tummy.

"You know what that position means, right?" I asked Wendy.

She chuckled and reached down to rub his belly. "And how's Detective Dickens doing? Have you stumbled across any clues we've missed?"

He raised his paw to let her know to continue the belly rub but didn't bark a word. I took that to mean he'd been listening but didn't have anything to add.

"I'm not rushing you, but when you're done with your drink, do you think we have time to run by the caravan park before we pick up your mum? I'd love to hear what the manager thinks about Max, the dearly departed tenant."

Wendy looked at her watch. "We should be able to manage that, and if Mum's done before we get there, I'm sure they'll treat her to another glass of bubbly. Just so long as she doesn't get bored and decide on blue streaks."

Once again, I plugged an address into my GPS and crossed my fingers we'd get there via a main road. Luckily, the caravan park wasn't far out of town, and the manager was in. It was my turn to sleuth.

"Good afternoon. We met one of your renters last weekend, and he recommended your park as well kept and reasonably priced. Do you have a brochure?"

"Sure, I'm Shirley, and I'll be happy to help you. Will you be bringing this cute little thing with you? What's his name?"

Dickens spoke up. "Another one! I'm not little, dang it."

"I think he likes you," I said. "His name is Dickens, and he never leaves my side."

"Plenty of our guests bring their dogs, so he'll be welcome. Will you be bringing your own caravan or renting one of ours?" she asked.

"Oh, we don't have our own like Max did, so we'd want to rent a two-bedroom if you have one available. And probably for a month, maybe over Christmas and into January."

"Max? Are you talking about Max Maxwell? You must have met him right before he passed away. I was sorry to hear about that."

"Yes, that's him. We met him at the Fall Fête in Astonbury. He put on a nice show, and it was a shock to find out he died that very night."

"It was a shock to me too. Though with the life he led, I can't say I was surprised."

I cocked my head and said, "Really?"

"A bit rough around the edges, he was. Kept his little yard tidy, but was always running girls in and out. Even had one girl come banging on his door yelling at him late at night. Read him the riot act about that."

"Gosh, seeing him perform and make the children smile, I never would have imagined that. And, somehow, I had the impression he had a regular girlfriend . . . maybe named Sparkle?"

"Ha! I think the girl banging on his door thought she was the one and only, from what she was yelling at him. She must've gotten over it, 'cause she was back all lovey-dovey not long after. Don't think it was a name like Sparkle, though. Maybe Patience or Prudence? I recall thinking the name didn't fit her behavior. Anyway, I doubt I'll have those kinds of problems with you ladies."

Wendy and I laughed and told her definitely not and asked about pricing.

The manager was quick to say, "I'm not sure what Max told you, but I need to let you know he had a special rate 'cause he rented for six months at a time. Not many folks do that. And it costs more to rent one of ours. Still, I'd have to agree we're reasonable. Even at that, Max was forever behind on the rent. For all his grumbling, he knew he wasn't going to find anything cheaper than £400 a month, and he always paid up in cash, so I mostly let it ride."

£400? That was a huge discount on high and mid-season rates, but a bit higher than those for the low season. Perhaps the long-term nature of the rental made it worth it to her. We thanked her for the information and made a show of taking a drive around the park.

"Well hell, how many girls did he have on a string?" I asked.

"We knew about Sparkle, and we've learned there's someone named Prudence or maybe Patience. Which gal was banging on his caravan door? Maybe Prudence? Given what the bartender told you about an on-again, off-again relationship?"

"Could be, but Leta, I don't get it. Sure, he was good-looking in a bad boy kind of way, but he treated women like dirt. Why would they stay around? At least Trixie wised up and got out."

"Who knows? Maybe there's something about a magician that's alluring. Anyway, it's probably past time to pick up your mum. I can't wait to get her report."

We could see Belle through the window when we pulled up to the Blue Hair Studio. She was sipping a drink and laughing with the receptionist.

"Mum, you look lovely," exclaimed Wendy. "Did you have your makeup done too?"

"Why yes, dear. I think you and Leta will have to take me somewhere special for dinner tonight. Can't let all this go to waste. And look at my nails."

"Belle, is that Bubble Bath pink? That's what I wear. I like it for its natural look. Did you have a pedicure too?"

"No, I went for the makeover instead. No one's going to see my feet. What do you girls think of my hair?"

"Love it, Mum."

"Me too," I chimed in.

While Wendy paid the receptionist, Belle placed her champagne flute on the counter, and I helped her put on her coat. Seeing her preparing to leave prompted her stylist, makeup artist, and manicurist to come running to give her hugs. They went on and on about how much they'd enjoyed her. Belle had been quite a hit.

She was beaming. "Oh, Leta, I almost forgot. Come with me for a minute, please."

I followed her to the back where several girls were washing hair. Belle motioned to a young girl and whispered in her ear when she approached. She pulled a phone from her blue smock and asked for my number. I had no idea what was going on until my phone pinged with a text.

I saw photos of Max in his tails and hat, and I could see people walking behind him and the waterwheel in the distance. These were from the Fête. There was one of Sparkle doing fairy hair, one of Captain Hook with little Michael, and a sweet one of Max and Sparkle hugging. It was the last photo that surprised me. It was Max lying down, eyes closed, on what looked like the riverbank, and it was nighttime. "Oh my gosh, where did this come from?"

Belle shushed me. "We'll talk about that later, dear. Let's be on our way."

Wendy was talking on her phone outside. "That's right, Peter, you can't believe what a hit Mum was in the Blue Hair Studio. They loved her, and she loved them. Yes, yes, I'll send pictures. Uh-huh. Our day of detecting is over, and we're going to the hotel. Leta and I need to freshen up before dinner, but Mum is already gorgeous. Yes, consider this our check-in for the day. Bye now."

Wendy gave me a questioning look, and Dickens barked. It must have been the look on my face. "I know, I know, I look as though I've seen a ghost, and I think I have. I'll explain once we're in the car—or perhaps Belle should do the explaining."

Belle was beside herself. "Okay girls, you'll have to hold your horses, because I want to start from the beginning. And thank you, Wendy, for my day of pampering. I'm not sure what was better, the beauty treatment or the clues I gathered."

I glanced at Wendy in the rearview mirror. "Seems you'll have to wait to hear about the shock I just had, but it's Miss Marple's story, so we'll follow her lead."

Belle smiled sweetly. "Once upon a time . . . just kidding. I found a huge clue as soon as I sat down in the hair washing chair and Tina noticed the sparkly blue strands in my hair. Had to pop my hearing aids back in so I could hear her. She asked where I'd gotten my fairy hair. When I told her it was in Astonbury at the Fall Fête, she said, "Oh, that was probably Prudence. She does the fairy hair here, and she's one of my flatmates.'"

"Prudence?" Wendy and I said in unison.

"Yes, girls. I told her I'd not met anyone named Prudence, that Sparkle and Summer had a booth and did a booming business. Tina looked puzzled and said she was positive Prudence had gone to the Cotswolds for two weekends of festivals. I thought that was odd, but I couldn't ask any more questions right then because my hearing aids had to come out so she could shampoo my hair.

"It was time for Priscilla to set my hair, and I pondered how to proceed as we talked. She commented on my fairy hair too but had a similar reaction about Summer and Sparkle. Hadn't heard of them. By the way, you may have noticed my hair is not as curly as usual. I like the way Priscilla used bigger rollers."

"Oh, is that what it is, Mum? We'll have to try that at home. It's a much more elegant look."

I glanced at Belle. "I think it makes you look younger."

Belle just chuckled. "May have to shop for curlers on the way home. Meanwhile, Priscilla sat me under the dryer, and the manicurist worked on my nails. She rubbed cream into my hands, applied oil to my cuticles, and stuck my hands in these marvelous warming gloves. I think I need some of those too. Wouldn't they be a comfort on chilly nights?"

"Belle," I asked, "is this the first professional manicure you've had?"

"Yes, but hopefully not the last," she replied.

Now I had an idea of something to get Belle for Christmas —a gift certificate for a manicure in Astonbury. I was eager for her to get to the part about Sparkle, but it was a joy to hear the wonder in her voice as she described her salon experience.

"Loved the hand and arm massage, and I like the look of my nails. Next, Priscilla combed out my hair and styled it in these soft curls. Sprayed something on it to make it shine too. Darn, should've gotten the name of that stuff. It was Priscilla who suggested a makeover, and I thought it couldn't hurt.

"It was while the makeup artist was pulling out colors that I had a brainstorm. I excused myself and went back to the hair washing station. Asked Tina if she by chance had a picture of Prudence. And she did. Someone had snapped a pic of Prudence doing fairy hair on Tina. Guess who it was?"

"Well, you just said it was Prudence, didn't you?" asked Wendy.

"Um, was it Sparkle?" I asked.

"Nailed it. Yes, Prudence and Sparkle are one and the same."

Wendy looked at me dumbfounded. "How on earth did you know that, Leta?"

"I wish I could say I was that smart, but I'm not. Let your mum explain."

"I had an inkling there couldn't be that many girls doing fairy hair in Totnes. That's why I asked for a photo. Still, I was surprised to find my hunch was right—that Prudence had a stage name, so to speak."

Wendy laughed. "Makes me think of that Beatles song, 'Dear Prudence.'"

The lyrics popped into my head, as did a piece of trivia I'd picked up who knows where. "Ha! Bet you didn't know the song was inspired by Mia Farrow's sister Prudence?"

"Honestly, Leta, you're forever coming out with strange crumbs like that. Funny how that brain of yours works."

"Now girls, let's get back to the story," said Belle. "The photo prompted me to go a step further and ask about Max. Told Tina I'd met him at the Fête too. That's all it took. She told me all about Max and Prudence's up-and-down relationship. Been going on for several years, according to her.

"When I told her about Max dying, she said Prudence had called her with the news and was pretty broken up. I couldn't believe my eyes when she pulled out her phone to show me a text from Prudence and said, 'She sent me a few pics from that day. Glad she got some to remember him by.'

"Remember, Leta, you told us he'd been found on the river-bank? That was the last pic, him lying there in the dark. He looked so peaceful. He had to still be alive when Prudence . . . or Sparkle took that picture, right?"

"Bloody hell," Wendy whispered.

I caught her eye in the rearview mirror. "Look at my phone. Your mum had Tina forward the message to me. Read the caption too and tell me what you think."

Wendy pulled out her blue reading glasses and didn't react as she looked at the first few photos of Max waving his magic wand and smiling. When she got to the one of him lying down, her reaction was identical to the one I'd had.

She turned my phone every which way, enlarged the photo,

made it smaller again, and then read the message aloud: "'Started the day sober and wound up dead drunk as usual. Looks a right fool, doesn't he?' Good grief, Leta, I don't know what to think. She was probably playing around, but what poor timing. How was she to know he'd wind up dead soon after?"

Dickens was ahead of us. "Looks dead to me."

"Dickens, are you trying to tell me something?" said Wendy.

He barked excitedly, knowing full well I was the only one who could understand him. "Yes, I am. He looks dead, dead, dead."

"Well, we don't call him Detective Dickens for nothing," Belle said.

Wendy leaned over the front seat to show the phone to Belle. "Surely he's alive, and she took the picture planning to show it to him later, right?"

Belle replied, "No matter. We're going to have to send this to Gemma. Maybe her technicians can tell for sure. Granted, I hardly know the girl, but I can't imagine she'd be fool enough to snap a picture of a dead man."

"Goodness knows, but you're right about forwarding it to Gemma," I said.

Belle was looking pretty smug. "Do I win the prize today? Or did you girls come up with something better at the pub?"

Thankfully, we were still able to laugh at ourselves. "Belle, I think your daughter would agree you've won the prize. We heard Max was often at the pub with a girl named Prudence, and now we know who she was. You cleared up that mystery for us. Let's discuss the rest over dinner. I have an idea for something special tonight."

Chapter Ten

A DICKENS & CHRISTIE MYSTERY

I stopped by the front desk and asked the concierge to make us a reservation at The Angel. It was fancier than the other places in town, and I thought it would be a perfect spot for Belle to show off her new glamorous look. She was in for quite a treat.

I took Dickens for a quick walk and promised to take him for a longer one after dinner. Explaining why he couldn't accompany us to our special dinner was a waste of breath.

As I left the room, he barked, "Fine, be that way."

It would have been a pleasant and invigorating walk to The Angel but difficult for Belle, especially after her day in Totnes. I had the car waiting and warmed up when Belle and Wendy came out.

"How festive," exclaimed Belle as she admired the lights on the river walk. "Is it always lit up like this?"

"I think so," I replied. "I wonder whether they add Christmas decorations in December? Surely they do."

The Angel was located in the Dartmouth town centre overlooking the River Dart, and our concierge had reserved us a table by the window where we could watch the Dartmouth to Kingswear ferry go to and fro. This one was larger than the one beside our hotel.

I sighed in contentment. "It almost seems a shame to discuss murder and mayhem in this charming setting."

"Leta, luv," said Belle, "why don't we enjoy ourselves and save the serious talk for later?"

Wendy nodded in agreement. "Yes, let's savor the sights and the meal. Nothing's going to change in the next few hours. And who knows? Letting the events of the day simmer in the back of our brains might produce a major aha moment!"

"Looks like we're all on the same page, and here comes our server, right on cue. What do you say to a round of Prosecco to kick off the evening?"

We made our request and listened to the specials. The restaurant offered a choice of a two- or three-course menu, and we splurged on three. I took advantage of being on the water and ordered roast diver scallops as my appetizer and roasted stone bass as my main course. Belle chose oysters followed by venison, and Wendy went for a beetroot tart and then salted cod. A bottle of crisp Sauvignon Blanc saw us through the meal.

Thank goodness we could order three desserts for the table, as choosing only one would have been impossible. When we told our server we'd be sharing the final course, she carefully arranged the banana and pecan souffle, lemon crème, and raspberry tart in the middle of the table.

Belle smiled as she sampled the lemon crème. "I'm in heaven. Perhaps we should return in the spring. I can see myself spending another afternoon at the Blue Hair Studio followed by dinner here at The Angel. Greenway's on tomorrow's agenda, but there's so much more to see. We could tour the Naval Academy one day. You know Queen Elizabeth met Prince Phillip there, don't you? And we could do the Round Robin ferry, bus, and train ride one day."

Wendy looked at me. "We may have created a monster. Before you know it, Mum will be booking massages and facials. But seriously, Mum, if you'd like to come back, let's plan on it."

We were paying our tab when my phone pinged with a text. I smiled when I saw it was from Deborah. She'd sent the photos she'd taken at the Fête with an apology for taking so long. I texted her back and told her the timing was perfect, that I was with Belle and Wendy and could share them when we returned to our hotel.

Belle dozed off on the short drive to the hotel, and she reluctantly suggested Wendy and I carry on without her. Chuckling about losing one-third of our brainpower, Wendy escorted Belle to their room while I went to get Dickens.

Dickens was good about being quiet when he was on his own, but when he heard me approach our room, he barked a greeting. "About time."

"My, my, and here I was ready to take you for a walk along the river. You'd better change your tune, young man, or you'll be right back up here instead of lying beside me while Wendy and I brainstorm."

"But you need me for brainstorming. How could you even consider doing something so important without Detective Dickens? Let's go."

I knew it would take Wendy a while to get Belle settled, so Dickens and I walked almost to town before turning back.

After a three-course meal, a walk in the crisp, cold air was just what I needed. I reflected on what we'd learned during the day, but if anything, I was more puzzled than I'd been before we explored Totnes. An idea did occur to me, though—not an idea about who the killer was, but one about how to organize our thoughts.

At the front desk, I asked whether the hotel had a conference room or office with a whiteboard or flipchart. The gentleman on duty thought for a moment and asked me to wait while he disappeared. He returned looking quite pleased with himself and asked me to follow him to the second floor.

There he unlocked the door to a large conference room overlooking the river. It had a whiteboard along the front wall and two flipchart pads on stands. "I didn't think the size mattered, miss, and this one has a view. We use it for staff meetings."

I wanted to hug him but refrained. Dickens showed no such restraint. He jumped up and put his paws on the man's legs and gave a joyful bark. "Thanks. Just what we need."

It didn't matter that Dickens had no idea why I wanted a conference room. It was enough that I was pleased. I texted Wendy to let her know where we were and asked whether she wanted wine or tea. I should have known what her answer would be.

By the time Wendy joined me, I had two glasses of wine on the table and the words "Case Map" written across the top of the whiteboard with "Max's Murder" in the center. Off to one side, I had a list of motives and on the other side, a list of suspects.

Wendy looked around in amazement. "We have an office and a *case map* too. If you're Maisie Dobbs, does that make me Billie?"

I had recommended Wendy read Jacqueline Winspear's books about the detective Maisie Dobbs, and she had thoroughly enjoyed them. Maisie had been a nurse in World War One and had embarked on a career as a private investigator when the war ended. Billie was the veteran who worked with her. For each case, Maisie and Billie would lay a sheet of wallpaper on her desk, blank side up. There they would create what she called a *case map*—a record of information they'd gathered during their investigation.

"Well, maybe you can be Sandra, her secretary who occasionally did some snooping. I don't think you can pass for a man."

Dickens barked. "I hope she had a dog. Every detective needs a dog."

"No, Dickens, she didn't have a dog," I said.

Wendy chuckled. "I know Dickens doesn't speak, but you do a good job of acting as though he does. Okay, let's see what you've got here. Are those motives in general or specific to our murder?"

"They're general categories. I found them online. One of my favorite authors, P. D. James, says, 'All the motives for murder are covered by the four Ls: Love, Lust, Lucre, and Loathing.' Don't you love the word lucre, like filthy lucre? Though I doubt there's any of that at stake in this crime."

"Only the roll of bills you found in the sugar jar, right?"

"True, but I'm still inclined to rule out lucre unless you feel strongly about it—or if Gemma uncovers something more about the drug angle. And if this list doesn't take us anywhere, there are plenty of others out there. What do you think of this one? Greed, Humiliation, Safety, Cheating, and War. I found it somewhere on the internet."

Wendy smirked. "I think we can rule out war, but humiliation and cheating could be factors with Max—we heard he humiliated or at least embarrassed Trixie at the book shop, and we know he cheated on her. And it sounds as though he cheated on Sparkle, or maybe it's just that they weren't exclusive in his mind. This is becoming awfully complicated."

"And, as if that's not enough, revenge and jealousy also crop up online as motives. "

Wendy studied the whiteboard while I added more motives. "Well, let 's look at the suspects: Trixie, Sparkle or Prudence, Jill, Phil, Barb, and some guy in a brown jacket. I know I'm repeating myself, but I can't believe Trixie did it. For that matter, I can't believe any of the girls did it."

"Neither can I," I said, "but we've got to be objective about this. Nothing would make me happier than to study the information we've gathered and find that a complete stranger committed this crime."

Wendy pulled out her phone. "Didn't I read somewhere that it's most often men who commit murders? Let me google women and murders. Here we go. One study found that 85% of murderers were male and only 15% female. I don't want to invent suspects, but we've only two males. Is that a problem?"

I had to laugh at her question. "Like I know? Let's start adding what we know about each of them and see what we come up with. When we feel like we've documented everything, we can transfer it to a big sheet of flipchart paper to take with us."

Wendy listed the five names in a circle around the words *Max's Murder*, leaving plenty of space. For good measure, she added Brown Jacket Man. She drew a circle around each name and wrote *MOTIVE* beneath them. For Trixie, we filled in Loathing, Humiliation, and Cheating but agreed that was a stretch.

"I can't see it," I said. "I didn't pick up feelings of loathing, and if she felt humiliated because Max had cheated her on while they were married, why would the feeling boil over into murder now? She sounded so sincere when she told me she didn't hate him."

Wendy nodded and wrote the same three words beneath Sparkle/Prudence. "The motives could be the same, but to me, they seem slightly stronger for Prudence. Was she humiliated because he dumped her for Trixie? Maybe, but she took up with him again regardless. Did she suddenly *loathe* him when she discovered he'd lied to her about being divorced? Did she kill him in a fit of rage? I can't see it."

"Neither can I. Things like that only happen in the movies."

I picked up a marker and wrote Loathing and Revenge beneath Phil. "I feel like I need something more descriptive like macho anger for Phil. That's the only reason I can see for him following Max and killing him. I mean Phil'd already knocked him around and given him a bloody nose. Wouldn't murder be overkill—so to speak?"

Wendy wrote the same two motives beneath Barb and Jill. "Jill had plenty of reason to loathe him, but I think she was scared to death after he grabbed her. I can't see her doing anything beyond what she told you—kneeing him and jumping on her bicycle and leaving."

"Right. And I'm not sure about Barb. She'd already taught him a lesson Friday night. Sure, he said something to her at the Fête on Saturday and to all the girls at the bar that night, but would snarky words provoke her to kill him? Of all the girls, she seems the most likely to let it roll off her shoulders."

Wendy grabbed another marker and added a big question mark beneath Brown Jacket Man. "Let's try something else,

PUMPKINS, PAWS, & MURDER

since motive doesn't seem to be helping us. How about a list of evidence?"

So we tried that angle. Off to the side, Wendy wrote EVIDENCE. Beneath that, she listed PIG written on the car, apple in mouth, apple core, missing top hat and cane, coroner's report he was strangled, and red scarf tied around his neck. That was it.

"Should we add the wad of bills, baggie of pot, and pills?" I asked. "I'm not sure those things count as evidence."

Wendy looked exasperated. "I think we need an instruction manual for sleuths, like *Detection for Dummies*. What's evidence versus things that tell us more about the players? Like the pot and the pills tell us about Max, but they're not evidence of anything to do with his murder, are they?"

"Could point to a killer if he was selling pot and pills, and his supplier or a client killed him. I don't know, but none of this seems very useful," I murmured. "Would it help to do a timeline?"

Wendy drew a line across the bottom of the whiteboard. "Couldn't hurt. It's all about the pub and the inn."

Wendy wrote,

Max bumps into Barb in AM
Max shoves Sparkle in apple bobbing bucket
Brown jacket guy accosts him
Trixie slaps Max
He threatens her
He's rude to the girls at pub
Phil jerks him up
Max leaves & drinks in his truck at the inn (Phil thinks)
Phil bloodies Max's nose
Max attacks Jill
Jill knees him & rides off

Max goes to the river

Trixie finds Max by river's edge & leaves him there

Sparkle finds Max in same spot, takes picture of him, and leaves him

I looked at Wendy. "It didn't hurt, but I'm not sure it helped. We still have no idea who stuck an apple in Max's mouth and strangled him. Neither girl who admits to being at the scene mentioned an apple. Sure, Sparkle took a picture, but that probably only proves she was there, which we already knew."

"And where's the hat? Only Trixie mentioned it, and it's still missing. Did the killer take it? And if so, why?" asked Wendy. "And where's the cane?"

That question got Dickens's attention. "Too bad Paddington missed that."

I repeated Dickens's observation as though it were mine. "If only Paddington could talk. Gavin says he prowls all night, so I bet he saw everything. But until he breaks his silence, I haven't a clue. I'm still as befuddled as I was. Either one of the people on this timeline is lying or there's a player we're missing. Or they could all be lying."

Wendy groaned. "So, what would be your best guess as to who's lying? My gut tells me to rule out Trixie and Jill. Barb? I don't know her that well. Yes, we see her all the time at the Ploughman, but I can't say I really know her.

"Sparkle, I know the least. In fact, most of what I know is from your chat with her at the Tearoom and what we've picked up here in Totnes. And what does that amount to? She has a stage name. So what? She's dated Max longer than she's let on. Again, so what?"

I wrote *temper* on the whiteboard next to Sparkle. "If she's the person who made a scene at the caravan park, could be she has a fierce temper."

Wendy wrote *sweet and naïve* next to Jill and Trixie. "That's my take," she said.

"What would you write to describe Barb?"

Wendy wrote *savvy and street-smart*. That seemed to fit.

I stared at the whiteboard. "If more men than women commit murder, maybe it's Phil who's lying, or at the very least omitting information?"

Dickens barked, "Why don't you list the key questions?"

As usual, I acted as though I'd had a brainstorm. I wrote as I talked. "I'm going to start listing our key questions. Who put the apple in his mouth? Where's the hat? Where's the cane? Who wrote PIG on the truck and drew the picture? Who is Brown Jacket Man? Who's lying?"

Plopping into a chair, Wendy put her head on the table. "Too many questions without answers. I can't take any more tonight. Let's take a picture of this and copy it all onto a big sheet of paper so we can add to it if we have any earth-shattering ideas later. And then let's call it a night. With any luck, things will be clearer in the morning."

"Or foggier," I mumbled.

I tossed and turned all night, my mind fixing on some random fact like Phil giving Max a bloody nose or the song "Dear Prudence," and I gave in and turned on the bedside lamp at 5:30. I fixed a cup of coffee in the Keurig on the dresser and sipped it as I looked at emails on my phone. Both Anna and Dave had written wanting to know the latest about the murder. Ugh.

Dickens stirred and stretched. I'd long been thankful that he wasn't an early riser. He barked softly. "What's going on? Why are you awake?"

"Couldn't sleep, so I figured I might as well get up. Well, I'm not exactly up, but my eyes are open."

"Can we take a walk, then? As long as you're awake?"

I nodded and threw on my leggings, a sweatshirt, and a parka. When I added a ball cap and picked up the leash, Dickens knew I was ready. It was not yet six, and the hotel was quiet. The sun wouldn't be up for another hour or so, but the walk along the river was well lit.

"Dickens, I'm stumped. There are too many possibilities as to who killed Max, and we can't seem to rule anyone out. Any number of people could have come and gone to the riverbank that night, and no one would be the wiser. Unless they raised a ruckus, that is. And, apparently, no one did. And where does my brain go? To a book title of all things—*Death Comes Silently* by Carolyn Hart. In this case, it sure did. Now, see, I can make connections to books but not to anything useful."

Dickens stopped walking and looked at me. "Maybe we should leave it to Gemma. By the way, have you called her yet about all the stuff our detective agency found out yesterday? I bet we uncovered plenty of information that will be news to her. Does she have any idea that Sparkle has another name, for instance? Here you are beating yourself up for not solving the murder yet, but we're making progress."

"As in 'Slow but steady wins the race?' It just feels so *very* slow to me. And I'm worried that leaving it to Gemma may result in Trixie being charged. She had the motive, the means, and the opportunity. But you're right, I need to contact her this morning. Maybe she learned more at the Ploughman."

We'd made it to town already, so we walked up Fosse Way

and glanced in the dark store windows. When we turned around to head back, we stopped by one of the kiosks. It wasn't open, but I made note of the ferry departure times for Greenway. The earliest time in the off-season was eleven, giving us plenty of time for a leisurely breakfast and a call to Gemma. Perhaps in the interest of time, we could call Trixie's landlady and speak with her instead of making a second trip to Totnes.

When I joined Wendy and Belle in the restaurant at eight, Belle looked as though she'd slept well, and I was surprised to see her in makeup. "Belle, that can't be yesterday's makeup, can it?"

She chuckled. "No, luv. Wendy let me use hers this morning. How'd I do?"

"You look smashing. I could get used to this new you. Does this mean we'll be shopping not only for new curlers but also makeup on our way home?"

"Could be," she replied with a smile. "I hear you girls could've used an additional brain last night. And here I thought you two would solve the case with all the clues I gathered at the Blue Hair Studio."

I sighed. "I wish. Dickens and I've been up since 5:30 because it was all swirling in my head. Taking a before-dawn walk didn't help, but it was a beautiful outing. I managed to do one productive thing, though. I found out the first ferry to Greenway is at eleven. Shall we try to make that one?"

"Yes, dear. I'm looking forward to both the ferry trip and the tour. I'm not sure I can manage the stairs to the second floor, but I'll enjoy whatever I can see."

Wendy refilled our coffee cups from the carafe. "Yes, Mum. I researched accessibility, and the good news is there's a car to take us from the quay to the house, and the first floor has step-free entrances to all the rooms. Could be we take turns doing the tour, as Dickens won't be allowed in the house. If you don't feel comfortable with the stairs to the second floor, perhaps you and Dickens can relax at the café outside the house while Leta and I do the second level."

"What do you mean, I'm not allowed inside? What's up with that?" barked my boy.

I rubbed Dickens's head and looked at him meaningfully. "Dickens will have a full day, what with a ferry ride and exploring the grounds, the gift shop, and the second-hand bookstore—he's allowed in all those places. I'm hoping they have something I can take home to Christie. Doesn't seem right that she's missing this."

"Mum," Wendy said, "what do you think about popping in a few shops in Dartmouth before we board the ferry and then lunch in town when we return? Too full a day or doable?"

Belle chucked. "You girls take such good care of me. I think I can do all of that. What's on the schedule for after lunch?"

"I'm struggling with that," I said. "Sometime today, we need to call Gemma and bring her up to speed and find out how her investigation is progressing. And we need to speak with Trixie's landlady. I've entertained thoughts of driving home this afternoon, depending on what you ladies would like to do. You mentioned the Naval Academy, Belle, but could you do a second tour in one day?"

Wendy wore a puzzled expression. "Is there a reason you want to go home today?"

"Not one I can put my finger on. I don't think there's more

to discover here, and I don't know what we'd do in Astonbury to push this case along either. So, no, I don't have a reason beyond feeling at loose ends."

Clearing her throat, Belle spoke up. "Girls, I suggest we enjoy our stay and return home on Saturday as we'd originally planned. I can't see any urgency about getting home. This afternoon, I'll take a nap. You may recall I didn't get one yesterday. Didn't you say there was more to see in Dartmouth? Isn't there a castle? And more shops? Why don't you two enjoy yourselves this afternoon while I rest? And if Dickens wants to nap with me, he's welcome."

Dickens had something to say about that. "Let's see how I feel after two boat rides. It's nice to have a choice—snuggle with Belle or explore more of the town."

Belle snuck him a scrap of toast. "Is that a hard choice, Dickens? Bark once for yes, twice for no."

And he obliged with a single bark, which made us all laugh. The couple at the table next to ours had been taking it all in and commented on Dickens's obvious intelligence. If they only knew.

I had to admit Belle was right about returning to Astonbury. Yes, we'd likely learned all we could in Totnes, but that didn't mean we couldn't enjoy more of the sights before traveling home. I gave in and suggested to Wendy that she meet me in my room so we could get Gemma on speakerphone before we drove to the shops. She knocked on my door at nine, and I hit speed dial.

"Gemma Taylor. Oh hi, Leta, glad you called."

I never knew what kind of reception I'd get, and I was relieved. "Hi. I've got you on speakerphone, and Wendy's with me. And Dickens too, so be careful what you say."

"Right, wouldn't want to offend the little hero dog. So, I've got some news on this end. First, they tested the apple core and apple for DNA, and guess what?"

Dickens barked and Wendy and I said, "What?"

"Well, the DNA on the apple belongs to Max and both bite marks match his teeth, but—and this could be a lead—the DNA on the apple core belongs to someone else."

"But, let me guess," said Wendy. "There's no DNA match in the database, right?"

"Right you are, but if we have good cause, I can gather DNA from our likely suspects. Not that eating an apple is proof of murder. But it would place someone at the scene."

"How 'bout what you learned at the Ploughman? Anything beyond what Peter gleaned from Phil the other night?" I asked.

"Now, that was a good lead, Leta. I got plenty more detail. Barb was working, and she admitted to having a fling with Max in Totnes and thinking she'd never see him again. She wasn't happy to see him on her home turf and definitely wasn't up for a repeat. Her story explains the bruising on Max's torso that came prior to Saturday. And I was able to solve one more mystery."

"Oh! And what's that?"

"Brian, Barb's cousin, is the brown jacket man. He's the gardener for The Olde Mill Inn and quite a few country estates around the area. He was at the pub drinking with his mates, and as soon as I saw him, it clicked. You know him, right, Leta?"

"I don't think I do, but maybe I should. I could use a gardener for my cottage."

"You'd probably recognize him if you saw him. Anyway, it hit me that Barb was his cousin and she probably told him about the episode with Max on Friday night. It fit that he'd be riled about it, so I asked him about Saturday afternoon. He had no problem admitting he'd told Max in no uncertain terms never to come near his cousin again."

Wendy laughed and said, "Even though Barb did a good job of taking care of Max herself."

"Right," I said, "but some macho posturing for reinforcement couldn't hurt."

Gemma sighed. "We see a lot of that in the pubs around here."

I thought again about the Friday evening altercation. "It's a wonder Max could work the Fête, though he didn't appear any worse for the wear. No one said he winced when Brian poked him or when he pushed Sparkle or Prudence's face in the water."

The words Sparkle or Prudence got Gemma's attention. "What do you mean 'Prudence'? Has the girl got a twin?"

"A twin," Wendy said. "Now, that'd be one for the books, wouldn't it? A mystery book or BBC show. No, Sparkle doesn't have a twin—it's just that her real name is Prudence."

Gemma cleared her throat. "I might use another name too if Mum had named me Prudence or Patience or the like. Doesn't it mean to be careful and disciplined? And then people would call you a prude, right? Yuck. But never mind that. What exactly did you find out?"

It was my turn. "Remember I said how surprised you'd be at what people would tell Belle? Well, she got the story from one of Sparkle's flatmates who works at the Blue Hair Studio in Totnes. Sparkle—or Prudence, as she's known there, works in the same place. Belle had herself a wash and set yesterday and came away with all kinds of news."

"Blimey. What else?"

Wendy continued. "We heard Mum's story after Leta and I

visited the local pub and heard that a girl named Prudence had been carrying on with Max off and on for quite some time, as in before Max ever married Trixie. Can you believe it? You know, it's occurred to us Sparkle's a bit inconsistent when she talks about how long she's dated Max."

Gemma was in an amazingly good mood today and surprised me when she said, "Is this where I'm supposed to say 'the plot thickens'?"

I'd saved the best for last. "Yes, and there's more. This blew us away. Prudence sent Tina, her flatmate and co-worker, several texts on the day of the Fête—with photos. No big deal, shots of Max doing tricks and such until the final text—a photo of Max lying on his back at the river. And, let me pull up the caption she texted. Here it is. 'Started the day sober and wound up dead drunk as usual. Looks a right fool, doesn't he?'"

"Bloody hell. You're sending me all that, right? Surely he's alive in the photo. I mean, how stupid can the girl be?"

"Our exact thoughts," I said. "It's hard to be sure, but I'd bet he was fine when that photo was taken. Guess it proves Sparkle was there, but we already knew that. Of course, there's no apple in his mouth. I suppose she could have taken the pic and then finished the job. That idea seems ridiculous when I say it out loud, though. Why even put yourself at the scene?"

"You're right," said Gemma. "The picture doesn't prove anything, and the idea of her killing him after that seems far-fetched. Still, anything's possible.

"On this end, I'm still checking alibis for Barb and Brian and Phil. So far, not one of the people we've identified with a motive has a decent alibi, but I'm not through yet."

Wendy sat forward. "Gemma, I know you found a laptop in Max's caravan. Anything useful on it?"

"Not a thing. I was hoping it would have an email saying

'I'm the killer. Come find me here,' but no such luck."

We all chuckled at that comment. If only.

"Based on his search history, looks like he mostly used it to find magic tricks and watch how-to videos. And, as Leta probably told you, he had tons of photos of Trixie.

"As for the little red book, not much joy from it either— notes on magic tricks mixed in with scribbled sums and dates. Small sums, at that, so if he was selling drugs, I think he was small-time. Could be the notes were for dates and payments for magic shows, but the amounts are too all over the board for that."

"Well, at least you've made me feel better, Gemma," I said. "I was feeling pretty low after Wendy and I captured every little thing we knew about this case and still couldn't make heads nor tails of it. The more we learn, the cloudier it becomes."

"Yes, that's the way it is more often than not, but what you've uncovered so far has helped push things along. Just don't you two get cocky and go getting yourselves in trouble. It's early days yet."

"We won't," said Wendy, "because we're taking today off. Going shopping and visiting Greenway before we drive home tomorrow. Wouldn't it be lovely if we arrived in Astonbury to the news that you'd had a break in the case—or better yet, arrested the killer?"

"Lovely for all of us, I'd say," responded Gemma. "Time for me to chat with Constable James and see where he is on both the alibis and the drug angle. It's a long shot, but we could find something that says Max was a major player in the drug world. Doubtful, though. *Do* call if you stumble across anything else, and don't forget to forward me the texts from Sparkle or Prudence or whatever name she's using today."

Chapter Eleven

I dropped Belle and Wendy in front of the Community Bookshop on Higher Street and parked across from the ferry dock. I was a born shopper, but this morning I preferred to get our ferry tickets and relax on a bench by the water while Dickens explored. Wendy had promised to text me if she found anything she knew I couldn't live without. And if Belle needed a lift down to the dock, I'd get a text about that too. We wanted her to save her energy for touring.

What the heck, I thought. *Perhaps I can get Wendy's landlady Carol on the line and be done with that.* The phone was answered on the second ring.

When I explained who I was, Carol responded enthusiastically. "I've been hoping you'd call. My entire family loves Trixie, and we want to do anything we can to help."

"Well, really I'm looking for background about Trixie and Max, anything that would paint a picture of them and their relationship. Did Trixie move out before they married or after?"

"Oh! They lived here for a few months after the wedding,

but I had to ask them to leave. I hated to do it, but Max and his friends weren't people I wanted around my children. Trixie understood."

"I had no idea they'd lived there as a couple. So his friends were trouble?"

"Not to speak ill of the dead, but Max was no prize on his own, and when his friends were over, he was worse. He denied it, but I know they were smoking more than cigarettes in my garden, and I think they were into drugs. Saw some money exchanging hands a few times. There was no way I was allowing that on my property."

There was that phrase again, "Not to speak ill of the dead." Was there no end to the bad news about him? "Had you met Max before?"

"Yes, but it was like he had a split personality. He was a delight when they were dating—bringing flowers, doing card tricks for the kids, an absolute prince. Then it was as though a switch was thrown, or he had an evil twin."

"Oh my goodness, poor Trixie."

"Yes, if you know her at all, you know she's a sweetheart. Didn't deserve to be treated that way."

"What way?" I prompted.

"I guess you'd call it verbal abuse. If he'd spoken to me that way, he'd have been out on his ear, but I think Trixie was in shock. I can't imagine he didn't show some signs before the wedding, but I never saw any. Like I said, could have been his evil twin.

"I was proud of her, though, when she left him and moved back here. The few times he came around, she stood up for herself. Got right in his face and told him to get lost. That was a Trixie I'd not seen before."

I was wishing I'd taken Belle's advice and left my detective work for later. Her story was more of the same, except for the drug angle. Yes, I'd found a small amount of pot and pills in the caravan, but possession was not the same as selling. Not that Gemma had turned up anything about drugs in the background check. Had he been lucky or was he so small-time he wasn't on the radar of the local authorities?

I thanked Carol and assured her we were doing everything we could to help Trixie. Before I rang off, she asked about Trixie's health. "Please tell me she's got her asthma under control. I worry about her," she said.

"Well, I know she had an attack earlier this week, but I think she's okay now. Did she have them often when she lived with you?"

"She had two, and they were after Max moved in. Could have been the friends smoking that aggravated it. And the worst was the day she tripped at work and sprained her ankle. Max was good about wrapping it and waiting on her, but after he gave her something for the pain, she had a severe attack. So bad, we had to ring 999."

"Omigosh. I don't know much about asthma. I wouldn't think Advil or such would be harmful."

"I'm not sure what it was, but I know she has to be careful with headache medicine that the rest of us take like candy. Anyway, I'm sure her aunt is looking out for her. And it sounds like you are too. Thanks for calling, and please tell Trixie we miss her."

How depressing. I was having a roller coaster day. Disheartened about not being any closer to identifying Max's killer, then up because Gemma was encouraged by the information we'd unearthed, now down again after hearing Carol's tale. I could only hope the ferry ride and Greenway tour would cheer me up.

At least Dickens was having a ball. He'd taken to chasing the flocks of birds that landed on the bank of the river. He didn't seem bothered that he'd chase them off only to see them return. It was a new game. When he saw me put the phone down, he dashed over, panting.

"Is our ferry here yet? Are the birds going too? How 'bout Belle and Wendy?"

As I was chuckling at his excitement, I spotted my companions approaching. I didn't see a shopping bag, but Belle was sporting a new blue-grey hat. "We *have* created a monster," I said. "A new hairstyle, makeup, and a new hat. What next?"

"Have to look my best to visit Dame Agatha's home," said Belle with a smile. "And here comes the ferry. I'm rather excited about this, as I've been reading her books since before you two were born."

"And don't forget, Mum, we adore all the Hercule Poirot stories on the BBC—the ones starring David Suchet. I think we've watched them all and more than once."

That reminded me of the costume party I'd thrown in September when Toby had come as the famous detective. He'd had the devil of a time keeping his curled mustache straight as the evening progressed.

"Well, we may not encounter the Belgian detective, but we've got our very own Miss Marple, right Belle? And I think the original would be envious of your new hat."

We joined the crowd queuing for the ferry and were able to get seats inside. I took Dickens up top as the crew cast off. This was his first time on a boat of any kind. He'd been timid about the metal gangplank but once aboard seemed right at home. Standing on the top deck, he faced into the wind as we powered toward Greenway. He was a sight to behold with his ears and his long white fur blowing in the strong wind. I, on the other hand, was tugging my red beret over my ears and snugging my wool scarf beneath my chin.

The ferry captain entertained us with facts about the river and waved at the students from the Royal Naval College conducting man overboard exercises. It took me a moment to realize they were practicing with dummies dressed in orange. Not far from Greenway, the captain pointed out a small boathouse whose stone pillars had originally formed the foundation of Sir Walter Raleigh's house.

When we arrived at the Greenway quay, Belle and Wendy found seats in the sun. They would wait for the quay car to take them to the top, while Dickens and I climbed the steep path to the house. We planned to meet outside the Barn Café.

Dickens pranced along taking in the sights. The climb didn't faze him, but I was winded long before we arrived up top.

Dickens cocked his head at me. "Leta, are you panting?"

"Why yes, I am. All those walks to see Martha and Dylan didn't prepare me for this terrain."

"Does that mean we'll start walking hills when we get home? And take Christie with us in your new backpack?"

"Yes, we will. Maybe a picnic lunch too."

Greenway welcomed dogs with tether rings and water bowls available in the courtyard, and I was happy to leave Dickens there while I got coffee in the café. Without the wind from the river chilling me to the bone, I was able to remove my coat and scarf while we waited for our companions. When they joined us, we agreed they'd tour the first floor while Dickens and I took in the garden and made our way to the boathouse. I'd about decided to forgo seeing the house again so I could concentrate on the grounds.

Because Henry and I had only toured the house, I was eager to walk the path to the Dart Estuary and see the Boathouse, the scene of the crime in Christie's novel *Deadman's Folly*. I had heard that the garden, the boathouse, and the main house were easily recognizable in the book as those at Greenway. How appropriate that the TV movie starring David Suchet as Poirot was filmed here. I wished I'd had time to read the book before this trip. I'd be sure to do that when I got home.

The winding path and the views were breathtaking, and I could imagine Agatha Christie with family and friends whiling away the summer playing croquet and meandering the many pathways. When Dickens and I returned to the courtyard at the house, we found Belle relaxing with a pastry.

Dickens barked a greeting, and Belle gave him a nibble. "Enjoyed that no end, but I sent Wendy along to the second floor on her own. She promised to take pictures."

"I was afraid the stairs would be too much. When you're rested, would you like to visit the gift shop with me? I'm in search of Christie paraphernalia."

"That would be grand, luv. Are you looking for anything in particular?"

"As a matter of fact, I have in mind something from the Detection Club. I stumbled across an article about the group and was fascinated. A handful of London-based mystery writers formed the club in 1930, and Agatha Christie was a founding member, along with Dorothy Sayers. Gotta love the fact that two women were there at the start. New members had to be invited and had to be voted in. Then they had to swear an oath. Just a sec. I have a screenshot of it on my phone."

Do you promise that your detectives shall well and truly detect the crimes presented to them using those wits which it may please you to bestow upon them and not placing reliance on nor making use of Divine Revelation, Feminine Intuition, Mumbo Jumbo, Jiggery-Pokery, Coincidence, or Act of God?"

Belle read it aloud and exclaimed, "Oooh, I like that. I detest books where they take me for a fool, where there's no way the detective could possibly have solved the crime based on what I've read or the murderer isn't even in the book until near the end—kind of sprung on me. I feel cheated when that happens."

"Exactly. This club felt the same way, so they adopted "The Ten Commandments of Detective Fiction," a list of rules for mystery writers to follow. I think it was the very first rule that said the criminal had to be introduced at the beginning of the book. I'd love a framed print of the rules, and this seems the perfect place to find something like that."

I could tell Dickens wanted to loll in the sun, so I found him a water bowl and hooked him to another tether. Belle and I spent a pleasant thirty minutes shopping. They didn't have the Ten Commandments, but the clerk found a small version of the oath framed in gold. I could think of several places in my cottage where it would fit. I purchased two, thinking I'd give one to Beatrix for her shop.

I hadn't forgotten about a gift for my prissy black cat, but I couldn't find anything I thought she'd care for. Plenty of bookmarks with black cats, but she didn't need one of those. She chose to mark her place by chewing the corner of a page in the book. She also chewed the corners of newspapers, magazines, and notebooks anywhere she found them.

Wendy greeted us when we emerged from the gift shop. Dickens was lying by her feet with a little girl rubbing his belly and a toddler lying with her head on his rump. The mum was snapping photos of her children and my adorable dog.

Belle laughed. "We often charge for pics."

The mum smiled and wanted to know all about what kind of dog Dickens was. When she heard the typical 140-pound size of a Great Pyrenees, she groaned. "Not happening, but this one has a lovely temperament. Come along, girls. Your father will be wondering where we've gotten to."

Though we'd snacked on coffees and pastries, we were ready to sit down to a real lunch. Wendy and Belle hailed the quay car, and Dickens and I took the downhill path. It was much quicker going down than it had been coming up. We'd planned to take the ferry back to Dartmouth, but Wendy suggested we take the shorter ferry ride across the river to Dittisham. From the Greenway quay, the colorful buildings on the village's Manor Street looked inviting, especially the pink Ferry Boat Inn.

What a treat. The FBI, as the locals call it, had a huge picture window looking out on the river sparkling in the sun plus several local ales to choose from.

I raised my pint for a toast. "Cheers, ladies. This has been a grand adventure for a mystery fan like me. Even before I moved here from the States, I adored British mysteries— books and television shows—and all these bits of trivia make my day. Like seeing the actual boathouse Agatha Christie describes in her book and knowing that a Poirot movie was filmed there."

"Look," cried Belle, pointing to a framed poster near our table. "I'd never made the connection between Lady Dittisham and this village."

"Huh?" said Wendy. "Who's Lady Dittisham? Oh, I see." The poster depicted the cover of Christie's novel *The Five*

Little Pigs and proudly proclaimed that the character Lady Dittisham was named after the village.

"Belle, have you read *everything* Dame Agatha wrote?" I asked.

"Honestly, Leta, I'm not sure I have, but I've seen most of the Poirot movies, and *Five Little Pigs* was one of them."

"Gee, Mum, maybe we should have you join us as the speaker at Beatrix's book club for an Agatha Christie night. Wouldn't that be fun?"

"No, luv. I prefer to read books, not discuss them. But maybe between the three of us, we could come up with an Agatha trivia game for your club. Now, I'd get a kick out of helping with that."

We continued to discuss Christie trivia as we enjoyed our lunch and Dickens happily chewed the knucklebone the waitress had given him. He didn't want to leave it behind when we left to catch the ferry to Dartmouth, so I tucked it in a napkin and promised to give it back later.

I was looking forward to the captain's informative talk as we traveled downriver, and I wasn't disappointed. This time he pointed out a small building as the spot where the *Mayflower* and another ship, the *Speedwell*, put in for repairs before proceeding to Plymouth to set sail together for America. When it was decided the *Speedwell* was too leaky for the trip, only the *Mayflower* made the voyage. This one small stretch of river was packed with history.

It was late afternoon when we docked in Dartmouth, and I was glad I'd acquiesced to staying the night. It wasn't only Dickens who chose to join Belle in a nap. Dickens carried his knucklebone, we ladies grabbed mugs of hot chocolate, and we all retired to our rooms. I enjoyed naps on the best of the days, and after a restless night, I needed one.

When I awoke refreshed, I rang Wendy to see if she was up for a walk to town and a glass of champagne at Platform One on the river. I loved the quirky story of how the train station was built before the railway was granted permission to build a bridge over the River Dart. Permission never came, and the train runs only along the other side of the river. Travelers have to take a ferry from Kingswear to Dartmouth for the final leg.

Dickens and I met Wendy in the lobby. We were glad we had our gloves and had donned our quilted coats, as the wind had picked up. Dickens, of course, was in heaven. His Great Pyrenees brethren have been guarding herds of sheep in the Pyrenees mountains for centuries, and his coat, like theirs, is well-suited to cold and windy weather.

We ordered flutes of champagne and a dozen oysters and settled in to enjoy the view with Dickens ensconced beneath the table.

I turned to Wendy. "This turned out to be a lovely day— once I managed to put the whole Max the Magnificent issue out of my mind, that is. I think I can honestly say it didn't enter my head from the moment we boarded the first ferry until just now."

"And what brings it to mind now?"

"For some reason, I remembered I hadn't shown you the photos Deborah took at the Fête, and that made me think of Max and the rest of the story. Let's continue ignoring that tale and focus on Deborah's photography. There are quite a few shots of your Peter Pan group."

We oohed and aahed and laughed over the images. Wendy thought she'd get copies of one of the Wizard of Oz group to frame for both Peter and Belle for Christmas. I suggested she give her mum a copy of the Peter Pan group too. After all,

Belle had done a masterful job on the Peter Pan and Cowardly Lion costumes for her twins.

She asked my opinion on which Peter Pan shot to choose. "Hmmm, I like this one, but isn't that Max in the background?" I said.

"Yes, but maybe I can crop him out if it doesn't ruin the picture. Wait, who's that with him?"

I studied my phone. "Not sure. Let me make it larger. It's a man poking his finger in Max's chest. It must be Brian. He *does* look familiar to me. Guess I've just never met him, only seen him around."

Wendy studied the photo. "I've only met him once or twice, but I think you're right. So, happy photos and one pic Gemma can put in her files. Are you going to send it to her?"

"Yes, and after I do that, I'm making this whole Max murder thing a taboo topic, at least until tomorrow."

Wendy looked at me and rolled her eyes. "We can try. You should put in the text 'Do Not Disturb tonight' or 'Little Old Ladies signing off until tomorrow.'"

I thought for a moment. "Don't want to rub Gemma's nose in the fact that she's always on duty and we're not."

"Right. Better left unsaid. How about one more glass of champagne before we fetch Mum for dinner?"

We'd decided on a more casual evening at the Floating Bridge, the pub next door to our hotel. Wendy rang her mum and asked her to meet us in the lobby and told her to bundle up for the short walk. We chose not to tell Belle about the photos, and we felt fortunate that we didn't hear from Gemma.

We shared an order of calamari and ordered burgers for the main meal. Dickens got a few fries, or *chips* as they call them in the UK. And Belle gave him a chunk of her burger. He and I would have to get in some long walks at home to make up for the goodies we'd both indulged in.

The only murders discussed were those in our favorite mystery novels. I hadn't gotten very far in my Tommy & Tuppence book, and already I'd added two more Agatha Christie books to my To Be Read list—*Five Little Pigs* and *Deadman's Folly*. I planned to stop by the Book Nook to get them and knew Beatrix would order them for me if she didn't have them in stock.

We'd had good weather for several days, so it was no surprise when we woke to a rainy day on Saturday. Gemma called while we were eating breakfast. "Are you ladies on the road yet or are you having another day of leisure?"

"Today, it's a quick breakfast and the drive home. How are you?"

"Well, I wish I could say I had the day off as I did last Saturday, but no such luck. I got the photo of Brian and Max. Thanks for that. Thought you'd get a laugh out of another bit of information that came my way. Mum and I are sitting here in my kitchen chuckling about it. Doesn't push the case along but does answer a question."

"And which question is that?" I asked.

"Who scrawled PIG on the truck? I got a call from Barb last night. Said she did it."

"Why on earth would she own up to that?"

I could almost picture Gemma rolling her eyes. "Said she didn't want me to waste time trying to figure it out when I could be looking for a murderer. Remember, Leta, when you saw her and Max pass each other Saturday morning? She'd seen him approach from his truck and had the spur of the moment idea to get back at him one more time. The nose of the truck was almost in the bushes, so she could complete the artwork unseen. Really, all I could do was laugh."

"Guess there's no one to file a complaint?" I said.

That got a laugh from Gemma. "Right. Just going to document it and let it be. Like Barb said, one less question to worry about. Wish all the answers would come my way that easily.

"Anyway, safe travels. Mum says give her a call when you get home."

I put the phone down and turned to my companions to share the Barb story. "Gemma is so unpredictable. This is two days in a row she's been perfectly pleasant, no snide comments, no insults. Do you think she's beginning to see how valuable we little old ladies are?"

"Based on recent history, I wouldn't bet on it," quipped Wendy. "Her behavior is a bit erratic. Can't tell whether it's only when she's stressed about a case or it's her usual personality. Maybe as more time passes after something awful like murder, she gets calmer and more patient."

I nodded in agreement. I hoped my relationship with Gemma would continue on its current pleasant path. *Pleasant and productive*, I thought. We might come at things from different angles, but together we seemed to make progress. What was the harm in our putting our heads together?

Chapter Twelve

We pulled out of the parking lot shortly before ten and were in Astonbury by one despite the rain. As I dropped Belle and Wendy off, I realized I was more than ready for some quiet time with Christie and Dickens.

Dickens echoed my sentiment when I pulled into the driveway. "Home at last," he barked.

We heard Christie meowing as we approached the side door. "Hurry up. I need food."

"Lovely greeting," I replied as we entered the mudroom. I kicked off my wet shoes, hung my parka on a hook, and grabbed a towel to dry Dickens. "I know Peter fed you while we were gone. Can't you admit it was our company you missed?"

"Well, maybe just a little. It gets lonely around here when you two are gone."

Dickens barked and butted her with his head. "I missed you too, silly girl."

Dickens chased her into the sitting room while I carried my suitcase upstairs to unpack. I laughed as my four-legged companions dashed up the stairs and down again while I unpacked my suitcase and changed into leggings and an oversized heavy sweater.

In no time, I had a fire going in the fireplace, a cup of tea in my hand, and my Tommy & Tuppence book in my lap. Yes, indeed, home at last.

I must have dozed off because I was awakened by the phone ringing. It was Rhiannon calling to see if I was up for dinner in Stow. She was in the mood for a meal at the Old Stocks Inn.

I yawned and stretched. "Oh my, let me get my wits about me. I've been lazy this afternoon. What time are you thinking?"

"Not before seven at the earliest. Toby wants to go and can't leave until he closes the Tearoom for the day."

I glanced at the clock and saw it was 3:30. "I should be able to make that if I can shake myself awake, though I can't say I'm looking forward to going back out in the rain after this morning's drive from Dartmouth. On the other hand, I have nothing in the house for dinner after being gone for three days. What's one more meal out?"

"That's the spirit. And the forecast calls for the rain to start tapering off after dark, so maybe it won't be too bad. Do you plan to bring Dickens?"

I looked at my boy. He was lying on his side with his paws stretched toward the fireplace. "I think I'll leave him home this time. I've managed to keep him mostly dry today, and I'd like him to that way. Let's say I meet you guys at 7:30 so Toby isn't rushed."

The conversation with Rhiannon made me think about Beatrix's shop across from Toby's Tearoom, so I called the Book Nook. Trixie answered the phone and told me Beatrix had gone to Manchester to shop for used books at the flea markets there and would be back Sunday afternoon.

"So, Trixie, you're in charge this weekend? How's it going?"

"It's been slow today due to the rain. At least I'm warm and dry here, not like poor Summer and Sparkle at the Burford Fair. They're going to close up their booth early, and Aunt Beatrix suggested I do the same with the shop. I haven't had a single customer in the last hour."

"Are you bored to tears?"

"Not at all. Being here alone is like having my own private library. I've rearranged a few displays, and I've been browsing the art section. I've got a few ideas for books to add there. Hey, I'm going to Bourton-on-the-Water to meet the girls for a pint. I invited Jenny too, but she's opening the Tearoom early tomorrow and said she'd have to pass. Want to meet us? I'd love to hear about your trip to Totnes, and I bet Sparkle would too."

I wasn't too sure Sparkle *would*, but what the heck. "That's a thought. I'm meeting Rhiannon and Toby in Stow-on-the-Wold for dinner. Stopping off with you girls would be a nice start to the evening. But, so as not to catch anyone off guard, I need to ask you something. Has Sparkle told you she goes by a different name in Totnes?"

"Oh, you mean Prudence? Yes. I didn't know until the Knitwits luncheon, though. When they were clearing up, Summer called her Pru. That took me by surprise. Sparkle explained she chose a name to sort of line up with Summer so folks would remember them. You know, 'The Fairy Hair Girls —Sparkle and Summer—something like that. Not to mention, she hates her real name."

"Okay, good to know. I'll have to show you the photos of Belle after she had her hair and makeup done at the Blue Hair

Studio where Sparkle works. Belle had a ball. And we all enjoyed Greenway. It was a fun trip. Anyway, what time and where in Bourton-on-the-Water?"

"They want to try the Ale House, and we'll be there around six."

I promised to stop by. I was glad I'd gotten a short nap, though I was still tired. A shower would perk me up. The phrase "No rest for the weary" came to mind. An amateur sleuth can't afford to pass up any opportunities to do more digging.

Christie made her displeasure known when she saw me putting on makeup. "You're not leaving *again*, are you? And taking Dickens too?"

I glanced at her as she stood in the doorway to the bathroom. "Will I be forgiven if I leave Dickens here with you? And I promise to take you for another outing in the backpack this week, okay?"

She chose to give me the silent treatment. Instead of responding, she proceeded to wash her paws and her face. Christie was adept at communicating without words.

Dickens, on the other hand, was all about chatter. "Who're you going out with? Is it a date? Or is it girlfriends?"

"Silly boy. Who would I have a date with? Dave's in New York, and he's the only man I've dated since Henry died. To answer your question, I'm having dinner with Rhiannon and Toby. And before that, I'm meeting up with the young girls, as I think of them. Can't imagine why they want me tagging along—someone old enough to be their mother—but I'm going."

Dickens watched me pull out my skinny jeans and my black suede knee-high boots. I debated between a hip-length cranberry sweater and a longer black velveteen top. The pub would be casual and the Old Stocks Inn a bit dressier. I chose the velveteen top for its touch of elegance and because I could wear my new red plaid wrap with it.

Christie broke her silence as I finished dressing. "You know, you and I both look ravishing in red. Maybe I need a matching collar."

I laughed at my fashion-conscious cat. There was no doubt she was a pretty thing, and I liked the plaid collar idea. "Why, I think you do, Miss Priss. Should we get Dickens a coat to match?"

She rubbed against my boots. "He's got all the coat he needs, but it would be cute if we all dressed alike. We could have a photo made of the three of us in our matching outfits. That could be our Christmas card this year."

Was I wrong to think I had the cleverest animals in the world? Adorable and smart and loving—I couldn't imagine life without their companionship.

Rhiannon had been right about the rain. It had stopped and all that remained was a heavy mist. I was glad I'd grabbed my black cloche to protect my hair. Cute and functional.

When I walked into the pub, Summer saw me and waved me over. "Love the hat, but we can't see your fairy hair."

I removed my hat and shook out my hair. "Better? Have to be sure people see your handiwork, right? The red strands are perfect with my wrap. And I see Trixie has fairy hair now too."

Trixie turned her head back and forth. "Yes, Sparkle added the gold threads when I went to lunch with the Knitwits, and every person who's walked into the Book Nook has commented on the look. I may have to get a few more strands."

Sparkle looked much improved since I'd seen her last, almost like the girl I'd first met a week ago. She grinned. "Tell us about your trip. Trixie says Belle had a makeover."

I showed them a picture of Belle all dolled up and regaled them with the story of Belle's time at the Blue Stair Studio and our tour of the High Street shops. "Sparkle, I understand I was the only one in the dark about your alias. How was I to know your real name was Prudence?"

"You weren't to know. I really don't like my name, and working with Summer was a chance to be called something besides Pru, at least some of the time. Imagine being called Prudence the prude in high school. Pru was only a small improvement."

"Ugh. I wouldn't have liked that either. Guess the folks who called you that didn't know that the term prude has nothing to do with being prudent. Then again, I'm a word nerd. Prudent means to be cautious and careful, not such bad things. A prude is someone who is prim and prissy."

Sparkle looks surprised. "Gee, I never thought to stick up for myself by using a dictionary. Wish one of my English teachers had helped me out."

I laughed. "I think my family had a dictionary in every room of the house when we were growing up, and my sisters and I are all word nerds and grammar geeks. Funny how that happened. Bet you didn't know I'm named for Aleta, the Greek Goddess of Truth. Imagine telling a white lie with a name like that."

The girls chuckled at that. "But you *can* tell one, can't you, Leta?" asked Summer.

"Yes, I've adjusted. I mean, there's not much upside to

being brutally honest when someone asks you how you like their new haircut or new outfit. For important things, though, I'm known to be pretty direct, which gets me in trouble from time to time."

"Okay then, I'll put you on the spot, Leta. How'd you like Totnes?" asked Sparkle.

"Oh, we enjoyed it. The shops on High Street were fun. Loved the bookstore and lunch at the pie shop. And we got Timmy a magic set at the White Rabbit and had a nice time chatting with Chrystal."

"I adore Chrystal," Trixie said. "You know, she taught Max quite a few of his magic tricks."

Sparkle frowned. "Well, not exactly. He learned most of them on his own, and he was as good, if not better, than she was."

Trixie looked taken aback but didn't argue the point. "Anyway, I met her when I was taking classes at Sharpham Hall. She was the one who introduced me to Max. Seems like another lifetime."

Sparkle looked uncomfortable. I'd wondered at Trixie and Sparkle spending time together given their separate relationships with Max. Unless they were bonding over their love for him, I couldn't see them becoming friends.

"Who's for a round of shots?" Sparkle asked. She didn't wait for a reply before heading to the bar.

Summer watched as Sparkle placed the order. "I'm worried about her. I know it's an emotional time, but her highs and lows seem extreme to me. One minute she's quiet and teary, the next she's angry and almost belligerent. She smiles over happy memories and then rants about how badly Max treated her. Is it that way for you, Trixie?"

Trixie hesitated. "Not exactly. I mean, I tear up because I

do have some happy memories, mostly from before Max and I married. Maybe it's because we'd been separated for almost six months, but I'm not angry anymore. Could be she just needs more time."

We all looked up as Sparkle returned with a tray of shot glasses. Goodness knows I didn't need to start doing shots. I'd never been much of a drinker even when I was their age, and I was driving to Stow tonight.

Sparkle held her glass high and said, "Here's to Max. May he rest in peace." We all raised our glasses. The three of them tossed back their shots, and I took a small sip. Then I nudged my glass toward Sparkle. She chuckled at me and downed it.

The shots seemed to clear the air, and we chatted about the Burford Fair and how the day had gone. Despite the nasty weather, the girls had enough customers to make it worth their while. Many had booked appointments at the soap shop for the next week, rather than sit in the tent in the rain—so many that Sparkle planned to stay on at least through Wednesday. Plus they had the Twitchy Stitchers lined up for another luncheon.

Trixie smiled at the mention of the luncheon. "I had so much fun with the Knitwits. It's sweet that they make booties and hats for newborns. I like working with paper but never took to any kind of needlework."

Summer and Trixie chatted about how cute the knitting group had been and how excited they got about their fairy hair. One of the Knitwits was making a winter scarf for Summer and was going to experiment with weaving in some of the silk threads.

Sparkle looked thoughtful. "I wonder whether there are similar groups in the Totnes area? Surely there are. I could check Paignton and Dartmouth and other neighboring towns."

Trixie offered to ask her former landlady and the manager of the bookshop. "I know you can google knitting groups, but they don't always have a presence on the internet. More often they're groups set up via church connections. I'll see what I can find out for you."

"Could be one in Dittisham," I offered. "Belle, Wendy, and I had lunch there when we finished touring Greenway. It seemed an adorable village, but we didn't get a chance to explore it."

That led to my describing the Greenway visit. Sparkle and Summer had never been to the mansion, though Trixie had. I mentioned Christie's archaeological trips with her second husband, and we all agreed the author had led an amazing life.

As the conversation swirled, I noticed Trixie growing increasingly quiet. She shook her head and said, "I'm going to get a glass of water and take a Panadol. I've got the beginnings of a headache, and I need to nip it in the bud before it gets worse."

Sparkle studied Trixie as she left the table. "Are headaches an indicator of an asthma attack coming on? Max told me Trixie had those, but not all that often. What does she do for an attack?"

"I've read that headaches can be a sign, as can nausea or coughing. To use Trixie's turn of phrase, using her inhaler should 'nip it in the bud.' If the headache doesn't go away, that will likely be her next step."

We continued to chat, and Summer explained that the fairs and festivals brought in lots of money for them and also resulted in repeat customers. Sparkle was booked up for the holiday season in Totnes, and Summer would join her there for the Christmas Fair at Sharpham Hall in December.

"That will be our last gig for this year. The winter months

KATHY MANOS PENN

can be slow, so we have to make a killing while we can," Sparkle explained. "Oi, bad choice of words. Can't escape the topic of Max, can we?"

Trixie had returned to the table, and my next words were for the widow *and* the girlfriend. "Ladies, I promise it will get easier. The tears will flow less often, and someday you'll be able to smile at the memories."

I raised my pint. "Here's to treasuring the good times."

We all had unshed tears sparkling in our eyes, but we also had tremulous smiles on our faces. I donned my hat and pulled my plaid wrap close around me. As I said goodbye, my lower lip was trembling.

The mist was still thick as I walked to my car. Chances were the mist would be followed by fog, and I'd need to be especially careful driving tonight. In the best of conditions, I had to constantly remind myself which side of the road was mine. Now was no time to let emotion cloud my judgment.

The Old Stocks Inn was more crowded than I'd expected for a rainy night. I was speaking with the hostess when I saw Toby waving from a table near the back. Rhiannon was already pouring me a glass of red wine when I sat down.

"Glad you could join us," she said. "We tried to get Libby and Gavin to come too, but they've got another full house this weekend and preferred to stay put."

"Yes, autumn's a busy season for all of us, but it will be a different story after Christmas," Toby explained. "Beatrix and I and the other shop owners will be slow in January and February and part of March. If it's a warm spring, business will pick up in April."

The waitress approached to see about our orders and rattled off the specials. It didn't take me long to settle on lamb

208

as a shift from the seafood I'd consumed for three days on the coast.

Toby grinned. "I'm with you tonight, Leta. I think I'll go for the lamb."

Rhiannon attempted to look aghast but couldn't quite carry it off. "As a vegetarian, I know I should be appalled at both of you, but to each his own. I'm going for the root vegetable casserole."

Orders placed, the two were eager to hear what I'd been up to with Belle and Wendy. I shared the assortment of clues we'd picked up on our trip along with the fact that we were no closer to knowing who the killer was.

Rhiannon was intrigued by Prudence's change of name. "Gosh, I don't see it as a bad name. Makes me think of 'Dear Prudence.'"

"That's exactly what I thought of when I heard it," I said. "I should have known you'd make that connection, since your yoga studio is named for a Beatles song."

Rhiannon shook her head. "Funny about names. I've lived most of my life with people asking me if I was named for the Fleetwood Mac song 'Rhiannon.' The song hadn't even come out when my parents named me. The real Rhiannon was a Celtic Goddess, and the name translates to White Witch or Great Queen. I'll take either one. I like having a powerful name."

"Just like I get a kick out of my namesake being the Goddess of Truth. I can think of worse things."

"Okay, ladies," said Toby. "Will you think less of me if I tell you I have no idea what my name means, and I've never been curious?"

We laughed and assured him we'd keep him as a friend. I wondered aloud about writing a column on names and where they came from. I thought it likely it was mostly expectant parents who researched names and their meanings while trying to decide what to name their newborns. I doubted most adults were that curious unless they'd been saddled with what they saw as an odd name.

We drifted into a conversation about business. I knew October through December could be a make or break time for small businesses, and I wasn't surprised when Toby shared how apprehensive he was about the next several months. His impending divorce only heightened his anxiety, as he was faced with having to buy his wife out of the business. Though he'd been able to secure a bank loan, money was still tight.

I asked him how Jenny was working out at the tearoom. It was clear Libby and Gavin were delighted with Jill, and I wondered if he felt the similarly about her sister.

Toby grinned. "Oh! You cannot believe how amazing she is. The customers love her. She's punctual. She does everything I ask and more." We all agreed that the sisters had a down to earth practical approach to most things and that Toby and Libby and Gavin were fortunate to have found them.

"You know," said Toby, "I haven't had a weekend off in several years, and with Jenny on board, I'm seriously considering visiting my family in Cornwall over the New Year's holiday."

"Good for you," I exclaimed. "I haven't decided yet what I'm doing for the holidays. I'm getting a fair amount of pressure from my sisters to go home, but I just don't know."

"Have you thought of going to see them for Thanksgiving instead?" asked Rhiannon. "Since Thanksgiving isn't a big deal here?"

I was sure my face lit up. "That's brilliant. Then I could spend my first Christmas in the Cotswolds as I've been longing to do. I'll have to think how to broach that topic so they'll go for it."

Our freewheeling conversation continued on through coffee, and once again I marveled at how fortunate I was to have made new friends so quickly.

When Toby suggested we order aperitifs, I quickly declined. "No way. I've already sipped a shot tonight. Wouldn't allow myself to down it. Those young girls—Sparkle, Summer, and Trixie—are more hardcore than I am or ever was. That reminds me, I think I'll check on Trixie. She was getting a headache after that shot of whiskey. With Beatrix out of town, I just want to be sure she's okay."

Rhiannon chuckled. "Bit of a mother hen, aren't you? I bet she's fine."

I rang Trixie. It went straight to voicemail, so I tried again. This time she picked up on the first ring. She sounded breathless. "Hello . . . Aunt Beatrix?"

I heard what I thought was wheezing. "Trixie, it's Leta. Are you okay?"

"No . . . my asthma . . . can't get a breath . . ."

"Where are you? Do you have your inhaler?"

"Home . . . inhaler . . . not . . . helping."

"Trixie, I'm going to hang up and call 999. I'm on my way. Where does Beatrix keep her extra key?"

Trixie coughed several times. "Doormat."

Toby and Rhiannon looked at me in alarm as I called 999 and described the situation. When I grabbed my purse, Toby stood up.

"I'm going with you. Rhiannon drove me here, so I can drive your car. Let's go."

"Bless you, Toby."

Chapter Thirteen

Thank goodness Toby was driving. He was faster and more comfortable on the road than I was. We arrived at Beatrix's home in record time, and I was fumbling with the doormat when the ambulance pulled up. I unlocked the door and rushed in with the EMTs behind me.

Trixie was sitting on the floor, back against the couch, her inhaler in her left hand. An overturned teacup lay on the floor beside her. She was conscious, just barely, and she was breathing in short gasps.

The EMT asked about allergies but I had no idea. I knew only that she had asthma. It was clear she'd tried her inhaler to no avail. The EMTs put her on a stretcher and loaded her into the ambulance. I watched as they strapped on an oxygen mask and hooked her up to an IV. I heard words like albuterol and steroids.

"If she doesn't respond quickly," said the other EMT, "we'll use the EpiPen."

As she began to breathe a little easier, he asked questions

about her evening activities. Had she been drinking? Had she done any drugs?

I was able to tell him she'd been at a bar and downed at least one shot. "No way she does drugs," I said. "She probably drank too much tonight, and she had the beginnings of a headache earlier in the evening, if that tells you anything. She took Panadol. I think there are some headache meds she can't take."

"That's right. Some of them can trigger an attack in people who have asthma. We're going to draw some blood so it's ready for analysis in the event we take her to hospital in Cheltenham. Are you her mother?"

"No, a friend. She lives with her aunt, but she's out of town this weekend. I can stay with her."

They suggested Toby and I wait inside. I was worried sick. Should I call Beatrix or wait until I knew more? Toby searched the kitchen and located the same bottle of brandy I'd found when I visited Trixie the week before. He poured me a shot and pushed me to drink it.

I obliged. "Toby, is it just me, or is it odd that she's had two asthma attacks in less than a week when she pretty much has her asthma under control? Beatrix figured it was stress last Sunday, and that made sense. Hearing your husband was murdered and the police asking you not to leave town has to be a double whammy. But what happened tonight? What could have triggered another severe attack?"

"Don't know much of anything about asthma, Leta. Did I hear him say certain drugs can trigger an attack? Is that why they're testing her blood?"

"Yes to both questions. I heard she had a severe attack in Totnes, and they had to call 999. The landlady mentioned Max giving her something for pain when she sprained her ankle.

Wonder what it was?" I started out the door, and then it hit me. "Wait. Gemma and I found a supply of oxycodone in Max's caravan. Is it possible some of those pills got mixed up with Trixie's Panadol?"

I went outside to mention the Totnes incident to the EMTs. They thanked me but kept their focus on Trixie. I waited a beat and asked, "Excuse me, would oxycodone trigger an asthma attack?"

That got their attention. The EMT closest to me looked up. "Yes. What made you ask? Any chance she took oxy?"

I tried to explain about Max and the availability of the drug. "Maybe unintentionally? I'm grasping at straws, I know, but I want to be sure you've got the whole picture. Oh, if it means anything, she had a severe asthma attack on Sunday."

I wandered to the front door and back again. The EMT exited the ambulance and called to me. "We're going to take her in. They may not keep her, but we'd feel better if they did a complete workup."

I explained the situation to Toby and offered to take him home when he said, "I'm in for the duration. Let's go."

I grabbed Trixie's phone and purse on the way out and then locked the door, pocketing the key. We were in for a long night.

At the hospital, it wasn't long before Trixie resumed breathing normally and the wheezing disappeared. She'd come in still wearing the oxygen mask and hooked to an IV, but those were soon removed. She was resting comfortably when the doctor came in.

He looked toward me and nodded at the side of the cubicle. "Are you her mother?"

"No," I repeated for what seemed the umpteenth time. "A friend."

"Well, we have the bloodwork back. We've started drawing blood in the ambulances because we've learned early analysis helps in possible heart attack and overdose situations. For this young lady, we wanted to know what could have triggered such a severe asthma attack. Could have been as simple as mistakenly taking ibuprofen—simple but potentially deadly. It wasn't. We found oxycodone in her bloodstream."

"I wondered," I murmured.

"And why is that?" he asked. "Has she been known to take it for pain? Can't imagine her doctor prescribing it, given her asthma."

How could I explain my hunch to him? I could hear Carol, Trixie's landlady, describing her attack after the sprained ankle —after Max had given her something for pain. And I was seeing the tablets in Max's caravan. Had some of those gotten mixed in with her Panadol? Was that even possible?

I did the best I could to make my thoughts understandable. And I dug through Trixie's purse to find her pill case. I held it out to the doctor. "Is there anything in this besides Panadol?" I asked.

He emptied the pills into his palm. "Yes! Three of these are oxycodone. She should know better. Now that she's coming around, let's ask her where she got them."

I moved to her side and held her hand. "Trixie, the doctor found signs of oxycodone in your blood. Can you tell us what happened tonight? Did you take anything besides the pill I saw you take at the pub?"

She looked at both of us. "Oxycodone? No, Leta. I took

that one pill, and I guess I should have stopped drinking, but you know how it is when you're out with friends. We had appetizers, more cider, and another round of shots. My headache got worse and I felt nauseated. The girls knew I didn't need to drive, so they offered to take me home. I rode with Sparkle, and Summer drove my car."

I was glad to hear she hadn't driven herself home. I had an inkling she wasn't accustomed to drinking that much. "What happened when you got home?"

"The car ride made me queasier, I think. Sparkle settled me on the couch and made me a cup of tea. I told her to go on. I wasn't worried about my asthma. I wasn't having any problem breathing—just the headache and upset stomach. Oh, I forgot. I thought it had been long enough since the last pill, so I took another with my tea. The girls hadn't been gone long when my wheezing started—much worse than I've experienced before."

I looked at the doctor. He nodded and asked, "Well, young lady, we found not only Panadol but also oxycodone in your pillbox. Why is that?"

Now Trixie was near tears. "I . . . I have no idea. I don't do drugs."

The doctor looked skeptical, but there wasn't much more he could do. He admonished Trixie not to take oxycodone—ever—and told us we could go home shortly, no need to remain for observation. He suggested Trixie get an EpiPen to have on hand in case of another severe attack.

Toby had been in the waiting room all this time and was asleep with a magazine open on his lap. I shook him gently, and he took a moment to get his bearings. "Everything okay?" he asked.

"Yes, thankfully. Can you handle one more stop at Beatrix's before I take you to your place?"

"Sure, whatever it takes. Jenny's opening tomorrow—I mean, this morning, so no worries."

On the way to Beatrix's, I explained to Trixie that I didn't think she needed to be alone after the night's ordeal. She'd be spending the night at my cottage. While she and Toby waited in the car, I gathered comfy clothes, a robe, and a nightgown.

We traveled down High Street and dropped Toby off in front of the Tearoom. "Don't hesitate to call me if you need anything, ladies. I'll be in my flat snoozing."

We thanked him and headed to my cottage. By now, it was three am and still dark. I suspected Dickens would greet us but Christie would stay curled up on my bed. I was right.

Dickens was slow to wake up but was barking by the time I entered the mudroom. "My goodness. What time is it? Where have you been?"

I reached down to rub his head. "Now behave yourself. We have a guest. You remember Trixie, don't you?"

He cocked his head and seemed to think for a moment. "She's the one Max grabbed that day at the Fête. She smacked him good, too."

We trooped upstairs, and I made Trixie comfortable in the guest room. Christie finally roused herself and put in an appearance. In the bedroom doorway, she stretched one front paw and then the other. "Who's this?"

"Hello there, Christie. Meet Trixie. I bet she'd enjoy a snuggle."

Trixie smiled and extended her hand for Christie to sniff. "Yes, I would. If I crawl into bed, will you join me?"

How is it cats know cat people when they meet them? Christie licked Trixie's hand and rubbed against her legs. When Trixie sat on the bed, Christie hopped right up and stretched out.

"Leta," meowed my sleepyhead cat, "I think this is our first overnight guest. Is this what you call a spend-the-night party?"

"I'm sure you understood her," I joked with Trixie. "She thinks we're having a pajama party."

"Then I need to get into my jammies quick, don't I?" said Trixie.

I was happy to hear my guest sounding cheerful. Hopefully, she'd sleep soundly and feel good as new when she woke up.

"Okay, then. Let's change into our pajamas and try to get some sleep. We have no reason to get up early. We can go to bed and sleep as long as we like.

"I'm just across the hall. If you start to feel bad or need anything, call me. I'm a light sleeper, and I'll hear you. And if I don't, Christie or Dickens will, and they'll let me know."

Christie stayed in the guest room, and Dickens went with me. He was full of questions, and I was wide awake. As I washed my face and put on a nightgown, I gave him the short version of the night's events.

"Goodness gracious, Leta. That poor girl. You must both be worn out."

"Yes, but I'm keyed up too. Maybe reading a few pages of my book will put me to sleep. I wonder whether I should text Beatrix now or wait until the morning? Hold on a moment."

I stuck my head in the door to the guestroom. "Trixie, is Beatrix expecting to hear from you? Have you checked your messages? I don't want her to be worried about you."

"It's okay, Leta. I texted her when I got to the pub last night and told her I'd talk to her tomorrow—I mean today, I guess. We don't open the shop until eleven on Sundays, and she'll expect to connect with me around that time, I'm sure."

"Good, then we can sleep in and not worry about explaining all this to her until a reasonable hour. Sleep tight."

I wouldn't say I woke up refreshed, but I didn't feel too bad. My guest and Christie were still sound asleep when I tiptoed down the stairs followed by Dickens. I let him out and started the coffee. It was 9:30.

Should I make a Sainsbury's run? I thought. I studied the contents of the refrigerator, which didn't take long. No eggs and no bacon. The pantry yielded better results. *I can treat Trixie to cheese grits,* I thought. *I bet that will be a first for her.*

I started a fire in the sitting room and let Dickens in. "Martha and Dylan! Let's go see them", he barked. "We can take Christie and Trixie. Don't you like the way their names rhyme?"

"My, my. You're perky today. When everyone's awake, I'll make breakfast. Then, yes, we can all go for a walk."

I poured my first cup of coffee and took it and my phone to the couch. Time to call Beatrix. She wasn't surprised to hear from me.

"I've been expecting you to call, Leta. Did you discover anything useful in Totnes?"

I shared all the glowing comments we'd heard about Trixie and the news that Sparkle had a different name when in Totnes. Rehashing the trip with Beatrix only served to remind me that Wendy, Belle, and I hadn't unearthed any clues that pointed to Max's killer.

"The Totnes trip isn't the only reason for my call," I said. "I wanted to let you know that Trixie spent the night with me last night."

There was a pause. "What? She spent the night?"

"Yes, it's a long story." I laid out the night's events for her, and I assured her that Trixie was fine. As I expected, she wanted to come straight home.

"Well, let's talk about that for a minute. I've been thinking about you being in Manchester and the plans you have for the day, and I've got an idea. First, once Trixie wakes up, I plan to make her cheese grits."

Beatrix laughed. "That's your idea?"

"Hey, at least I made you laugh, but I'm serious. After breakfast, I thought I'd leave her here to rest, and I'd go to the Book Nook. I'll put a sign in the window saying 'Closed due to illness.' You know the shops in Astonbury and the neighboring villages don't all open on Sundays. And, even if they do, they sometimes close on short notice. How does that sound? Oh, and I'll feed Tommy and Tuppence too."

"Okay, and I can get on the road and be back by one or so and open up."

"No, that's not what I'm thinking. Why don't you visit the flea markets and used bookstores as you'd planned? Is it really worth it for you to rush back to open for only a few hours? Trixie said it was dead yesterday."

Beatrix hesitated. I thought she was tempted. "I don't know. I feel like I should come home to check on Trixie. And the weather is better today. There might be more customers."

I bit my tongue, hoping she'd work her way around to taking my suggestion.

"What does Trixie think?" Beatrix asked.

"She's still asleep upstairs with Christie snuggled in the crook of her arm."

"Oh, that's so sweet. Sounds like you're taking good care of her."

"Yes, Beatrix, I think I am. So how about it? Finish out your trip and I'll bring Trixie home after you get in."

"Okay, you've convinced me. But you'll call me if anything changes, right?"

"Absolutely. Have a successful shopping day."

Funny how I could be so calm about Trixie's attack as I spoke with Beatrix. I wasn't lying when I said there was no need for her to rush home. There wasn't anything she could do to change what happened last night, but the whole chain of events seemed off to me. I just couldn't put my finger on why.

Chapter Fourteen

Not long after I hung up, Christie came down. She strolled into the sitting room yawning, and I took the hint. I went to the kitchen and poured her a dab of milk and fixed myself another cup of coffee.

As I stood there with my hip propped against the counter, Trixie appeared. She rubbed her eyes as she came down still in her robe.

She saw Christie lapping her milk and smiled. "You're the best sleep buddy ever, Christie."

"Well, of course, I am," meowed the princess.

Hearing that conversation, Dickens bounded in the kitchen. "Right. If only I were allowed on the beds, I could be the best sleep buddy. It's not fair."

I chuckled at my four-legged roommates. *Just a tad competitive*, I thought.

I poured a cup of coffee for Trixie, and she sipped it and sighed. She looked a little pale to me, but I don't think anyone else would have suspected she'd visited the emergency room last night. I had to wonder if I'd ever been capable of bouncing back like that.

She was eager to try grits and sat at the kitchen table while I pulled out milk, cheese, and butter. They were simple to make, and measurements were hardly necessary since I'd been making them for years.

I explained as I cooked. "Grits are hard to mess up. If they seem too thick, add more water or milk. If they're too soupy, cook 'em until they thicken. You boil the water and milk first —more water than milk. Add grits and salt. Cook and stir on medium heat until they're the consistency you like. I like mine thick, not quite like oatmeal, but not soupy either. I like to add plenty of salt and pepper too."

Trixie looked surprised. "Not sugar?"

"Nope. Grits aren't served like porridge or oatmeal or cream of wheat. I had a college friend from Ohio who grew up on cream of wheat, and when I saw her add sugar to her grits in the cafeteria, I almost gagged. We straightened her out pretty quick."

I held up the grated cheddar cheese. "You can serve them plain or at the last moment, add cheese and butter and stir. And, voila!"

I dished them up into bowls and sat down at the table too. I watched as Trixie tried her first spoonful.

"Yum. I need to make these for Aunt Beatrix. Has she tried yours?"

"No. She may have had them somewhere else, but I doubt it. I haven't found anywhere to buy them here, so I order mine from Amazon."

She looked around the kitchen. "Leta, I love your cottage. The reds and golds in here are so cozy and cheerful. And the little touches of green are subtle."

"Coming from someone with your art background, that means a lot to me. I had help pulling it together, but I chose much the same colors I had in my Atlanta home.

"Would you care for a second helping?" I asked.

She nodded yes, and I filled both bowls again. As we ate, I filled her in on my conversation with Beatrix and the plan we'd agreed on for the day. I think she was relieved she didn't have to go into the shop and that her aunt could still finish out her shopping weekend. I shooed her into the sitting room while I washed up and then joined her in front of the fireplace.

"Comfy?" I asked.

"Are you kidding? I could spend all day in here, dozing and drinking tea. I like the way you continued the red and gold color scheme in here."

I pulled a fleece throw from the large basket by the couch and offered it to her. "My aunt made two of these for me, this one with cats on it and another with dogs. Each of my sisters got a set too. Best snuggle blankets ever."

I left her ensconced on the couch with the throw tucked around her, Dickens at her feet and Christie in her lap. I showered, applied minimal makeup, and dressed in jeans, a silver sweater and a purple patterned scarf highlighted with silver threads. As I'd entered my fifties and my hair had begun to grey, I'd added that color to the blacks, whites, reds, and purples I favored.

I should have known Trixie would have something to say about my outfit. "You know your colors, don't you?" she asked. "I'm always amazed at the people who have no clue the colors they should wear. But you're not one of those."

I laughed. "If you can believe it, I and several girlfriends had our colors done years ago. And, I never vary from my recommended palette. Red is my favorite, but I enjoy the other jewel tones too.

"Now, can I get you anything else before I head to the book shop? From there, I plan to go to Sainsbury's, since the cupboard is almost bare. I'll be gone for a few hours. And we can still get in that walk to see the donkeys, maybe after lunch."

"No thank you. I'm fine, and I can make a cup of tea if I feel like one while you're gone. Are you taking Dickens?"

I was sure I was, but I paused for a moment. "You know, I think I'll take them both if you won't be too lonely. I'm trying to get Christie accustomed to riding in a backpack. I took her to meet Paddington at the inn. It's time she met Tommy and Tuppence."

"I'll be fine, but a backpack? This I've got to see."

When I pulled out the backpack and placed it on the floor, Christie jumped down from the couch and came right over. "You're serious? I get to go with you—again? What are we waiting for?"

In a flash, Christie crawled in, turned around, and stuck her head out. Dickens ran to the door and looked back at me, as I grabbed my coat and his leash. I hollered goodbye, and we were off.

Plenty of cars were parked in front of Toby's Tearoom but none across the street at the Book Nook. As I parked my taxi, I admired the librarian scarecrow propped by the door. The lights glowing in the window display provided ambiance day and night, but I switched on a few more as I let myself in.

Dickens set off in search of Tommy and Tuppence as I released Christie from her backpack.

"Leta, you said there were friendly felines here? Where are they?" asked my curious cat.

"I *think* they're friendly, though they've kept their distance from Dickens. With all the room in this shop, you three can either make friends or go your separate ways. Up to you."

Dickens came running from the back room and slid to a stop by the counter. "Tommy and Tuppence are awake now, thanks to me. I told 'em all about you, Christie, and they said for you to come on back."

Tommy was a plump black and white tuxedo cat, and Tuppence was a petite white kitty. I'd never had a conversation with either one. They mostly lounged around the shop, occasionally approaching customers and getting a tickle, but they weren't talkative. I wondered what my little princess would think of them.

This should be interesting, I thought. Christie followed her brother, and I turned my attention to making a sign for the front door. I decided a simple "Will Open on Monday" taped to the Closed sign would do. No need to worry Beatrix's regulars that anything was wrong with her or Trixie. I was searching for tape when my phone rang.

It was Trixie. "Hi, Leta. Sparkle just called to check on me and to tell me I'd left my coat in her car. She offered to bring it by your cottage, but I thought it'd be easier for her to find the Book Nook. Will you be there a while longer?"

"Sure. Not a problem. I can occupy myself browsing the Agatha Christie books. After my visit to Greenway, I added two titles to my never-ending 'To Read' list. Might look for a biography too. When do you think Sparkle will get here?"

"I'll ring her right back to let her know you're waiting. It shouldn't be more than twenty minutes. And, oh, if you find the books you want, just bring them home and leave Aunt Beatrix a note. You know you can settle up with her later. Thanks for waiting."

With the note firmly attached to the sign on the front door, I decided a cup of tea was in order. Beatrix kept an electric kettle in the back room, so I plugged it in and found some Earl Grey.

I carried my cup to the mystery section and sat it on a shelf. What a treat to have an entire bookshop to myself. *Who knows?* I thought. *I could spend the afternoon here.*

I was paging through *Murder on the Orient Express* when my phone rang again.

Toby was calling. "I saw your car," he said, "and I was hoping I could get a report on Trixie. Is she over there too?"

I updated him on how the patient was doing and how I'd convinced Beatrix to finish her shopping trip. "I only came in to put a sign on the door. But since I'm here, I couldn't pass up an opportunity to browse. Oh, and now Sparkle's bringing Trixie's coat by—Trixie left it behind last night—so I have an excuse to stay a little longer."

Toby chuckled. "I have this image of you sitting on the floor, your back against a row of shelves, with a book in your lap. Maybe with Tommy and Tuppence on either side. If you're not gone by dark, should I come chase you out?"

He knew me too well. "Nope. I promise as soon as I take delivery of Trixie's coat, I'll be gone. The grocery store awaits."

"Right. I predict your departure won't be quite that fast. Shall I bring over a pumpkin latte and a scone to fortify you?"

I had to laugh. He was tempting me not only to indulge my book habit but also my love of coffee drinks. "Okay. I can't resist that offer. No hurry though. I can tell from all the cars that you're doing a booming business this morning."

I continued browsing and found *Five Little Pigs* and *Deadman's Folly* before turning to the biography section. My search was interrupted when three cats tumbled through the doorway from the back room, followed by Dickens.

"Leta, look at these cats, will you?" barked Dickens. "I haven't seen Christie this playful since she was a kitten."

He was right. Neither had I. They were a sight running over and under tables, hiding beneath rugs, doing that funny butt wiggle cats do when they're about to attack something. When the three skidded to a stop by the wall of children's books, I grabbed my phone to see if I could capture their antics on video. I was in luck, as they chose that moment to collapse in a pile.

"Leta," meowed Christie. "Can Tommy and Tuppence visit us? This is great fun."

"Hmmm. It may be better for us to come back here. After all, I bet you're the only kitty in Astonbury who travels in her own backpack."

I could tell she wasn't listening to me. Almost simultaneously, the frisky felines flopped and rolled, exposing their bellies as they stretched. This was going to make a great video to send my sister Anna. Her videos of her five cats were a hoot, and I never had anything to share in return.

A knock at the door got Dickens's attention and he barked hello. "Leta, it's Sparkle. Oh look, she's wearing a bowtie like mine."

I laid the phone on the counter. *How odd*, I thought. She wasn't just sporting a bowtie. She was also wearing a top hat and a red-lined black cape and carrying a black cane. I'm sure my surprise was obvious as I unlocked the door.

She came swirling in and asked, "What do you think?"

It took me a moment to reply. "You look stunning. The black and red with your dark hair? It's lovely, but . . . but . . . what's going on? Are you going to a party?"

"Not likely," she retorted. "I'm taking up where Max left off. We had plans, big plans, but now I'll be doing it without him."

I was stunned. "Oh! You mentioned he'd taught you a few tricks, but I didn't realize you were a full-fledged magician."

"I am. And a better one than Max ever hoped to be. I learned what he showed me in no time, and I've been studying videos on my own. I always was a quicker study than he was. Together, we could have played big parties and theatres, not these small-time village fairs."

I felt as though I was seeing Sparkle's—or Prudence's— alter ego. Weird. And I wasn't sure how to respond. "Wow. I wish you the best."

"That's it?" she snapped.

What did she expect me to say? Dickens must have been as shocked as I was because he growled. I reached down to touch him, and he stopped, but I could tell he was still disturbed.

I tried to laugh it off. "Well, I'm in complete shock, so I don't know what to say. But before I forget, thank you for taking such good care of Trixie last night and for bringing the coat by today."

Sparkle looked contemptuous. "Silly girl, she can't hold her liquor. I mean, Max told me about her asthma, but I didn't really understand what a wimp she was, how sickly she was."

Sickly wasn't the word I would have used. "Well, she's not exactly sickly. She has a condition lots of people have. I suspect, though, that she's not used to partying like you and Summer."

Her expression switched from contemptuous to angry. "What's that supposed to mean?"

Why was she so touchy? "It means I think she led a sheltered life until she went to Totnes. She's experienced all kinds of new things these last two years, and drinking with girlfriends is one of them."

"Not much of a life, I'd say. You know it's only because I felt sorry for her that I invited her along."

Sparkle's responses were getting stranger by the minute. "Uh-huh. It's been kind of you and Summer to include her while you're here. And you'll be returning to Totnes next week, right?"

"Yes. Can't wait to get back. Totnes is more my kind of town. It's younger, not as hoity-toity as this place."

I didn't want to be having this conversation, but I couldn't see how to get out of it. "I'd have to agree the Dartmouth and Totnes vibe is different than what we have here. They're both livelier than our quaint little village."

She looked indignant. "Think you know all about Totnes, do you? After sticking your nose in my business all around town? What gave you the right to ask questions about me—and about Max?"

Huh? Where was this coming from? I hadn't detected this attitude last night.

"Nothing to say?" she screeched. "It wasn't only Tina who told me the questions your lot asked, it was the bartender at the Whistling Pig too. What were you playing at?"

I was alarmed at the change that had come over her, and so was Dickens. He was growling again. I edged back toward the counter, hoping to put it between us. "Sparkle, we were trying to find out more about Max—so maybe we could figure out who would have a reason to kill him. We didn't think it could have been you or Trixie."

Could she tell I was lying? That I'd considered her a suspect, just as I had Trixie, Jill, Barb, and others?

She continued to advance on me as I tried to put distance between us. "Liar. You were trying to pin Max's murder on me. Of course, it couldn't have been Trixie, the little angel. It could only have been me. That's what you thought, right?"

My brain was screaming *yes*, but I kept my mouth shut.

"You and Trixie. You ruined everything. First, she steals my Max away with her Little Miss Innocent act. We were together again, and things were going well between us until she showed up at the Fête. I knew he wasn't divorced yet, but not that he was hoping she'd come back.

"Still, we'd have gotten through that. We'd have had another row and made up. We were good at making up. But not this time. I was ready to forgive him when I found him on the river-bank. He'd have gotten a kick out of the picture I took. I sat there with his head in my lap, wiping his brow, being sweet. Until . . . until he looked up at me and said 'Trixie, I love you, girl.'"

Oh my God. It was her. She strangled him.

"And you! You couldn't leave it alone. You stupid cow!" she screamed.

And before I could react, she swung the cane at me like a baseball bat. It struck my left temple, and I staggered against the counter. Dickens lunged at her and must have connected because she screamed. But she kept coming. The next blow hit my neck, and I went down.

I lay on my side. A third blow fell on my shoulder. I covered my head with my hands, expecting another blow to fall. Instead, I heard hissing, screeching, and screaming. I heard guttural growls—but no barking. I looked up in time to see Sparkle crash onto a table of books, three cats pinned to her chest and a dog attached to her calf.

I must have passed out because the next thing I saw was Toby kneeling beside me. "Leta, can you hear me? Can you sit up?"

His image was blurry. "Did you bring my latte?" I croaked.

He called over his shoulder. "She's still got her sense of humor."

I heard him say "oomph" and saw a black shape land on his back. It was Christie. "You're awake. We got the magic lady. She went down in a heap."

Tommy and Tuppence weren't as vocal as my girl, but they came over to look at me and tentatively lick my hand.

"Where's Dickens?" I asked.

Christie licked my chin and meowed. "Oh, he's still standing guard over the magic lady. Toby tried to shoo him away, but Dickens wasn't having it. If she budges, he'll get her in the thigh this time."

I smiled at the image of Detective Dickens taking a chunk out of Sparkle. Toby helped me sit up and lean my back against the counter. As my vision cleared, I took in the scene. Jenny and Dickens were standing over Sparkle. She wasn't moving. Rhiannon was running in the front door.

She looked aghast, as well she should. "Bloody hell. Jenny rang me after she dialed 999. What happened here? Who's that on the floor with the books? Oh my gosh. Is it Sparkle?"

The blow to my neck must have done something to my throat. I was having difficulty speaking. Rhiannon put a cup of water in my hand, and after a few sips, I explained as best I could. Still, Rhiannon and Toby had to lean in close to hear me. I honestly wasn't sure how I'd come to be the victim of an attack.

I'd barely finished croaking out what I knew when Gemma showed up, followed by the EMTs. *Oh hell*, I thought, *not another trip to the hospital*. And then I remembered my phone. I pointed up to indicate the top of the counter.

Rhiannon looked at the counter and then at me. "What is it you want? Your phone? You want your phone?" Rhiannon asked.

"Video," I whispered. I'd been recording the antics of the cats when I put the phone down. If it was still running, it might have captured the confrontation—the conversation, not the visuals.

Rhiannon picked it up and pressed the right buttons. I was in luck. The earlier back and forth when Sparkle had first come in was faint and scratchy, but the dialogue near the counter was crystal clear.

At least I wouldn't have to replay that last scene over and over for the police, but I knew Gemma would still have plenty of questions for me. Heck, I had plenty of my own questions.

I was beginning to detest emergency rooms. This was my third trip to the Cheltenham ER since I'd moved to the Cotswolds. I'd rushed here a month ago when I'd gotten word a friend had been involved in an accident. I'd sat here with Trixie last night —was it only last night? And, here I was again, this time for myself.

The EMTs had explained they were worried about the blows I'd taken to my head, and to my neck. My fall to the floor and the blow to my shoulder, they assured me, would result in stiffness and major bruises but nothing worse. I rode to the hospital with my head elevated and an ice pack on my neck.

For me, the afternoon and evening were a blur. Examinations by multiple doctors led to a cat scan of my head. Thankfully, there was no bleeding on my brain, though I'd have a headache for a day or two. Wendy told me later they'd debated putting a camera down my throat to check my larynx. They finally decided they could do that in a few weeks if my hoarseness didn't improve. Thank goodness for small favors.

By the time Wendy loaded me into her car, I was more than ready to be home with Dickens and Christie. I was even a tiny bit hungry but knew I couldn't manage more than a bowl of soup. Questions ran through my brain—well, maybe the questions weren't running. It was more like they were floating.

"What made Toby come to the bookshop?"

Wendy glanced at me. "Don't you remember? You asked him to bring you a latte."

"Oh right. Wish I had one now. And Dickens and Christie? I'm guessing someone took them home?"

"Yes, Toby was happy to do that. And when he told Rhiannon you'd been planning to go to Sainsbury's, she looked in your purse for your list. You should have a fully stocked fridge by now."

"How's Trixie?" I croaked.

"She's fine. Beatrix picked her up, and she went home to get more clothes. She'll be your babysitter for a few days."

I turned my head slowly to look at Wendy. "How sweet of her."

"Well, you *were* looking after her, so she's returning the favor. By the way, Gemma won't be by until tomorrow afternoon. She said there was nothing urgent about interviewing you, given she had Sparkle in custody. I *will*, however, be meeting with her tomorrow morning at the Stow station to rehash our findings from Totnes. That case map we put together will come in handy."

I groaned. "I don't recall Maisie Dobbs being dumb enough to get beaten up. When will I ever learn?"

Wendy didn't have an answer to that question. Probably thinking if I hadn't learned by this age, I never would.

Another question floated through my brain. "Uh, I didn't even ask about Sparkle. Is she okay?"

"Ha! As okay as she deserves to be. It took seven stitches to close up the gash where Dickens bit her. And I wish I could have seen the cat scratches on her chest. I understand they were extensive. Who knew cats could inflict so much damage?"

When we pulled in my driveway, I sighed. "Home again, home again, jiggity jig. Goodness, you can't imagine how glad I am to be here."

Trixie opened the door, and Dickens came bounding out. "Leta, Leta, you're a sight for sore eyes. I was scared to death when they loaded you into an ambulance. Are you all better?" barked my boy.

Christie followed at a more sedate pace. "Pfft, silly boy. Of course she's not all better. She looks like something the cat drug in, as the saying goes."

How I loved my animals. I slowly walked inside while Trixie and Wendy fussed over me. I made it as far as the couch and sat down gingerly. The glow of the fire and the sight of my attentive four-legged friends were a comfort.

"The doctor said you needed to drink plenty of hot fluids, so here's a cup of tea to start with," Trixie said as she placed a mug on the table by the couch. "I've got a pot of homemade chicken noodle soup on the stove, compliments of Belle. Doesn't it smell delicious? Peter delivered it earlier."

I was touched by the ministrations of my friends. What a day it had been. When I finally made it to my bed, Christie snuggled against my ribs and Dickens lay on the rug in front of the nightstand. I gave thanks for my four-legged heroes and drifted off.

Chapter Fifteen

Monday morning, I awoke to Christie licking my face. "Leta," she said, "time to get up. You forgot to tell Trixie how I like my milk."

"Excuse me, aren't you the one who told Dickens I wasn't *all* better? Don't I get to sleep in?"

She gave me a look only a cat can, and I chuckled. I struggled out of bed and into my robe and went downstairs. Dickens was downstairs with Trixie, who was surprised to see me up so early. She poured me a cup of coffee, while Christie stared at her bowl, waiting for me to instruct Trixie on the proper presentation for her milk.

Christie got her milk, and Trixie fixed toast before we moved to the sitting room. I pulled my fleece blanket onto my legs, and Christie appeared in my lap.

"I appreciate you staying here to take care of me, but what is Beatrix doing without you?"

"It's okay. Mondays are slow days. I suspect she'll spend most of the day adding the books she found in Manchester to the Used Book section. Leta, I'm so, so sorry about what happened to you. If it weren't for me, none of this would have happened."

"What? What do you mean?"

"If I hadn't married Max, if you hadn't helped me speak with him, if you hadn't been trying to clear me . . . you wouldn't have gotten caught up in this."

"Oh, Trixie, Trixie. It's not your fault. There are plenty who would say it's my own fault, and it serves me right for sticking my nose in your business."

"Who would say that? You were trying to help."

"I bet if you're here when Gemma comes by, you'll hear her say it."

Trixie said, "Oh, I almost forgot. Gemma called and said she'd be here around two or three. I hope that's okay."

"No worries, Trixie. Maybe I can make myself presentable by then. Now, I don't think I can take a walk this morning, but would you care to take Dickens to visit the donkeys?"

Her face lit up and Dickens barked. "Don't forget the carrots. Martha and Dylan haven't had carrots in days."

Christie curled into a tighter ball in my lap. "I'm staying with you. Someone's got to keep you out of trouble."

This getting bruised and battered is for the birds, I thought as I stared into the fire. *I need to take better care of myself.* Fortunately, before I could get too deep into second-guessing myself, the phone rang. It was Dave. I looked at the clock. It was two AM in New York. *He must be working on his article for December*, I thought.

"Hey there, how was your trip? Did you ladies have a good time?"

Where to begin? "Um, the trip was wonderful, but there were some complications once I got home."

"Complications? Why am I thinking that's code for something bad, Leta Parker?" he asked.

I tried to explain what had transpired since I'd spoken to him Tuesday night, almost a week ago. We'd exchanged a few texts as we usually did but hadn't had a conversation. Dave was understandably incredulous and making noises about flying over to take care of me.

"You know I'd love to see you, but you're busy with your Sherlock Holmes article, and I've got more nurses than I know what to do with. Trixie's here. Belle and Wendy are on the way over. And, of course, I have Dickens and Christie."

"Right, now those two are not only your protectors? They're also your nurses? Okay, I won't come right away, but I'll call tonight to check on you. I may call you every night, and I may have to call Belle to get the real story about how you're doing."

Case map rolled up under her arm, Wendy showed up for lunch with Belle by her side. Trixie warmed the soup Belle had made, and we enjoyed it while I got the rundown on the morning at the police station. My friends wanted to be here when Gemma arrived, so we could fill in any blanks together.

"By the way, Leta," said Belle, "we've decided on our official name—the Little Old Ladies' Detective Agency."

I couldn't quite manage a smile. "Gee, Belle, we may have to retire that name before we get to use it. I can't say I'm eager to play detective again any time soon."

Belle let that pass. Perhaps she knew me better than I knew myself.

In the sitting room, Wendy taped the large pieces of paper

to the windows, and we sipped tea as we waited. Dickens sat leaning against my legs, and Christie chose Belle's lap. Soon, we heard Gemma pull up.

"Hello, Tuppence," Gemma called as she came in. "How are you feeling today?"

"A bit worse for the wear. Being beaten with a cane is a first for me."

"I can only imagine. And how are your little heroes, Christie and Dickens?"

For a change, Dickens didn't seem to take offense at the adjective *little*. He and Christie both looked up when they heard their names. Christie acknowledged the recognition by moving from Belle's lap to mine, and Dickens laid down on my feet.

We all laughed. "I think they're fine and taking their protector jobs seriously," I said.

"Good thing. Well, on that note, let's move on to Sparkle's story about killing Max, trying to kill Trixie, and going after you. It's quite a tale."

"What? She tried to kill Trixie? How'd I miss that?"

"According to Sparkle, 'cause you're nosy but not too bright. She mixed oxycodone in with Trixie's Panadol. Figured sooner or later, she'd take one by accident and die from an asthma attack. You ruined a good plan by calling Trixie in time to get the EMTs there."

Belle was shocked, but then, she hadn't seen the crazed Sparkle I'd experienced. "That's cold," she said. "She didn't care when Trixie died, just so long as she did?"

"Apparently," said Gemma. "Sparkle hated Trixie for coming between her and Max. She saw Max as falling prey to Trixie's charms. Why is it women always blame the other woman, not the man?

"When she got back with Max, he told her about Trixie's asthma attack—that he'd given her oxy for her ankle pain. He had no idea she shouldn't take oxy and was horrified he'd almost killed her. Sparkle recalled that bit of information and acted on it."

"And me? Why me?" I asked. "I even tried to console her by sharing my experience when Henry died. She seemed so sad and sorry that Max was gone. She had me convinced she was grieving."

Gemma tried to explain. "I think she *was* grieving. She was furious with him, and could be she killed him in a moment of blind rage. Maybe she wished she hadn't. Still, I think, in her mind, she was justified. She even blamed Trixie for that. If not for Trixie, she told me, none of this would have happened."

I still didn't get it. "Okay, I can see her blaming Trixie in her twisted mind, but what did I do? Sure, I asked questions, but I wasn't anywhere near figuring out she'd killed Max."

Gemma shook her head. "Well, Tuppence, you seemed too close for comfort, at least in Sparkle's estimation. You and your sidekicks asked lots of questions in Totnes, and she was worried about what you'd uncovered. She didn't hear anything worrisome from you Saturday night and was hoping you hadn't put two and two together. "

"And we hadn't," Wendy piped up. "We were as confused as ever."

"Yes, but Trixie surviving her asthma attack and then spending the night with Leta had Sparkle worried. She'd been cozying up to Trixie to keep an eye on her and maybe find a way to pin Max's murder on her. To no avail, mind you. But she'd spent enough time with Trixie, she was afraid Leta would hear something that would make her more suspicious."

I sighed. "I admit, I wondered if Sparkle was somehow

connected to the oxy, but it wasn't a fully-formed thought. I might have gotten there eventually—if she hadn't tried to kill me first."

Belle was deep in thought. "We weren't the only ones asking about Sparkle and Trixie and Max, though. Peter questioned Phil, which led you to question Barb. The field was crowded with suspects."

Gemma was always patient with Belle. "Yes, Miss Marple, it was. We traveled down plenty of blind alleys, as they say. But as you know, we had to check every possibility. We had the Totnes police trying to figure out if there was a drug angle because we found drugs and cash in Max's caravan. But drugs had nothing to do with his death."

I was getting angry about Sparkle. "If she only knew how hard we tried to give her the benefit of the doubt. Maybe she had two names, we said, but that's not a big deal. Maybe she had a sick sense of humor—like taking a picture of her boyfriend passed out—but that wouldn't make her a murderer."

Wendy spluttered. "We had an inkling she had a temper, based on what the caravan manager in Totnes said about her. Even then, we weren't absolutely positive she was the girl who ranted and raved at the door to the caravan. Taken all together, I still don't see anything that would have said she was a cold-blooded killer."

Gemma tried to explain. "I'd say she's unstable. I suspect if we could access juvenile records, we'd learn there had been early signs. It's also likely that moving from home to home in foster care would have made it difficult to detect a pattern. But we'll never know.

"We've now matched her fingerprints to the apple in Max's mouth. We'll likely match her DNA to that from the apple core too. And while she didn't quite admit to strangling Max when she spoke with you, Leta, it was pretty close. No one thing says she's the killer, but all the pieces together form a pretty convincing case for Max's murder."

Belle looked up from stroking Christie's head. "Can you prove she tried to kill Trixie?"

"If we can get prints from Trixie's pill case, we may be able to do something about that attempt. I'm betting those oxy pills are from the same batch we found in Max's caravan, meaning she had access to them."

Trixie was standing in the doorway with tears running down her face. She'd been sitting quietly in the kitchen listening to our conversation. "What about Leta? Can you prove she tried to kill her?"

"No doubt there. We have the video documenting the attack, at least the verbal part. We have the weapon with her fingerprints on it. Means, motive, and opportunity—we've got it all."

I was exhausted from listening to this horrendous tale. I'd read enough detective stories to know Sparkle wasn't a homicidal maniac. She didn't kill for pleasure. In her mind, she killed for good reason.

I thought back to Lust, Love, Loathing, and Lucre. She loved Max, and he'd betrayed her—guess that was the love motive. She attempted to kill Trixie because she blamed her for taking Max—could be love for Max or loathing of Trixie or both. She tried to kill me because I was a threat. That could be purely practical, though I'd seen hate and loathing in her eyes.

"Ladies," I asked, "would you indulge me for a moment? Can you help me understand what we missed? Was it obvious the whole time it was Sparkle, or was it always clear as mud?"

Gemma grimaced. "It wasn't obvious. We had a killer who

lied directly or by omission, and we had no way of knowing that. With her fingerprints, we would have gotten closer, but without her confession, I'm not sure we would have put it together. I hate to say that, but I'm being honest. Plus, I think some of the other suspects were as plausible."

Gemma looked at the piece of paper on the window. "You really did lay it all out. It reminds me of our board at the station where we pin photos and write notes. I may have to read one of those Maisie Dobbs books."

We all looked at the notes. It was easy to see the missing piece. We'd had it all except for the truth about Sparkle's final actions on the riverbank.

She didn't take a picture and leave him that way. She told Gemma she'd sat for a while with Max's head in her lap, just as she'd told me. He might still be alive if he hadn't looked up and called her Trixie. That was surely the nail in his coffin. She strangled him—with his red scarf.

"Oh my God," I said. "When did she put the apple in his mouth? Before or after she killed him?

"She didn't say," Gemma answered. "But the two sets of bite marks on the apple make it seem like it may have popped out—now that's a ghastly image—and she jammed it back in."

"How cold-blooded," I cried.

"And the hat," Belle said. "It was Sparkle who took Max's top hat. And she was wearing it yesterday."

"Yes," said Gemma. "His name was stitched inside. She must have snatched it and the cane after she left him lying dead on the riverbank."

Wendy couldn't get over Sparkle's lying. "Well, she lied to us. Think of the things she lied about. She wouldn't have dated Max if she'd known he was still a married man. Hogwash! She took up with him as soon as Trixie moved out. Said at first she'd only dated Max for months when really it had been for years. Without the lies, we'd have figured it out right away."

Gemma and I laughed at the same time. Then Belle joined in.

"What?" asked Wendy. "What did I say that's so funny?"

"'Without the lies.' Killers always lie, don't they?" I said. "At least on TV."

"And in books," said Belle.

Gemma looked amused. "And in real life, ladies."

Like the sleuths in Agatha Christie's books, we'd come across plenty of clues, a few pointing to the killer, others leading us in the wrong direction. But, unlike the fictional detectives, we'd never figured it out. We hadn't wrapped up the case in a neat package. We'd been *duped* by the killer. It was small consolation that the police had been similarly fooled.

Wendy had the final word. "The good news, to quote Shakespeare, is that 'In the end, the truth will out.' And so it has."

Psst... Please take a minute.

Dear Reader,

Writers put their heart and soul into every book. Nothing makes it more worth it than reader reviews. Yes, authors appreciate reviews that provide them helpful insights.

If you enjoyed this book, Kathy would love it if you could find the time to leave a good honest review. Because after everything is said and done, authors write to bring enjoyment to their readers.

Thank you, Dickens

Spanakopita Recipe

RECIPE

Yield: 12 3x3 pieces
Ingredients

- 10 ounces frozen spinach, thawed and squeezed dry
- 2 large eggs
- 1 ¼ cups crumbled feta (6 ounces—sheep's milk feta preferred)
- 1 cup finely chopped onion
- 2 tablespoons minced garlic
- Kosher salt and black pepper
- ½ cup grated Parmesan (2 ounces)
- ½ cup chopped parsley
- ½ cup/115 grams unsalted butter (1 stick), melted
- 8 sheets frozen phyllo dough, thawed and halved crosswise

Optional ingredients to taste

- 1/3 cup fresh basil, chopped

- 1/3 cup fresh dill, chopped
- 1/4 cup fresh oregano, chopped
- zest of 1 lemon

PREPARATION

1. In a medium bowl, combine the spinach, eggs, olive oil, feta, parmesan, basil, dill, oregano, lemon zest, garlic, crushed red pepper flakes, and a pinch each of salt and pepper.
2. Heat oven to 375 degrees. Lightly grease a 9-by-13-inch pan (2 inches deep) with butter. Lay one half sheet of phyllo dough in baking dish. Using a pastry brush, brush dough with butter. Repeat 7 more times to form crust. Spread spinach mixture evenly over crust. Brush one half sheet of phyllo dough with butter and lay on top of filling, butter side up. Repeat with remaining 7 sheets of dough. Using a serrated knife, lightly score top layer of dough into squares (this will make it easier to cut once baked). Bake until crust is lightly golden and filling is heated through, 50 to 60 minutes. Serve warm.

Tips

- *Can be served as a side dish, an appetizer, or a main course.*

Parker's Pen: Christie's Perspective on Black Cats

Columnist Leta Parker is out shopping for Halloween candy, so her cat is filling in for her.

I'm happy to be a beautiful black cat who is loved and pampered. But what about those poor black cats who don't have homes, who are shunned because people are foolishly afraid of them? How did black cats get such a bad rap? The answer requires a brief history lesson.

We cats started hanging around humans 10,000 years ago, when you first started growing food instead of hunting it. We were observant—still are—and noticed rodents wherever corn and wheat were stored. Rodents meant a meal. Soon enough, we grew to like people and vice-versa.

Most everyone knows that the Egyptians worshipped cats. They realized that we made fine pets but still had minds of our own. Doesn't that sound like the cats you know? I mean, do we come when called?

The Egyptians also worshipped gods and goddesses that were part human and part cat. The goddess of violence and fertility, Bastet, was one of those combos, and one of her favorite colors was black. Don't ask me how you combine violence and fertility. Humans come up with the strangest ideas, but Bastet is why black cats were seen as special. Note, I said *special*, not bad luck or evil.

Perhaps it was this pagan affinity for cats that caused medieval Christians to distrust us. Distrust is too mild a word. Heck, they accused us of participating in orgies with the devil. From then on, it got worse for cats, especially black ones. We were all described as favorites of the devil and of witches, and you know what happened to the witches, don't you?

Years later, cats were better appreciated, with intelligent people like Charles Dickens and Mark Twain holding us in high regard. Having a few admirers still didn't do away with most people's fear of cats, black ones in particular, and Edgar Allan Poe's horror story "The Black Cat" didn't help matters. I mean, honestly—he described a dead black cat driving some poor human mad, and people believed him.

Even today, black cats remain unpopular. Because we're the least likely of all cats to be adopted from shelters, October 27 is Black Cat Day in the UK. Similarly, August 17 is Black Cat Appreciation Day in the US. Both days are promoted in an effort to get more of us adopted.

I guess superstitions die hard, and just as people avoid walking under ladders or living on the thirteenth floor, some also avoid black cats. Seeing black cats as Halloween decorations along with witches and monsters like Dracula and Frankenstein likely reinforces this aversion.

There's never been any proof to support these wrong-headed beliefs about black cats, but then, when have humans ever needed proof? My friend Leta, of course, has never believed any of this hooey. As a child, she had a stunning black cat named Sheba and loved her dearly. Just because she went on to own a white cat and two calicos doesn't mean she thinks there's anything wrong with black ones.

The fact is all cats are magnificent creatures, and black cats are exceptionally striking. And me? I'm also highly intelligent and have come up with a marketing slogan to help my brethren —A black cat for every lap. I implore you to run out and adopt a black cat today!

Now, I know one lucky kitty who's worn out from too much thinking. Time for me to head to Leta's lap for a recovery snooze.

Christie Parker lives in the Cotswolds with her canine brother Dickens and columnist Leta Parker.

Acknowledgments

This journey began when Lisa Frederickson suggested I write a cozy mystery. Never in my wildest dreams would that idea have occurred to me. And so it began. When I balked, she pushed. When I faltered, she encouraged. When I encountered writer's block, she offered ideas.

Book one in the Dickens & Christie mystery series would not have happened without her, and here I am with book two under my belt and book three underway. She has stayed with me the whole way—coaching and cajoling. I owe her so very much.

The next debt of gratitude is owed to my marvelous critique group, a band of ready, willing, and able women who stepped up to read one or both books in the series in draft form. Their feedback and suggestions made both books infinitely better.

Many thanks to these well-read ladies who critiqued the books under tight deadlines: Beth Bush Bangs, Jeannie Chambers, Linda Jordan Genovese, Lucy Molinaro, Audrey Moran, Jan Slimming, and Katie Wills. I'm not sure they realized they'd signed on for life.

Of course, I have to thank my husband for giving me the freedom to write and write and write. When I finally retired, I know he envisioned me having lots of leisure time and being more available. It didn't quite turn out that way, but he's happily coming along for the ride. He keeps saying he can't wait to see me on *The Today Show*. I just humor him.

Though Banjo and Puddin' receive daily thanks—in the form of treats and belly rubs—let me officially say thank you to my four-legged muses. They not only keep me company in my office but also provide nonstop inspiration for the personalities of Dickens and Christie. There *really* is a drawer in my desk with kitty treats, and Banjo *really* does lie beneath my desk gently snoring.

Finally, the journey continues because of you—my readers. Words cannot express the joy I get from hearing that you related to one of my characters or recognized your pets in the antics of Dickens and Christie. As readers, you have innumerable choices, and I thank you for choosing to read my books.

About the Author

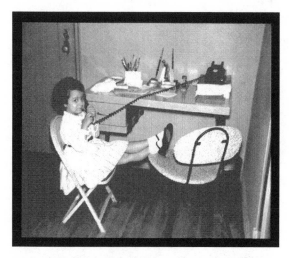

Kathy at her desk when she was four years old.

Picture me sitting serenely at my desk surrounded by my four-legged office assistants. The dog warms my feet, and the cat provides the purr-fict background music. I sip hot tea, sift through handwritten notes, and place fingers on the keyboard as thoughts take shape. Such is the joy of writing.

As a child, I took a book everywhere—to family dinners, to doctor's offices, and of course to bed. Years later, a newspaper article inspired me to put pen to paper and submit my thoughts—my words—to the editor. Before I knew it, I was writing weekly columns and blogs. Then came a book co-written with my dog. (What? Doesn't everyone do that?)

Now I'm living a dream I never knew I had—writing cozy animal mysteries featuring a dog and cat who talk to their owner. If a dog can write a book, surely animals can communicate. Naturally, my office assistants help with the dialogue. And, yes, they are angling to be listed as co-authors.

By the way, if you can't find me, I'm traveling in the UK doing research for my next mystery—don't judge.

—Kathy

www.KathyManosPenn.com

facebook.com/KathyManosPennAuthor
twitter.com/kathymanospenn
pinterest.com/kathymanos
amazon.com/Kathy-Manos-Penn

Also by Kathy Manos Penn

Just in case you haven't already had the pleasure of

reading the first book in the

Dickens & Christie Mystery Series,

here is your chance to get a copy.

Available in paperback also at regular price.

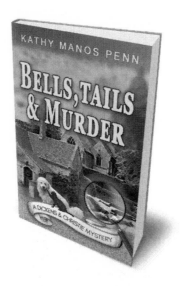

https://www.amazon.com/dp/B084X6546S

Book Three ~ Whiskers, Wreaths & Murder (Nov 2020)

Made in the USA
Columbia, SC
25 April 2021

36878322R00164